# NOBODY'S
## a novel
# IDEAL

# NOBODY'S IDEAL

*a novel*

Quill & Flame
**FIREBRAND**

# L. E. RICHMOND

Quill & Flame
PUBLISHING HOUSE

*Nobody's Ideal*

Copyright ©2026 by Laura Richmond

Published by Quill & Flame Publishing House, an imprint of Book Bash Media, LLC.

www.quillandflame.com

All rights reserved.

No part of this publication may be reproduced, digitally stored, or transmitted in any form without written permission from the publisher, except as permitted by U.S. copyright law.

This is a work of fiction. Names, characters, and incidents are products of the author's imagination or are used fictitiously. Any similarity to actual people, living or dead, organizations, business establishments, and/or events is purely coincidental.

NO AI TRAINING: Without any limitation on the author or Quill & Flame's exclusive copyright rights, any use of this publication to train generative artificial intelligence is expressly prohibited.

# NOBODY'S IDEAL

*a novel*

Quill & Flame
**FIREBRAND**

# L. E. RICHMOND

Quill & Flame
PUBLISHING HOUSE

*Nobody's Ideal*

Copyright ©2026 by Laura Richmond

Published by Quill & Flame Publishing House, an imprint of Book Bash Media, LLC.

www.quillandflame.com

All rights reserved.

No part of this publication may be reproduced, digitally stored, or transmitted in any form without written permission from the publisher, except as permitted by U.S. copyright law.

This is a work of fiction. Names, characters, and incidents are products of the author's imagination or are used fictitiously. Any similarity to actual people, living or dead, organizations, business establishments, and/or events is purely coincidental.

NO AI TRAINING: Without any limitation on the author or Quill & Flame's exclusive copyright rights, any use of this publication to train generative artificial intelligence is expressly prohibited.

This one is for my own personal Barton Drossel, the dark-haired young man with dimples and a cleft in his chin who chose to pursue a strong, opinionated girl. You are true steel and velvet, kindness encasing bulldog tenacity and unwavering convictions. Forever and always, Kyle.

And for Mom, because you believed in this story before anyone else, and because you raised me to know that womanhood and strength can go hand in hand. I love you.

# Author's Note

Dear reader,

This is a work of Christian fiction, but I imagine that as you read this book, you may notice some of the actions and speech included and think, "That does not reflect how Christians are supposed to live." And you would be right. The reason I chose to depict these things is because I believe that good art—especially Christian art—must walk the line between showing people and the world as they are and as they should be. Especially for my protagonist Chel, my desire was to show that people change after they encounter Jesus.

With that in mind, I hope you enjoy this story that holds examples of both the sinful brokenness of humanity and the gracious mercy of God.

L.E. Richmond

"A king had a daughter who was beautiful beyond all measure, but at the same time so proud and arrogant that no suitor was good enough for her."

~Grimm

# Chapter 1

## The Idea

**July 2008**

I don't want to wake up. Because, even now, with my eyes tightly closed against reality, I can feel the heaviness in my chest returning, as though someone showed up in the night and placed a block of concrete on my ribcage. I try to dispel the weight by drawing a deep breath, but as I do so, memory swells and despair pushes me deeper into my mattress. No amount of deep breathing is going to make this go away.

"Rachel!"

I squeeze my eyes tightly shut, hoping that if I ignore the summons, the voice will just leave me alone.

"Ra-chel!!"

My grandpa's voice. He's clearly getting ticked.

I sit up too quickly and let out a moan as my head throbs. The previous night comes rushing back, and I lean my aching forehead against my hands as the weight in my chest threatens to suffocate me. Rain slips down my window, like tears running down a face. But I don't cry. I haven't since the night my father died.

"Rachel." The voice of my mother is right outside the door. Her high-pitched tremolo grates on my nerves, and my headache worsens. "Are you up, dear?"

I grit my teeth and force myself to my feet. "Yep."

"What did you say?"

"Yes. I. Am. Up."

A pause. Then her voice comes again, falsely sweet and cheery. "Have you forgotten that we're going to have a family breakfast this morning, sweetie?"

I use the grandpa-free opportunity to roll my eyes. "Nope."

Another pause.

"We didn't know if you heard us calling." Only about ten miles away.

"God, Mom, I just woke up! Are five peaceful minutes in the morning too much to ask in this house?"

In my mind's eye, I can see her brown eyes swimming with tears, and I hate myself. I know she isn't trying to be annoying. I know she just desires a sweet, storybook mother-daughter relationship. I know she just wishes I could be her little princess. But I can't help lashing out at her because she doesn't understand me. She never has. And she keeps trying to relate to the person she thinks I should be until the person I actually am wants to scream and throw things.

Dad understood me. Dad knew when to talk and when to leave me alone. Dad knew how to buy just the right gifts, the kind that fill you up with warmth as you open them and show that the person who bought them really gets you. Dad knew that I'm nobody's princess. And I've never wanted to be.

I stumble into the bathroom adjoining my bedroom and grasp the edge of the sink for a moment, gazing down at my cracked eggplant nail polish. Mom keeps badgering me to come to the salon with her, but I always refuse. Even I'm not sure why because I love the salon. It's like I can't help hurting her, pushing her away, sniping at her, all the time.

I raise my head slowly and stare at my reflection in the oval mirror above the counter. There are purple shadows under my eyes, and my face has that white, peaked look it always gets with a hangover. I watch the me in the mirror bite her lip and then reach up to rub her eyes, smearing makeup until she looks like somebody's idea of a Halloween zombie.

Closing my eyes, I hang my head down, allowing my hair to fall into the sink. It used to be brown, (my hair, I mean) a color my dad called chestnut, rich brown with natural red and gold highlights. It's black now. One day after my mom had been going on and on about how lovely my hair was, I headed straight to the salon and dyed it jet black.

She'd cried the rest of the day.

I open my eyes wearily to survey my own reflection again. My mouth quirks up slightly as I reflect that even with a hangover, I'm pretty much a knockout. My skin is clear and light, but with the faintest natural tan—no idea where that came from since the sun never shines in Western Washington. I have a narrow face with high cheekbones, what my mom sentimentally calls "an elfin face". My eyes are dark blue, the same color as the Straits of Juan de Fuca. My hair is thick and the perfect texture, with loose natural curls that frame my face and hang over my shoulders. I contemplated hacking all my hair off that afternoon at the salon, but in the end, I couldn't do it. Dad loved my hair.

Unlike pretty much every other girl at my high school, I've never had a single complaint about my figure. I'm an effortless size two, with slight curves in the right places, and I never gain weight, no matter how much ice cream I eat (and I love ice cream).

There have always been guys. As a general rule, I like guys. Usually much better than girls. Guys are just more straightforward. Drama and clothes and weight pretty much never enter into the conversation when you're with a guy. There's never any stupid giggling. And unstated undertones are pretty rare. What you see is what you get.

Until they start getting interested in you. I would rather have ten airheaded, simpering petty girls than one guy who thinks he likes me. And that's how it always ends. The perfect, amiable comradeship ceases, and I run like the furies are after me.

Well, that's how every relationship I've ever had with a guy has ended. Except for one.

I give my head a little shake and force myself to stop thinking. I need to get ready quickly or Grandpa will be pounding on my door, demanding if I've been eaten by a boa constrictor coming up out of the shower drain.

As I strip off my clothes, I catch a whiff of something strange and feel my stomach clench. I had heard there might be a smell. I pull off my pajama pants and close my eyes for a second before peering down. My panties are streaked with dry, dark stains. I had heard that might happen too.

Breathing quickly and shallowly, I kick my clothes into a corner and wrench the shower handle around. Water comes pounding down, and I test the temperature with one hand for a moment before hopping in. I realize a split second later I forgot to turn on the fan. Shrugging, I pull the shower curtain closed. Grandpa will be mad. What else is new?

As the water cascades around me, I close my eyes and try desperately not to think. But memories of last night seem to come pouring over me with the water. I grab the bottle of Acqua di Parma shampoo and scrub a handful into my hair. *Why did I do it?* As the water rinses the shampoo out of my hair, I lather my legs and pull a razor in smooth strokes along my calves. *What was I thinking?* I use body wash and then a scrub which is supposed to leave my skin silky soft. *Will I ever be able to forget?* With another jerk, I switch the water off. And I stand in the steamy shower, gazing with burning eyes at the white walls and wishing tears would come to relieve the heavy, twisting ache inside me.

As I enter the dining room ten minutes later, wearing ripped skinny jeans, my oldest and most comfortable Beatles T-shirt and just enough makeup to disguise the remnants of my hangover, Grandpa glances up. His expression darkens.

"Could you look any more like a teenage boy?" he greets me.

"I don't know." I put a finger to my chin in a mock-thoughtful pose. "Most boys I meet don't seem to think I look like them. But I am a teenager."

"Eighteen, Rachel! An adult. I wish you would start acting like one."

I march to the table and pull out my chair, ignoring my mother's wince as the legs scrape along the oak floor. "In case you've forgotten, I turned eighteen yesterday. And it's Chel."

Grandpa scrutinizes me, his eyebrows raised over his reading glasses. "Rachel is a beautiful name. I don't understand why you prefer that diminutive nickname."

Chel. What my father had always called me. Rachel Elizabeth Corinne King. The name my mother and grandfather had given me in honor of my dead grandmother. My mom has actually had the last name King all her life. By coincidence, she and my father had the same last name before their marriage. Before my dad's death in 2001, Mom had always called me

Chel too. But now that he was gone, she had fallen in line with Grandpa in his use of my full name.

I take a deep breath and reach to serve myself three slices of bacon, a pile of scrambled eggs, and a mound of oven roasted potatoes.

I see Grandpa's lips purse together. Just yesterday, he had informed me that I needed to be careful since my metabolism wouldn't stay this fast forever. I had responded that if I ever turned into a human blimp, I would take care to stay out of his way so he wouldn't have to be offended by the sight of me.

Today, however, he swallows the reprimand and gives me a benign smile. Clearly trying to restart on a better foot, he asks, "How did you enjoy the party yesterday?"

My chest constricts. *I hated it. Is that what you want to hear? Every minute was a nightmare. So I went out and drank myself into a stupor to forget. Happy eighteenth birthday to me.*

Breathing deeply, I shovel a forkful of eggs into my mouth and chew before replying. "It was fine."

My poker face has always been lousy. My mother's countenance falls, and my grandpa's darkens again. "What was unsatisfactory this time, Rachel?"

I put down my fork and clasp my hands together in my lap, twining my fingers together. *Come on, Chel. Pull it together. They were trying to do something nice.*

I force my voice to sound light and cheery. "It really was fine, Grandpa. The food was delicious. You found a good caterer, Mom."

But Grandpa will have none of this. "Clearly, something did not live up to your expectations. I would like to know what it was."

I drag air into my lungs and squash down the rising anger. Maybe honesty is the best policy. "I didn't know anyone there very well. And I don't fit in with girls my age. Trying to small talk with hostile strangers isn't really my idea of a great time." *And I see myself through their eyes the whole time and know I sound stupid and awkward, and I hate myself.*

"Rachel, those people are some of our oldest friends."

"Some of *your* oldest friends, Grandpa. You refused to invite Cat, who is my oldest friend."

"I don't appreciate your tone, young lady," he snaps.

"And I don't appreciate being forced to have a formal dinner party for my eighteenth birthday when I told you ad infinitum that I would prefer a quiet dinner at home!"

Mom bursts into tears. Seething, I gaze down at my cooling breakfast, all hunger gone. I want nothing more than to run back up the stairs to my room and not come out for at least a week. Grandpa pats Mom's shoulder, glaring pointedly at me. I take another deep, calming breath.

"Mom, I'm sorry, okay? It was a beautiful party."

Mom hiccups. "Honey, all I ever want is for you to be happy, but nothing I do is ever good enough for you."

*Guess what the problem is, Mom? You don't know me! You have no idea what would make me happy! Even though I try and try to tell you!*

I survey my plate to avoid looking at either of them. I'm so tired of this. This whole mess they call family life. I wish I could go down to the docks and steal a boat and set sail for Alaska, Hawaii, China—anywhere that isn't here.

"Besides," Grandpa adds calmly, reaching across the table for the saltshaker, "you know I object to that girl Catalina. She is a very poor influence, as I'm sure you realize now."

Jumping up, I send my chair whizzing away from me and am halfway to the door when his shout reaches me.

"Rachel! I am not finished with you!"

I turn slowly. "Well, you wanna know what? I'm pretty much finished with you." The dam that has been holding back my anger bursts in a vicious tide, and words flood out. "Both of you! With you," I point at Grandpa, "and your criticisms and nastiness and thinking you're better than everybody." I whirl on Mom. "And you! Always trying to make me someone I'm not. Always saying you want me to be happy, but never actually bothering to find out what would make me happy." I am breathing heavily. "I'm eighteen. So, the second I can find a place, I'm gone! Maybe I'll go live with Cat, since *I* don't consider her a bad influence!"

Mom's sobs have been increasing in volume during my entire outburst, and now she buries her eyes in her napkin, positively wailing.

Grandpa's face is white, whether with fury or fear, I can't tell. But when he speaks, his voice is surprisingly measured. "I apologize, Rachel. I didn't know you would take what I said about Catalina so hard—"

"Why should I take it hard when you badmouth my best, and only real, friend?" My voice drips with sarcasm.

I see his hand clench around his fork handle, tendons standing out in sharp relief. He hates being interrupted. Taking a deep breath, he pries his fingers apart and lays the fork deliberately by his plate. "Rachel, please. Sit down. Things got off to a bad start this morning. And I have something I would very much like to discuss with you."

I hesitate, debating whether to storm out the door to Cat's to prove I'm not kidding. In the end, I grab my chair and spin it around backward so I'm sitting with my torso pressed against the chair back with my arms resting on top. I'll have to hear what Grandpa wants to say eventually. His tenacity and inability to take no for an answer have made him a legendary business owner. He takes in my posture, and annoyance flickers in his eyes, but he only purses his lips and then flips over the stack of papers sitting next to his plate.

"Rachel, I'm sure you know the economy is doing very poorly right now." That is perhaps the understatement of the 2000s. "I am going to be frank with you. The restaurant has been hit hard. With the crash in the housing market, people can't afford their mortgages, let alone a fancy seafood dinner. Sales are down nearly fifty percent."

I raise my eyebrows, surprised and dismayed against my will. "That sucks, Grandpa."

His lips quirk slightly as though he is resisting a smile. "That is one way of putting it." His face settles into lines of worry as he glances down at the papers. "Things are becoming somewhat crucial. If we can't bring the bottom line up soon, I may have to close down."

I bite my bottom lip. The restaurant has always been a point of contention between Grandpa and me. He inherited it from his father when he was twenty years old and completely revamped the place until he made The Morning Catch one of the nicest and most upscale restaurants in Port Angeles. It's the kind of place guys in tuxedos bring girls in cocktail dresses and pull out a three-carat diamond ring as they're enjoying their seared scallops in Cajun mustard cream sauce paired with a nice cabernet. Grandpa books jazz bands for the dancing under dimmed lights on Friday nights. The waiters and waitresses wear silver and turquoise uniforms that match the table settings perfectly.

Ever since I was eleven—when Grandpa accepted that Mom and Dad weren't going to produce any sons—he's insisted I'm going to take over the restaurant at his retirement. And no matter how many times I tell him I'm not interested (AT ALL), he persists in the notion. But the arguments about it are always fruitless. I can't tell him what I really want is to go to college and study voice and then perform. I know there's no money in it unless you're super talented, and I would definitely class myself in the moderately talented camp. But music loosens all the knots inside me.

When I sing at O'Hara's on Friday nights, like I've been sneaking out to do since I was fifteen, I forget about Dad's death. I forget about the drama at home. I forget about the ache I feel whenever I hear a certain guy's name. When I'm singing, there's a ball of warmth inside me that obliterates the darkness and the cold. When I'm singing, there isn't anything but me and the audience, the music connecting us. I'm no longer stiff and socially awkward and snarky and opinionated, but a girl they love because we all love the music.

But the fact that I can't tell him what I actually want to do means I don't have any alternative to offer when he presses me to take over The Morning Catch. All I can tell him is that I hate numbers and logistics and managing and seafood. Particularly seafood.

So, I don't know what to say. Because to be quite honest, I hate the restaurant, and I can't pretend it going under would mean a whole lot to me. But I know The Morning Catch means everything to him.

"That's awful. I'm sorry," is the best I can manage.

He nods slowly. "We are particularly struggling because the cost of fresh, high-quality seafood is so high. If we had access to a significantly cheaper source, our operating costs would diminish so much that we would be able to ride out this recession until people have more discretionary income, and our sales rise."

I frown. "And I'm assuming you have an idea for getting access to a 'significantly cheaper source'?"

He doesn't answer but instead slides a small stack of photographs toward me. I eye the top one and then gape at him, completely nonplussed. "I'm sorry, what?"

He waves his hand. "Look through them, Rachel. There are bios on the back."

I squint at him for a moment longer, then with a shake of my head, study the first picture. It's a headshot of a young man with a round face, slicked-back dirty blond hair, and light-blue eyes. He's not that photogenic, unfortunately, or else maybe just not a looker in general. Flipping the picture over, I scan the back.

<u>Cooper Vine</u>
Born: March 29, 1988
Parents: Dustin and Amy Vine
Residence: Port Townsend, WA

Bio: Cooper is currently studying Welding Technology at Lake Washington Institute of Technology. When not in school, he works with his father, Dustin, managing the family business, Key City Fishing Company. His interests include fishing, video games, and weightlifting. His goal in seeking a welding degree is to be able to help repair the family boats.

I glance up at my grandpa and open my mouth, but he waves his hand again. "Look through them all. Then we'll talk." Rolling my eyes, I peer at the next picture. This young man has a narrow face and wide, dark eyes. His hair is cut so short it's hard to tell what color it is, but if I had to guess, I would say light brown. Again, he's not eye-catching, but I like his smile—he has dimples and a gap between his front teeth.

<u>Grant Blaine</u>
Born: August 14, 1985
Parents: Robert Blaine and Kristin Sewall (divorced)
Residence: Bellingham, WA

Bio: Grant is currently enrolled at Western Washington University as a master's student in accounting and is also in the process of taking the CPA exams (he has passed two). Eventually he plans to take over from his father who is the CFO for Trident Seafoods. Grant enjoys reading, marathon running, and playing the drums.

I stick Grant under the pile. And a face I recognize stares up at me. My heart gives one bound and then seems to stand still. Bile rises in my throat, and for one horrific moment, I think I'm going to puke all over the table. *Stop it, Chel! Stop! Do you want them to know? Get it together!* I take a deep breath and rearrange my features into what I hope is a bored expression, praying my mom and grandpa have noticed nothing. The young man staring up at me has shoulder-length black hair and fair skin with high cheekbones and eyes the pale gray of a stormy sea. He is definitely photogenic, but the picture doesn't do him justice.

Gavin Fairchild
Born: December 6, 1983
Parents: Aron and Veronica Fairchild
Residence: Port Angeles, WA
Bio: Gavin graduated with a degree in Graphic Design from Washington State University in 2005 and has since started a successful photography business in Port Angeles. He often works with his father, Aron, who owns High Tide Seafoods, by shooting promotional material for the company. Gavin enjoys karaoke, swing dancing, and good wines.

With shaking fingers, I place Gavin at the bottom of the pile. *Is this some kind of sick joke? Do they know what happened last night? Is Grandpa going to try to send the cops after him? But who are these other guys then?*

I pick up the final photo, and my heart jumps all the way into my mouth. This young man has thick, wavy, dark hair surrounding a swarthy face. In the picture, his eyes are hard to distinguish behind his big, dark-rimmed glasses, but I know they are vibrant green, like grass after rain. His hard jawline tapers down to a cleft chin Cary Grant would be proud of. A butt-chin, all the high schoolers used to call it.

Barton Drossel
Born: May 7, 1987
Parents: Keith Drossel and Rosemary West (divorced)
Residence: Seattle, WA
Bio: Through dual enrollment and a rigorous home education, Barton graduated from high school with a bachelor's degree in market-

ing from the University of Washington. He immediately began working for American Seafoods, a company he had interned with in high school, working on their fishing boats in Alaska. He recently became the youngest Chief Human Resources Officer in the company's history. Barton enjoys nonfiction, old movies, and water of any kind.

I shove Bart under the pile and realize I'm back to Cooper. I drop the photos face down next to my plate and look up. Both Mom and Grandpa avoid eye contact, suddenly appearing fascinated by the food in front of them. "Grandpa..." The word is a growl. "What is going on?"

Grandpa clears his throat. "I'm sure you recognize a few of those young men, Rachel, but, as a matter of fact, all of them are family friends. I went to college with Cooper's father and his entire family stayed with us for a week a few summers back." Memory stirs, and I remember Cooper. The entire time his family stayed with us, we barely exchanged two words since he never unglued himself from his Gameboy long enough to hold a conversation. I had hung out with his little sister, Lily, who was sassy and cute and blonde—Tinker Bell in the flesh. "You've never actually met Grant, but Kristin, his mother, was a friend of your grandmother's, and I have been in contact with his father for several years now, since he handles the billing for Trident Seafoods. I hear Grant is an extremely promising young accountant and is being prepared to take over his father's position."

"This is all fascinating, Grandpa, but could we cut through the crap to whatever the point is?"

Grandpa gives me a look and then continues his narration. "Gavin lives here, as you read. He is a few years older than you, so you two would never have gone to school together. His company took the promotional videos last year that are on the restaurant's website, and I was highly impressed with his work. I have also frequently bought crabs from his father." Grandpa taps a finger on the stack of photos. "Barton you probably know best. Obviously, he lived here through high school with his mother, who is a good friend of your mother's, and he visited Port Angeles frequently even before then."

I draw a deep breath to keep myself from snarling at Grandpa. *He'll get to the point eventually.* I pick up a piece of bacon and nibble on the end.

"I've invited all these young men to come for a dinner party at the end of next month. I think it would be nice for you all to meet."

I cram the entire piece of bacon into my mouth and chew ferociously to work off steam. Swallowing, I speak as calmly as I can. "Okay. Why? First, the restaurant is on the rocks; then, you want to have a dinner party with these four guys. Is this some kind of bizarre Clue game? Am I supposed to discover who the murderer is?"

Grandpa raises his eyebrows. My sense of humor is always completely lost on him. I grit my teeth. "Mom?"

She regards Grandpa before giving me a tremulous smile. "Sweetheart, you're obviously a young woman now. A lovely young woman. I'm sure you've been thinking about some of the next steps in your life recently and... Well, anyway, all of these young men are extremely eligible and well, as I said, you are extremely lovely, so if you all meet, who knows what might happen?"

And everything clicks. Grandpa's restaurant is about to go under. He needs a cheap supply of fresh fish. Every single one of these young men is somehow related to a fishing company. And if I were to marry one of them, Grandpa would definitely have a cheap supply of fresh fish at his fingertips.

Sometimes, fury makes everything fuzzy, and sometimes it makes everything crystal clear. My voice, when I speak, is like ice. "So, if I understand you correctly, the goal is for me to marry one of these eligible young men?"

Grandpa's brow smoothes in relief that I've caught on without him actually having to say those words out loud. "You must see, Rachel, that it would be extremely advantageous for all concerned. Your mother and I are close with all of these families, and the benefits of linking a seafood restaurant and a fishing company are..."

His voice dies away as I spring to my feet. My chair topples over backwards and hits the floor with a crash. "Advantageous for all concerned? You mean it's advantageous for you! For you and your stupid restaurant!

And I'm just some bargaining chip you can use because I'm a 'lovely young woman' and have enough sex appeal that I might be able to seduce one of these losers into marrying me! This is the twenty-first century, Grandpa! In case you missed it, arranged marriages went out of fashion, oh, at least a hundred years ago!" I grab the stack of pictures and with one ferocious yank, rip them down the middle. Throwing them over my shoulder, I speak in my softest and deadliest voice. "So, no, Grandpa, I will not be attending any dinner party. I will not be marrying any of your eligible bachelors. And you and your restaurant can go to hell for all I care."

I stride to the door, yank it open, and slam it behind me, ignoring their calls to come back.

"Trust my Grandpa to think marrying me off to some fisherman would solve his problems," I finish, absently running my fingers through Serenity's downy hair. She snuggles against me, sticking her thumb in her mouth.

"I can't believe she's so calm with you," Cat says, a little enviously. "The only time she lets me cuddle with her is right before bed. Usually she's a crazy child."

"'M not crazy child," remarks Serenity from around her thumb, glaring at her mother, who wiggles her eyebrows and blows her a kiss. I stroke her hair away from her forehead.

"There's nothing wrong with being a crazy child, baby. You know your Auntie Chel adores you. That's why you snuggle with her, isn't that right?"

Cat smiles at me, and for a moment, I see the sheen of tears in her eyes. I know what she's thinking without her saying a word. Her parents and siblings have never even seen Serenity and have made it plain they couldn't care less about her existence. The thought makes me so angry that I squeeze the warm little body in my lap tightly, trying to infuse her with all the love she should have gotten from a dad, grandparents, aunts, uncles, and cousins. She squeals in protest and wiggles to loosen my arms.

"Sorry, sweetie." I kiss her forehead in apology, and she nestles into me again.

"Chel?"

"Yeah, Serry-Berry?"

"Mommy says I can have a party when I turn phree. You come. Mommy says we'll have cake, balloons. And unicorns! I want a unicorn for my birphday. My birphday will be in ..." she raises one chubby little hand and contemplates her fingers, raising and lowering them one at a time. "One, two, phree, five, eight weeks! Right, Mommy?"

Laughing, Cat corrects her. "In three months, sweetie. Remember what Mommy told you? Your birthday will be when the leaves turn orange and fall off the trees."

"Oh, yeah. Why the leaves turn orange, Mommy?"

Cat glances at me. "Um, I think it's because the tree isn't giving them nutrients anymore, baby."

"What's nutents?"

I stifle a laugh at the expression on Cat's face. "They're in food... Speaking of food, do you want a snack, Serry-Berry?"

The diversionary tactic works. "Yes! Yes! Animal crackers!"

"We don't have animal crackers, sweetie. I told you we couldn't get them at the store this month. But you can have a cheese stick or some grapes."

"No, Mommy! I want animal crackers."

"Serenity, listen to Mommy. I told you we don't have any. You can have a cheese stick or some grapes."

Serenity's lips begin to tremble, and fat tears start pooling in her eyes. Next instant, she collapses to the floor with a heartrending wail. My eyes move from the crying toddler to where my friend sits with exhaustion written all over her face.

"Cat," I say softly. "I can run to the store and get her some crackers..." But she's shaking her head.

"She's fine, Chel. It's not bad for a kid to learn that life doesn't revolve around their whims." Kneeling beside her sobbing daughter, she places a hand gently on her shoulder and speaks in a coaxing tone. "Serenity, do you want some grapes? You like grapes."

Serenity's only response is to whack at her mother with her small hand. Cat's lips tighten. "Serenity Dawn Michaels, you have two options. Either sit up right now and you can have a snack, or you are going to your room until you can be happy." The toddler's wails only increase in volume, until she sounds like a fire siren. Sucking in her breath, Cat leans down and picks up her daughter, who flails and kicks, screaming the whole time. The sound retreats down the hallway, a door shuts, and Cat returns.

"We're having a bad week," she says grimly, waving in the direction of the hall from which muffled wails are still coming. She sinks onto the couch and puts her head in her hands, her short blonde hair tangling in her fingers. "What am I doing wrong with her, Chel?"

In a moment, I'm kneeling on the carpet next to her. "Nothing, Cat. You're a great mom. She's a good kid. It's just that she's two. She doesn't know how to control her emotions."

"But she does, though, Chel. Her teachers at daycare tell me she's never a bit of trouble. Sweet and quiet. The embodiment of her name. That's how they describe her. And every single day for the past two weeks, she has meltdowns like this, sometimes three or four times a day. Screaming at the top of her lungs and trying to hit and kick me when I won't give her what she wants. And she does it in the grocery store so that everyone stares at me, and I know they're thinking, 'You stupid woman, why can't you get your child under control?' I don't know what to do, Chel. Sometimes I feel like I hate her." Her voice drops and she groans, burying her face in her hands again. "I'm a horrible person to even think that, I know."

She bursts into ragged sobs, and I sit next to her on the floor with my hand on her shoulder, my own nerves frayed to shreds by the continued screeching from the bedroom. I can't imagine dealing with this on a daily basis. Just one of many reasons I am not cut out to be a mom.

"Cat," I start feebly and then realize I have no idea what to say. Serenity is the only small child I've ever been close to. I don't know what's normal.

She takes a shuddering breath and tries to pull herself together. "I'm sorry."

"No, seriously, Cat, it's fine. You don't have to apologize to me."

She shakes her head, a bitter smile twisting her lips. "I just wish for once I could be a good friend and listen to your problems rather than always droning on about mine." Her eyes stray to the kitchen counter, and I follow her gaze to the enormous pile of bills sitting there. My lips tighten and a jolt of fury stabs through me.

"Has that bum Derek not sent you child support *again* this month?"

Cat's family moved to Port Angeles from Kansas City when I was ten. Her father ran a successful IT business from home and had wanted to be closer to Seattle, the hub of Microsoft. The family had six children, of whom Cat was the youngest, the exact same age as me. Her oldest brother had joined the army when he was eighteen, but the rest still lived at home. Cat's mother and father were strict and religious. The children were homeschooled, and all the girls wore skirts all the time. My grandfather was fairly conservative in his views of appropriate feminine dress, but I resembled a hooker in comparison to Cat. Cat's family didn't watch movies or listen to anything but religious music.

Although I preferred boys to girls when it came to friendship, I fell in love with Cat the first time I saw her. The day after her family moved in, she was sitting in her parents' driveway, drawing with chalk. It was one of Port Angeles's rare sunny days, and I was perched in the oak tree in our yard, with a good view of everything going on next door. She was the best artist I, at ten years old, had ever seen. An enormous, twisting design of flowers, leaves, birds, and sunbeams soon surrounded her. I was leaning out of the tree, trying to see better, when I felt the first telltale drop hit my cheek. I scrambled out of the tree as rain began to pelt down and made a dash for my front porch. Under cover, I pivoted and froze. Cat was standing in her driveway, her golden-blonde, waist-length hair streaming down her back, her face lifted toward the sky, eyes closed, as rain beaded on her skin. While I watched her, she threw up her arms and danced in the rain, laughing and opening her mouth to catch the water. From that moment, I knew I wanted to know the girl next door.

Cat and I became best friends almost immediately. Despite their strictness and their bizarre obsession with Christianity, I liked the whole family. Cat's parents were kind to me and welcomed me into their home. Her older siblings were nicer than any other kids their age I had ever met and often helped us with games and crafts. Then, the summer Cat and I turned fourteen, her mom was diagnosed with breast cancer. In an uncharacteristic move, Cat's father enrolled her, and her two older siblings left at home at the local high school to remove the burden of their education from his wife.

I was thrilled. The first year of high school was more bearable than my entire previous school career because for the first time, I had a friend. But a snag quickly appeared in the form of Derek Allen, the junior class president, who almost immediately moved in on Cat. Despite her long skirts, Cat had been turning boys' heads since the day she started at Port Angeles High. Barely five feet, with a tiny, fairy-like figure, even long skirts and modest tops couldn't disguise how breathtaking she was. She could have worn a burlap sack, and guys would have run after her. But it wasn't only her looks. Unlike me, with my charming, porcupine-like personality, Cat's sweetness, sunny disposition, and general goodness endeared her to everyone. Like me, however, she spurned all romantic advances, but for a very different reason. Cat believed in courtship, or intentional dating, as she explained it to me. She told me she didn't just want to go out with someone for fun. Instead, she hoped to use dating to find a man to spend the rest of her life with in marriage. Also, waiting for someone who shared her Christian beliefs was very important to her.

At first, she rejected Derek as well, telling him kindly, but firmly that she wasn't looking for a relationship at the moment. But I knew she liked him from the first. Derek could be charming when he wanted something, and he wanted Cat badly. I hated Derek. I had been in school with him since kindergarten, and I had seen him cheat on tests, bully younger children in the playground—in elementary school, but still—suck up to teachers, ruin anyone he didn't like with malicious gossip, and pursue girls avidly and then icily ignore them if, as I did, they spurned his advances.

But, I had to admit, he acted his part perfectly with Cat. He agreed they would just be friends, since she didn't want a relationship, and proceeded to walk her home after school every day, carrying her books for her. Flowers started to appear in her locker. He began volunteering at the local soup kitchen after learning she went there every Saturday afternoon. He would text her each morning to see how she'd slept. He introduced himself to her father as a friend from school and charmed Mr. Michaels with his politeness and maturity.

In the middle of freshman year, she began going out with him behind her parents' backs. We argued about it. I didn't think her parents should dictate to a fourteen-year-old whether or not she could have a boyfriend, but I didn't like her lying to them. She flared up and asked how it was any different than me sneaking out my window on Friday nights to sing at O'Hara's. There was nothing I could say without sounding like a hypocrite, but I knew why this bothered me when my own wrongdoing didn't.

Cat wasn't me. Cat was good. I had always been a rebel. She overall had a good relationship with her parents. My relationship to my mother and grandfather could barely be called a relationship. Her Christian faith had always meant everything to her, and now she was violating her own principles for a boy I personally considered a scumbag. I was violating none of my principles by breaking an overreaching rule of my grandfather's.

For the rest of the year, I watched in silent discomfort as her relationship with Derek grew increasingly serious. I suspected they were going further physically than I thought prudent or Cat thought right. But I knew I couldn't say anything. She was head over heels for Derek by now. All I would gain by trying to interfere in their relationship would be the loss of my friendship with Cat.

Then, a few weeks before the end of the semester, I awakened to a sound like hail on my window. Cat stood outside, throwing pebbles. I immediately opened the window, and she crawled through. She was a mess. Her puffy, red-rimmed eyes indicated she'd been crying for hours.

My first thought was maybe Derek had broken up with her, and mixed with my hatred toward him, I felt a burst of hope for my friend. But the news she confessed made me feel as though someone had dumped ice water over me. She was pregnant. Derek had informed her that unless she "took care of it" he would break up with her. And she was terrified to tell her parents.

I held her as she cried and cried, my own heart aching for her hurt and blazing with fury at Derek and her parents. She asked me what she should do, and I told her we should find a crisis pregnancy center. I promised everything would be all right. I knew the words were empty, but I didn't know what else to say.

We visited the crisis pregnancy center together the next week and watched in amazement as a tiny, but perfect baby, appeared on the screen. Cat was further along than she had realized—almost sixteen weeks. I went with her to tell her parents. It was awful, worse than I could ever have imagined. Her mother, bald and wasted from the cancer treatments, burst into heartrending sobs, while her father, ashen faced, thundered that unless Derek married her or she "got rid of it," he would kick her out of the house. What kind of image would she give the name of Christ as a single mother?

Derek, as good as his word, broke up with her. And I, as good as mine, kneed him as hard as I could the next time he passed me in the hall. Cat dropped out of high school and got a job at Daily Bread. A kind older woman from her new church rented Cat her basement spare room, since at barely fifteen, there was no way that she could qualify for a traditional apartment. She grew bigger and bigger. I went with her to her OB/GYN appointments and her ultrasounds. We laughed and cried together when we learned she was having a girl. And the night she went into labor, I stole my grandfather's car and drove to the hospital so I could hold her hand as she groaned and writhed, struggling to bring her daughter into the world. The labor terrified and disgusted me. But I had to be there for Cat—there was no one else. And when, wrapped in a hospital blanket, tiny and wrinkled and red, Serenity was placed in my arms, a love so deep it was almost painful filled my heart. I knew Cat had made the right choice.

Despite her parents' behavior, Cat hasn't broken with her Christian roots. She and Serenity go to a local nondenominational church every Sunday, and she says everyone there loves and accepts them. "They don't deny I messed up, but they remind me over and over that Jesus's blood covers my sins, and He loves and forgives me. They adore Serenity and never treat me as inferior because I'm a single mom."

I, on the other hand, can't forgive her parents for the way they acted. And if I hadn't hated God already, I probably would have started after seeing the way they completely cut Cat and Serenity out of their family in God's name.

Cat silently shakes her head, her face crumpling. "I don't know what to do, Chel. Daily Bread is a dead-end job, and I know it, but what other options do I have? I would love to go to school, but I don't make enough right now to cover my bills, let alone to afford tuition. If Derek consistently sent child support, I could use it to cover daycare expenses. Then I would be able to save a little every month, and I might actually be able to afford college someday. But he only sends the checks about half the time and, God knows, I can't afford a lawyer to make him cough up. Daycare is one of my biggest expenses, but I can't work if someone doesn't watch Serenity, and I don't like her going anywhere that isn't reputable."

"Cat, come on. I know your goal is to take care of yourself and your daughter, but let me help you. My grandpa gives me a huge allowance every month, and I make a little off my singing gigs. I have no bills right now. I want to help you. Let me loan you the money to start taking night classes."

She's already shaking her head. My temper flares, and I leap to my feet, "God, Cat, let me help you! Why do you have to be so freaking stubborn?"

I see a shadow cross her face at my language, but I don't care. "Cat, I love you and Serenity more than anyone else on earth!" Her face softens, and she opens her mouth, but I plow on. "Let me do this for you! What else am I going to spend the money on? New music? Concert tickets? Designer clothes? Eating out? Spa appointments? If I don't have anything better to do with it, I blow every penny I have on frivolous stuff. Wouldn't this be a better use of my money?"

She still shakes her head, and I turn away from her with an inarticulate growl of frustration.

"Chel, shhhh! You'll wake up Serenity." Only now do I realize the screaming has stopped. She gets up from the couch and comes toward me, looking like a model in her skinny jeans and tea-rose-colored T-shirt.

She takes both of my hands. "Chel. I don't think you'll ever know how much your friendship has meant to me. You've been my family after mine abandoned me. You've loved my daughter while my family ignores her. You've listened to and sympathized with my struggles. You've defied your grandfather to remain my friend. I'm so grateful God gave you to me." I stiffen a little, uncomfortable as I always am when she casually brings up God in everyday conversation. "But, Chel, please, try to understand." Her blue eyes lock with mine, pleading. "I feel like a failure every single day of my life."

I open my mouth to interrupt, but she holds up her hand. "Let me finish. I didn't have enough sense not to fall for a loser, even though my best friend warned me against him over and over. I didn't have the self-control not to sleep with him, even though I knew it was wrong. I'm working a minimum-wage job at Daily Bread, hardly able to afford my bills, and unsure if I will be able to buy my daughter the twenty-dollar unicorn from Walmart that she desperately desires for her birthday. I have no prospects for career improvement, and it's my own fault. My daughter will grow up without a dad, and it's my fault. Chel, I barely have any self-respect left. I can't accept handouts from my friends, or I'll fall apart."

I open my mouth and then close it again, unable to think of a single thing to say. Cat's lips quirk a little at the corners as she watches me struggle for speech. "Come here," she says, tugging me toward the battered sofa. "Let's talk about your issues instead of mine for once. What's this about your grandfather wanting you to marry a fisherman?"

I give an involuntary laugh and sink onto the couch next to her. Then I fill her in on Grandpa's grand plan. As usual, her response is much more level than mine.

"Do you know the guys he's proposing as suitors?"

I raise my eyebrows at her. "Even if I was madly in love with one of them, I would refuse to marry him on principle. Didn't you hear me? My grandpa is trying to use me as a bargaining chip! He cares more about his stupid restaurant than about his only granddaughter."

Cat glances at me sideways. "Even if you were madly in love with one of them? You don't mean *he* is one of the options?"

I glare at her. "As a matter of fact, the person you're referring to was mentioned, but I am not madly in love with him." Cat gives me a look. "What? I'm not! I got over him ages ago. And besides I haven't seen him in over two years."

Cat laughs and shakes her head. "You know, I've never met your equal for cutting off your nose to spite your face. You refuse to go to the salon with your mom even though you love going, just because you can't bear to let her treat you. You go off and dye your hair black even though you know your natural hair color is gorgeous just to irritate her. You won't sing in your grandfather's restaurant but sneak out the window to perform at O'Hara's, which is frankly a dive. Now you're refusing to even consider dating a guy you've been crazy about since you were ten just because your grandfather happened to suggest it."

I grin. "I've never been able to take the easy way through life. You know that. It goes against my constitution."

She laughs again but then grows serious. "What are you going to do? Your grandpa isn't really one to take no for an answer."

"Lock myself in my room on the night of the dinner party? I don't know." I brighten. "Oh! Maybe I'll go and be so horrible to the guys he's invited that they'll all tell him they wouldn't touch me with a ten-foot pole. Yeah, that would actually be really fun..."

"Chel, come on. Don't you think that might be a little hard on the guys? What have they ever done to you?"

"Nothing, yet. And I'd like to keep it that way."

I stroll away from Cat's apartment, feeling cheered, like I almost always do after a visit with her. I haven't bothered to get a car yet, because one: I can always borrow any of Grandpa's four vehicles, and two: I wasn't lying when I told Cat I have the bad habit of spending any ready money on the first little thing that catches my eye. Besides, today I would have walked anyway. It isn't raining and, for Port Angeles, is quite a nice day, with gray clouds scudding along high overhead, allowing brief shafts of sunlight to pass through.

I reach into my pocket for earbuds and plug them into my iPhone, slipping the buds into my ears. James Taylor's "Fire and Rain" fills my ears, and I slow dance alone on the sidewalk, eyes closed, bent arms raised.

*I remember him, riding home from school with me and my mother one day and asking for one of my earbuds. His eyebrows rise as Bob Dylan's "Tambourine Man" comes through. "What?" I ask, defensively. He shakes his head, "You just always seem like a hard rock kind of girl to me. I didn't peg you as the folk type." I ignore him for the rest of the drive, sure that his words were an insult.*

Someone bumps into me and curses. My eyes pop open, and I jump aside, mumbling an apology. I've reached downtown. The Morning Catch is just ahead of me. I always forget how close Cat lives to grandpa's restaurant. I try to walk sedately, but "How Sweet It Is" has started playing, and I can't keep myself from swaying to the music as I walk. As I near The Morning Catch, I hit pause and pull out my earbuds. There's different music to listen to. The busker is here today.

He's average height and an average build. His dark hair hangs in skinny braids halfway down his back, a wannabe hipster. Diamond studs glitter in his ears, and there is a tattoo on his cheekbone: a single word, Redeemed. He has a short beard, which helps to soften his sharp chin. The blackness of the letters contrasts sharply with his golden-brown eyes, eyes like a big cat. His clothing surprises me a little bit: his jeans have a rip in one knee, but they fit him well and are—if I'm being honest—super flattering. His belt is old, but it's actually around his waist as opposed to wrapped around his knees. His hoodie, although faded, is clean and has no graphics.

He appeared outside The Morning Catch with his violin about a month ago, at the beginning of the summer. I remember Grandpa striding outside to send him away and stopping to listen as "Theme from *Schindler's List*" poured from his violin.

Usually, I don't enjoy violin music. The instrument is too high, and most violinists just sound squeaky and wailing to me. But this guy's music makes my heart throb. His tone is warm and golden and pure, like liquified evening light.

He doesn't have a set schedule, but three or four times a week, he shows up outside Grandpa's restaurant. Every time I peek into his case, I'm surprised how little money he's gotten, and I wonder why he hasn't given up and found a different and more lucrative street corner. I guess Grandpa's customers don't appreciate good music. So, I put five bucks into his case every time I pass and smile to let him know someone's listening.

I pause near him. The piece is one I don't know. Something simple and sweet, repeating like the verses of a song. His eyes are closed, and I can tell this piece means something to him. Not wanting to interrupt, I slip over and drop my money into his case, then turn to walk away.

"I saw you dancing, you know." I whirl around. The busker's eyes have popped open, and he's grinning at me. His voice is deep, even for a guy's, but his eyes crinkle at the corners, and I don't think he could be creepy if he tried.

Grudgingly, I smile back. "I sort of got cussed out for that. Serves me right for acting like a fool in the middle of the street."

"What song?"

It takes me a second to realize what he means. "Wha— Oh, 'Fire and Rain.' James Taylor."

"A classic."

He scratches his chin under his beard, then gives me a half smile as we stand in awkward silence, both struggling for something to say.

"What song were you playing? Just now?"

"'Abide with Me.' It's an old Irish hymn." He hesitates. "It's always a little hard to get the true meaning of hymns without the words."

There's another awkward moment, and I scuff my shoe against the sidewalk. I know I should walk away and allow him to keep playing, but for some reason, I'm inclined to keep talking.

"You must really like seafood."

I glance up in confusion and catch his half smile again. "Uh, no, I hate seafood. Absolutely ABHOR it."

"So, how come you spend so much time at a seafood restaurant then?"

I nod as understanding dawns. "Oh. My grandpa owns it. It's his baby. Probably the most important thing in his life." I add under my breath. "Definitely more important than me."

Cocking his head, he makes a skeptical noise. "Dramatic teenage self-pity?"

I glare at him, incensed. "Excuse me, I happen to be an adult. And it's true."

"Well, excuse *me*." He's laughing.

His laughter infuriates me more. "You don't believe me? Well, guess what? This morning, he told me the restaurant is floundering because of the recession. His solution? Marry me off to some owner of a fishing company so he can get cheap, high-quality seafood."

His smile is gone. "Not really."

"Yes, really." I can't keep a hint of smugness out of my tone. *Still think I'm a dramatic teenager?*

A smile quirks one corner of his mouth. "I pity your grandfather. I can't imagine trying to force you into anything you don't wish to do."

Stung, I turn on my heel. "You're never likely to have to. Because you don't know me." I move down the sidewalk.

He's laughing again. "I'd like to though!" he yells after me. "What did you say your name was again?" I wave dismissively as I continue to walk away.

"Once the king sponsored a great feast and invited from far and near all the men wanting to get married. Then the king's daughter was led through the ranks, but she objected to something about each one."

~Grimm

# Chapter 2
## The Party

**Two months later**

I sit on the toilet, staring at two little pink lines. I can't remember how long I've been frozen here. It occurred to me two days ago that I hadn't had my period in a long time. Trying to ignore the horrible sinking in my stomach that came with the realization, I told myself my period would probably start any day. I just needed to be patient. But tonight, I decided I needed to know. When I ripped open the pink packet I had smuggled home from the Dollar Tree, my hands were shaking with nerves. Now I feel nothing. Absolutely nothing.

*It was just the one time. Just the one time.*
*This cannot be happening.*
*Maybe it's defective.*
*Why did I do it? Why? What is wrong with me?*
*Please, let this be a dream.*

I taste something salty and realize I've been biting down on my lip so hard that I've created a line of puncture wounds. Somehow the physical sensation of pain causes my frozen stupor to evaporate.

Hands shaking, I drop the incriminating pink stick into the garbage can and push it to the very bottom. I stand and force myself to flush the toilet and wash my hands. Then I stand stock-still in the middle of the bathroom as a torrent of thoughts and emotions race past, slamming into me as they go.

A young man's face, darkly handsome and slightly blurred.
*My grandpa is going to kill me.*

*I could get an abortion.*
The thought makes my stomach twist.
*But I'm horrible with kids. I CANNOT be a mom.*
The darkness of a bedroom and an act that causes shame to wriggle all over me.
*What if Grandpa kicks me out?*
I don't feel pregnant.
*Oh God, I drank so much that night. What if the baby has fetal alcohol syndrome?*

I sink to the bathroom floor, feeling as though someone punched me in the gut. The thought of bringing a child into the world who is severely disabled because of my stupidity makes me feel like I'm going to hurl.

Oh no, I think I really am... I crawl to the toilet and manage to get the lid open just in time. Trembling and sweating, I lean against the chilled porcelain. Where did that come from? Could it be the pregnancy? I thought it was called *morning* sickness.

For a few seconds, I wish there was a God. I wish there really was some Higher Power who could help me out of this mess. Or at least Someone out in the universe who would hear me if I called for help.

I open my lips. Then I clamp them shut, cutting off the words. No one is there. And if Anyone is, He doesn't care.

"Rachel?"

I jerk awake, my arms still wrapped around the toilet bowl, cheek stuck to the lid. I sit up straight and let out a low moan as my cramped body rebels against the night spent on the bathroom floor.

"Yeah?"

"Honey?" My mom's voice sounds hesitant. "Are you okay?"

"Why on earth wouldn't I be okay?" I shoot back. Pulling myself gingerly to my feet, I twirl the shower knob, and warm water pours down.

"Sweetheart?" My mom is shouting now to be heard above the pounding water. "Are you sure you're not sick? Your bed doesn't appear slept in..."

I flick a switch, and the bathroom fan whirrs on. "Sorry. Can't hear you!" I yell and hop into the shower.

When I finally crack open the bathroom door, peering warily into my room to make sure my mom isn't sitting on my bed, the clock on my nightstand reads 10:08. Mom is nowhere to be seen, so I slip into the room and pull clothes out of my dresser. A gleam of red sparkles in the corner of my eye, and I turn toward the bed and let out a groan.

A cocktail dress is spread across the coverlet. The color is one of my favorites, a deep purplish red, what my grandpa would call burgundy. I walk forward and run my hand gently along the skirt, feeling the silky chiffon of the fabric. A ruffled waistline joins the skirt to the bodice, which is lace applique with tiny gems scattered over it. A sweetheart neckline and long sheer sleeves complete the stunning concoction. I have to hand it to my mom. The dress is tasteful, but at the same time alluring. I will look gorgeous and desirable in this dress without even a hint of sluttiness.

Or I would if I was going to wear it.

Two minutes later, clothed in a baggy shirt and cutoffs, I barge into the dining room and fling myself onto my chair. "What's the deal with the dress, Grandpa?"

He raises his eyebrows. "Good morning to you too."

His tone provokes a hot and irrational blast of fury. The intensity of the emotion shocks me. We go through a similar scene most mornings, and usually I feel mild irritation, but nothing more. I force myself to speak evenly. "I'd like an answer to my question."

Grandpa reaches across the table to lift the cover off the dish of sausages and potatoes. The smell hits me, and I know what's going to happen. Shoving my chair away from me and choking, "I'll be right back," I sprint up the stairs, praying I make it to my bathroom. I do, but only just. Puke splatters the edges of the toilet seat as I choke and retch.

*Dear God, how am I going to make it through this?*

Breathing heavily, I use the edge of the sink to pull myself to my feet and survey myself in the mirror. Yep, I look as awful as I feel. Plugging my nose with one hand, I clean up the toilet and flush. Then I dab blush onto my cheeks and quickly brush my teeth.

I can't throw up again. They'll get suspicious if I do.

I pull my iPhone 3G out of my pocket, Google *what to do about morning sickness* and click the Mayo Clinic page. Skimming through the recommendations, I frown. I guess I'm going to be substituting dry toast for my usual six sausages. I stuff the phone back into my pocket, shaking my head. *Let this be a dream. Please, please let me wake up soon.*

As I re-enter the dining room, Mom scans my face, worry etched on her brow. "Honey, are you okay? Are you sick?" Grandpa glances up as well, his eyes questioning.

The smell of sausages is urging me to hurl again, and irrational fury is still coursing through me. "I'm fine, okay?" I snap, sinking into my chair and picking up a piece of toast. Hurt tears fill her eyes, but she blinks them back and reaches across to serve me some sausages. I smack her hand away, hard, as it nears my plate and two sausages fly onto the table, splattering grease stains. She gasps. "I'm not three! I can serve myself!" I snarl at her.

"Rachel!" Grandpa's voice is like thunder. But it's the sight of Mom, sobbing as she tries to scrub out the grease stains with her napkin that really gets to me.

"Mom," I say, catching at her wrist. "Don't. I'll do it."

She shakes her head, crying harder.

"Mom, please stop. I'm sorry. Let me do it."

"I don't understand why you hate me so much," she gasps, still rubbing violently, as tears pour down her cheeks.

"I don't hate you, Mom."

"You do!" she wails. "I try to show you I love you. I try to buy you gifts. I try to do things with you. But you push me away. Every time. I think you wish I had died instead of your father."

My heart plummets. Sometimes, on my worst days, I have thought that very thing.

"Mom," I start weakly, unsure how to finish the sentence.

"You won't go to the salon with me. Any clothes I buy you, you stuff in the back of your drawers and never wear. You grudgingly have breakfast with us in the mornings and leave the house as quickly as you can as if you can't wait to get away from me." Tears are sloshing onto the tablecloth by now, and Grandpa grimly reaches into his breast pocket for a handkerchief to hand her.

"Mom, I'll go to the salon with you today."

She shakes her head, tears still falling thickly. "You don't want to."

I force a bright, cheery note into my voice. "I want to, Mom. Come on. Let's go together."

She sniffs. "You really do?"

Something in the pit of my stomach twists at the lie, but I give her my most disarming smile.

"Of course, Mom. I'm sorry I was horrible. I...I'm not feeling well. A little queasy. Must be something I ate last night." Mom catches hold of my hand and gives it a squeeze. I resist the urge to yank my hand away. I hate physical touch.

Grandpa gives a slight cough, and I turn expectantly toward him. "I'm glad to hear you are going to the salon with your mother, Rachel. I'm sure you remember the little dinner party I was telling you about in June. It's tonight. The dress is for you to wear. The gentlemen will be here at 6pm."

He is avoiding me, concentrating deliberately on the sausage he is cutting up. I stare at him. I had told him no dinner party. That I'd rather die than marry some random person. I thought I had been clear and he'd given up on the idea. But no. He had gone behind my back to get his own way. And he thought I would just go along with it?

Usually, my anger is red. Bright and flashing. Screaming and shouting. Quickly there and quickly gone. But now, my anger is white. Icy and cold, slicing underneath my consciousness. Instead of blurring my ability to think, it seems to sharpen all my senses. My grandfather is dabbing his mouth with his napkin, slowly and deliberately, clearly poised for a fight. I feel my mother gazing at me, gripping my hand, terrified and imploring. Clenched in my opposite hand, I feel the sharp ridges of the toast dig into my palm.

And one thought pounds through my mind over and over and over. *I am pregnant. I am pregnant. I am pregnant.*

They don't know. They don't care. None of them. Not my mom who yearns for a perfect daughter. Not my grandpa who views me as a pawn. Not the jerks who are coming to my grandpa's dinner party to find out if I'm hot enough to consider marrying.

I know what I'm going to do.

I smile charmingly at Grandpa. "six o'clock it is. Should be fun."

Downstairs the doorbell rings. I sit up on my bed, rubbing my eyes. I don't remember falling asleep. But that must be the guys downstairs.

"Damn!"

I catapult out of bed and race to the mirror to check that I haven't completely wrecked my eye makeup. I sag with relief as I realize it's still perfect. Then I shoot upright as I hear voices downstairs. Ripping off the flowy top and jean shorts I wore to go to the salon with Mom, I gently pick up the burgundy dress and pull it over my head. The chiffon slides around me in whispering waves, and with a pang, I wish the circumstances were different. If things were different, I could be ecstatic in a dress like this.

But things aren't different. I reach back to pull up the zipper. What I need is to talk to Cat. I need to figure out what to do. But first I'm going to deal with this situation. And after the night I have planned, I don't think Grandpa will mind if I'm out of the house. He might prefer it to keep himself from committing murder.

There is a light knock on my door. "Rachel, dear? The gentlemen are here."

Gentlemen. Ha.

"I'll be right down, Mom," I say sweetly. I slide into the black high heels with swirling cutout designs encasing each of my feet and turn to survey myself in the mirror. My ebony hair is freshly washed and styled, hanging in natural curls around my face. My makeup is perfect. The chiffon skirt rustles around my knees, and paired with the shoes, creates the illusion my legs are longer and more slender than they actually are. I'm ready.

"So, Cooper," I say, swallowing a mouthful of succulent steak. "I hear you're still interested in video games?" I keep my tone light and pleasant. For the moment.

So far, the dinner has been just that. Light and pleasant. The half hour before the meal was easily filled with introductions and desultory chitchat. Appetizers and drinks were served. Luckily, my age prevents my abstinence from alcohol being remarked upon. I managed to stay away from the two men I wanted to stay away from, focusing my attention on the others. Now everyone is seated around the dining room table while two of grandpa's best waiters from the restaurant hover silently in the background to replenish dishes.

I can tell all the young men are impressed with me. Fine feathers apparently make this bird fine. Their admiration gives me a heady sense of power. And it makes me reckless.

Cooper swallows his mouthful of gruyere mac and cheese too quickly and chokes. I smirk slightly, watching his round, red face grow redder as he retches and swigs water. "Yes, yes, I do," he gasps.

I raise my eyebrows slightly. "Do tell."

Cooper has finally managed to catch his breath. He glances around the table and then gives me what I imagine he thinks is a charming smile. "Well, right now I'm really into *God of War: Chains of Olympus*. I like how it incorporates Greek mythology and monsters and stuff. Basically, how it goes is that you as the player are Kratos who has teamed up with Athena to find the Sun God and restore light to the earth. And I'm super excited for *Star Wars: The Force Unleashed* to come out. In that one,

Vader takes on this apprentice named Galen, also known as Starkiller, to try to conquer the galaxy..."

I give a pointed yawn and cut through his prattle. "You know, I was reading an interesting article about video games today."

He trails off and adopts a polite, attentive air, but I can see the annoyance in his eyes.

"It drew a strong correlation between video games and the current obesity epidemic." I pointedly inspect his stomach, which protrudes well over his belt. Grant gives an unwilling snort of laughter which he quickly suppresses. Cooper turns bright red. I continue smoothly, "I thought you might find the information interesting, Cooper, given your fascination with video games and your..." I pause significantly to eye his paunch again, "your build."

A muscle jerks in Cooper's jaw. He puts his knife and fork down with a sharp click on his plate and pushes back his chair. "Mr. King, may I ask where your bathroom is?"

Grandpa turns the glare he was giving me into a painful smile. "Certainly, Cooper. Right down the hall. First door on the left."

Cooper strides out of the room, shutting the door significantly harder than necessary. Grandpa is trying to catch my eye, but I ignore him.

"Grant, how are the CPA exams going? I hear you've passed two."

Grant grins at me, and I'm disarmed for a moment by his gap-toothed smile, but I harden my resolve. "They are tough, let me tell you. I failed the first one before passing it, and I barely scraped a pass in the second. Studying like mad for the third."

"So is marathon running a coping mechanism?"

His brow furrows. "I'm sorry, I'm not sure what you mean by coping mechanism?"

I give a light laugh. "Well, I've always considered accounting the most boring career anyone could possibly have, so I thought maybe you needed something to vary the monotony. But, picking marathon running as something to vary monotony...oof, maybe not your brightest move. Arguably, the most boring sport in existence. Running. And running. And, just for variety's sake, a little more running."

Clearly miffed, he tries to pass it off. "Well, you know, when you put it like that—"

I steamroll over him. "Or maybe you just needed a sport conducive to those legs. You must be able to go a mile a minute with those props. Ooh, and I bet you can jump! I'm sure Doc Rivers has been calling your number. Or maybe," I study him critically, "maybe he needs a little more...musculature? The gangly, daddy-longlegs impression is perfect for an accountant, or maybe even a marathon runner, but the NBA might want a little more brawn."

Not the most original insults, but Grant appears at least mildly affronted.

"Rachel!" Grandpa hisses between his teeth, but I pretend not to hear.

"Gavin," my voice trails away as his gaze locks on me. He really is handsome, in a very Edward Cullen kind of way. It wasn't just my alcohol-soaked brain. My insides start to tremble as his gaze slides over me. A very slight smile twists the corners of his mouth. He knows who I am. And he knows what I look like without this dress. The thought makes me want to vomit my steak all over the pristine white tablecloth.

"Yes, Rachel?" His voice is soft and silky. Maybe he really is a vampire.

As always happens with me, fear turns to anger. I make my smile steely. "You enjoy alcohol. Or so I've heard." It isn't really a question.

He gives a mild chuckle, clearly wise to what I'm trying to do. "It's no crime to enjoy alcohol, Rachel. You enjoy certain kinds yourself. Or so I've heard." The danger in his voice is clear.

I toss my hair over my shoulder. "You must have been misinformed. I'm only eighteen. Be that as it may," I wave a hand lazily, "I would never have guessed you work as an outdoor photographer. Your complexion doesn't exactly reflect your career." I decide to use my spastic thoughts as insult fodder. "Or maybe you have a secret? Western Washington is the place, after all, for sun-hating, snow-white folks."

He throws back his head and laughs. "A vampire? Is that really the best insult you can come up with? Not exactly original, Chel."

His use of my nickname, which I must have let slip that night at the bar, only adds fuel to my fury. But I know he is smarter than Cooper and Grant. He knows that for whatever reason, I am being offensive on purpose, and he is refusing to be offended.

I decide another angle might work better on him. I give my best sorority girl giggle and bat my eyelashes exaggeratedly. "Oh my God, you got me!" I put a hand to my throat affectedly. "But it's not an insult, sweetheart. Girls *love* men like that."

He raises his eyebrows at me, and I see a flicker of doubt behind his eyes. He is trying to deduce how much of my sappiness is real.

I give him a simper. "No, really, your complexion is *so* hot. I'd totally choose you over Taylor Lautner. Oh, geez!" I clap my hand to my mouth and let out another high-pitched giggle. "I shouldn't have said that!"

I am nauseating myself with this performance, but it's working. I can see it in the contemptuous smile twisting his lips.

I turn to the man on my right, whom I have ignored the whole evening. *Let's get this over with. Might as well keep up the ditsy routine.*

He isn't watching me but his fork, which he is twirling between his fingers. When he feels my gaze, he glances up. My stomach drops. His bright-green eyes are sparkling with mirth behind his square glasses. He is clearly choking back laughter. And in that moment, I know none of my tricks will work on him. Which makes me hopping mad.

"Bart— I mean, Barton." I kick myself mentally but give another giggle to cover my mistake.

"Bart is fine, Chel. We have known each other since you were six." He's smirking at me, and for some reason, the expression seems familiar. I give myself a mental shake. Of course, it seems familiar. I saw him every day for his last two years of high school.

I ignore the memories. "So, Barton, I hear you're quite the celebrity these days. Youngest Chief Human Resources Officer in American Seafood's history? Wow." I give an exaggerated sigh. "So intimidating to poor little me."

Bart chokes. Everyone at the table stares at him as he gasps and splutters. He laughs so hard that he has to use his napkin to wipe his streaming eyes. The whole situation is slightly ludicrous. Grandpa is sitting at the head of the table resembling a bear that was stuffed with a snarl on its face. Mom is emitting nervous, polite little giggles, as though trying to ease everyone through Bart's awkward moment. Cooper is gawking at Bart as though he's not all there. Grant is grinning, eyes scanning between Bart and me as though trying to decipher the joke. Gavin is gazing out of the darkening window with a bored expression.

But I don't find it funny. My heart is hitting my ribs so hard, I think it is trying to get out. Scars I thought had healed three years ago tear wide open. Without consciously deciding to, I find myself on my feet, and he's not laughing anymore.

"Go on! Laugh!" I hurl at him, and he stares up at me, wide-eyed, an indecipherable look on his face. "Isn't that all you've ever done? Because I'm just the snarky, opinionated little girl you've known since she was six, who's not pretty enough or easygoing enough for the handsome, overachieving Bart Drossel to take any notice of."

He's on his feet now, moving toward me. "Chel, listen..." We've both forgotten that we're not alone in the room.

I stumble away from him, catch my stupid high-heeled shoe, and feel my ankle turn. Reaching down, I yank the shoe from my foot, ignoring the twinge of my ankle. I hurl the stiletto away from me and hear a splintering crash. It must have hit a piece of expensive bric-a-brac.

There is a collective gasp, and Mom squeals.

"It doesn't matter, Bart!" I'm shouting. "I'm over you! I'm over your green eyes and your weird sense of humor and the way you're nice to everybody and your stupid butt chin! You can't get to me anymore. Just stay away from me!"

He starts walking toward me again, beginning to say something. But I whirl and tear from the room, wobbling in my one high heel, ignoring the pain in my ankle, knowing only that I need to get away from Barton Drossel. As far away as humanly possible.

# Chapter 3
## Memory Lane

I sit on the docks and stare out across the Straits. My earbuds are in, and Josh Groban is crooning "So She Dances" in my ears. My throat is so thick it hurts, and my eyes keep stinging, but the tears still won't come. I don't think I know how to cry anymore.

Flashes of memory are breaking across my consciousness, and I try vainly to shove them back. I've pushed those memories into the back closet of my mind for years. I can't take any more pain tonight. My heart is bleeding already.

But maybe I need to remember. Maybe it's like Cat says. You can't be free of a thing until you acknowledge it first. Or maybe I'm just too tired to keep fighting.

Sometimes it feels like I've been in love with Barton Drossel my whole life. We met when I was six and he was nine. He was staying with his mom for the summer. Our moms introduced us one day at the park, and I immediately challenged him to a contest of who could swing higher on the swing set. He agreed good-naturedly, but my legs were no match for his nine-year-old ones. Determined to impress him somehow, I launched myself off the swing at the height of its arc. Landing badly, my ankle wrenched, and I cried. He hoisted me onto his back and carried me to where our moms were visiting. Later, when I was peering miserably out of my bedroom window and wishing Dad would come home to cheer me up, I heard a patter of rocks on my window. Seeing Bart smiling in the tree outside, I hopped out of bed—-with a sharp howl as my ankle took the full force of my weight—and let him in. He was clutching a handful of dandelions.

"How're you doing?"

"Okay, I guess." I got gingerly back into bed and propped my ankle back up. "Show-off," I added as an afterthought.

He grinned. "I probably should have let you win, since you're a little kid. That's what my mom said."

I spluttered with indignation. "I am NOT a little kid!"

He cocked his head side to side in a clear expression of skepticism. I huffed and crossed my arms, glaring away from him. "Well, you can have these anyway," he finally said, thrusting his handful of dandelions under my nose.

I spared them a glance and then returned to my glare. "Dandelions aren't even real flowers."

"Yeah, they are. George Washington Carver said, 'A weed is only a flower in the wrong place.'"

I didn't plan to display my ignorance by asking who George Washington Carver was. "My dad buys my mom roses. Those are pretty."

He scoffed. "I wouldn't bring you roses. They mean you're in love with somebody."

I stiffened. "I don't want dandelions. If you're going to bring somebody flowers, at least do it right!"

Incensed, he stalked to the open window and chucked the dandelions out. "Happy?"

"Not with disgusting boys in my room!" I shot back.

"I don't particularly like hanging out with stuck-up babies," he returned, climbing out the window. I stuck my tongue out at his retreating form and waited in bed until I was sure he was gone. Then I limped downstairs and snuck outside to gather up the dandelions and put them in a glass of water for my room.

The next summer, my front teeth are missing, and Bart is obsessed with fishing. Every afternoon after I'm done with my homework, I run down to the docks to sit with him as he uses the new fishing rod his dad gave him for his birthday. He won't let me touch it because he says I'm too young and might break it.

"How come your mom and dad don't live together?" I ask him one day.

He shrugs. "They're divorced."

"Do you wish they did live together?"

He ponders for a moment. "They lived together until I was eight and toward the end, they fought all the time. Constant screaming and stuff. It was horrible. It's quieter now that they don't live together." He reels in his line for another cast. "I wish my dad was like yours," he says slowly.

I swell with pride. "My dad is awesome."

His gaze flickers to me and then out across the Straits again. "Yep."

"What's your dad like?"

"Loud. Ambitious. Successful. Never satisfied."

I frown. "What does ambitious mean?"

"He's always pushing for the next thing. A bigger promotion, a bigger house, a bigger salary. I wouldn't care so much if he was just ambitious for him, but he wants me to be the same way. I have to get straight As or he yells. He wants me to be class president next year." He jerks his line irritably. "I couldn't care less." He glances at me again. "Your dad likes you how you are. My dad wishes he had a different kind of son than me. He insists I should be into football and stuff, but I hate football. It's stupid. Just guys shoving each other around a field. I might like soccer or track, but Dad says those aren't real sports, just running around in circles."

I frown at him. "Football isn't stupid. My dad likes football."

He shakes his head wearily. "Your dad likes watching football. Nobody's forcing him to play."

"Does your mom like you how you are?"

"Mom likes writing. I'm not sure if she would ever care about me as much as her books. She didn't fight Dad for primary custody."

I feel a pang of pity for him but don't know how to express it.

"Do you need something to take your mind off things?"

He grins at me. "Sure."

I jump to my feet and give him a hard shove so he topples into the water. He comes to the surface, spluttering furiously and clinging to his fishing rod with one hand. "What is wrong with you?"

I smirk at him from the dock. "I know you know how to swim. And you're not thinking about what mean jerks your parents are anymore, are you?"

"Don't call my parents... Oh never mind. Give me a hand, Chel!"

I lean over to him and then quickly draw my hand back. "You're going to pull me in, aren't you?"

"No, I'm not. Come on, Chel!"

Satisfied, I lean out to him. Quick as a flash, he grasps my fingers and jerks me off the dock and into the water with a splash. Coming up, spitting water and coughing, I see that he's hauled himself back onto the dock and is laughing at me.

"Fingers crossed!" he crows, showing me the hand not holding his fishing rod. I glower at him through my streaming hair and grab the edge of the dock to pull myself up. He reaches down to help me, but I shove his hands away.

"Leave me alone!" I struggle fruitlessly to get a leg over the edge of the dock, before suddenly feeling hands under my armpits. Bart drags me up onto the dock, scraping my knees in the process.

I jump to my feet, giving him my best death glare. "I could have gotten out myself!"

He eyes me skeptically. "Oh, yeah?"

"Yeah!" I stomp away from him.

That night, I hear a familiar patter against my window and find him sitting in the tree outside. "What?" I demand.

His demeanor is contrite. "I'm sorry for pulling you off the dock, Chel. That was mean."

His capitulation takes the wind out of my sails. "It's okay," I mutter. "I started it, I guess."

"Hey, to make it up to you, I'll let you use my rod tomorrow. But if you break it, I swear I'll dunk you again."

"Really, Bart?"

"Really, Chel."

When he leaves at the end of August, I cry.

The summer I turn ten, I'm shocked when I first see him. He's different. His voice is deep, even deeper than my dad's, and there's a cut on his cleft chin, like he's been shaving. His arms and legs are super muscular, since his dad's been taking him to the gym to get him ready for freshman football. Oh, and he's like a foot and a half taller than me, when we were always about the same height.

When I just gawk at him instead of saying hi, he smirks at me. "Cat got your tongue?"

"Razor got your chin?" I shoot back.

He roars with laughter, and for the first time, puts out an arm and pulls me into a side hug. Something warm explodes inside my chest. "Still the same old crotchety Chel." I push him hard in the side and feel weird butterflies as my fingers brush the ridges of muscle underneath his shirt. Discomfited, I step away from him.

"There's a new girl next door. I think you'll really like her."

"Trying to set me up?" he chuckles.

I reach out to shove him again, but memory of the last time makes me curl my fingers into a fist and drop it to my side. "Fat chance. She's way too good for you."

He raises his eyebrows. "Oh, really? I'd like to see this angel."

I point behind him. "You got your wish." Cat has just come around the side of her house, carrying a bucket of gardening tools. She's singing under her breath, and her hair hangs in a long blonde braid down her back. Bart stares at her for such a long time that something unpleasant stirs inside me. Cat isn't that much prettier than me. And he's never looked at me like that.

At last, he turns back to me. "You're right. She is much too good for me."

Suddenly, I don't care to introduce them. "You wanna come watch *Back to the Future* tonight? Mom's out of town visiting Grandpa, so Dad and I are getting Chinese. Mom doesn't like time travel movies anyway."

He bites his lip. "Sorry, Chel, I won't be able to hang out as much this summer. I'm taking Business 106 online. And Dad's got me on this really strict workout schedule. I'm not gonna have a ton of time."

My heart sinks, but I force my face to remain neutral. "Whatever."

The corner of his mouth twitches. "How come you aren't with your mom? My mom said she was going to visit your grandpa, and she thought you were going too."

I feel a flush raising up my neck. "I...I had stuff going on..." I mumble. "Stuff I didn't want to miss..."

He nods slowly and turns as his mom calls that they need to go. As he's walking away, he yells over his shoulder. "*Back to the Future*'s a good movie. I think I'll make an exception from school tonight."

Bart moves in with his mom just in time to attend Dad's funeral. The whole evening is weirdly disjointed for me. Broken glass snippets of pain, cutting me over and over and over.

The sight of Dad in the casket, and the feeling of unreality. *Dad can't be dead. He can't be.*

The feeling of Mom next to me, shaking with her hysterical grief, while I sit ice cold and still, staring straight ahead with burning eyes.

The sound of the pastor talking about how Dad is with his Savior, Jesus Christ.

The taste of blood in my mouth as I clamp my tongue between my teeth to keep from yelling at the stupid people who come through the receiving line to tell me and Mom that this was all part of God's plan.

The sickly scent of flowers, rising in cloying waves until I'm sure I am going to pass out.

The sight of people stuffing their faces full of the extravagant buffet Grandpa had catered.

The feeling of paper napkins as I shred them unconsciously in my hands until the carpet around my chair looks like it's been snowing.

The sound of Dad's favorite hymn "It Is Well With My Soul" pouring from the loudspeakers, causing my throat to close up as I remember what a lousy singer he was.

The taste of bile rising in my mouth as people tell funny stories about Dad and laugh. Laugh.

The familiar smell of Old Spice from the man next to me, reminding me so forcefully of Dad that I can't stay there anymore.

I bolt from my chair, pushing through the crowded tables and chairs. Ignoring the onlookers and their whispers, I fight my way to the doors, yank them open and run down the long, carpeted hallway outside the fellowship hall. I pound up the stairs into the foyer and pull open one of the heavy front doors. And then, mercifully, I am outside in the cool night air. There is still a faint gold line on the edge of the horizon and the sky is smoky blue with stars just beginning to spark into being.

The back of the church is surrounded by trees. Like a wounded animal, I stumble into the shadows, yearning only to go somewhere where I can be alone with my terrible pain.

I want to cry. But the tears won't come.

My heart feels as though red-hot knives are being stabbed into it. I clutch my chest, trying desperately to still the pain, begging silently for tears because I know they will bring temporary relief.

Dad is gone. Dad with his high-pitched, dolphin's laugh. Dad with his glasses perched on the bridge of his nose. Dad with his enormous smile that seemed to light up the whole world. Dad whose warm arms around me made trouble melt away. Dad with his wisdom and ability to talk seriously. Dad with his goodness and his love for God that led him to treat everyone around him as though they were royalty. Dad with his anger over injustice. Dad with his romantic soul that made him bring home red roses for Mom as though they were still dating. Dad with metal shards in his hands and oil in his hair talking about a particularly ferocious battle with a tractor he had been trying to repair. Dad who had recognized my love for music and persuaded Mom to let me have voice lessons.

And memories flood me. Dad and I laughing over Garfield comics on Saturday mornings. Dad with tears in his eyes listening to me sing "Yesterday." Dad, Mom, and I running along the beach together with the wind in our hair. Dad acting as the intermediary between Mom and me, trying to help us understand each other better. Dad slow dancing with me at the Daddy Daughter Dance at school, tears slipping down his cheeks, as they play "Butterfly Kisses." Dad letting me drive a tractor around the lot at the agricultural repair shop he works at after everyone else has gone home.

I let out a ragged groan and lean my forehead into the trunk of a tree, relishing the bite of the rough bark into my skin, distracting me from my inner pain. A twig snaps behind me, and I spin around. Bart is standing a few feet away, his face faintly illuminated by the light coming from the church windows. His eyes are swollen and puffy.

"I'm sorry," his voice sounds husky. "I didn't mean to...disturb you...I just wanted to make sure you're all right..." His voice trails off and he shakes his head, angry at himself. "Of course you're not all right."

He stands for a moment, rubbing the back of his neck. "I'm really sorry," he says again and turns to go. I let out a strangled noise, and he turns quickly.

"Stay. Please." I manage to croak out as I collapse with my back against the tree.

Immediately, he sinks to the ground next to me. His knee brushes against mine, but he doesn't try to hug me or anything, for which I am supremely grateful. Our eyes lock, and then he glances away, like I'm naked or something. The silence stretches between us. He doesn't say anything. Our eyes meet again, and this time he gives me a faint grimace, his lips twisting as though he's trying not to cry again.

Finally, I whisper, "Talk to me."

"What?" He leans toward me.

"Talk to me. About anything. Just talk."

For a moment he bites his lip, and I wonder if he's going to ask a stupid question like, "What do you want me to talk about?" But then he says,

"I saw this movie the other night. *How To Steal A Million*. With Audrey Hepburn and Peter O'Toole. It was really funny. You see, the main girl's dad is this master forger, so he has tons of forged art pieces at his house—fake Van Goghs and Monets and stuff. And he sells them and gets tons of money because people can't tell the difference. Then a museum asks him to allow them to display the 'Cellini Venus' he has, and he lets them, but of course it's a fake. And he signs paperwork without realizing it, saying the museum is allowed to run a bunch of diagnostic tests on it which will reveal it's a fake. When the daughter hears about it, she's SUPER upset. And she decides to steal the Venus back before the tests can be run on it. But she needs help. One night when her dad was gone, she met this guy breaking into their house, and she thought he was an art thief because he was holding one of her dad's pictures. So she asks this guy—Peter O'Toole—if he will help her steal the Venus. And he agrees, not because he's an art thief—he's actually a private investigator of art fraud—but because he likes her..."

I allow Bart's voice to wash over me, forcing myself to follow every word, trying to fill my mind with images of Audrey Hepburn and Peter O'Toole to replace the ones of my father.

When he finishes the story, he goes on to talk about the trip he took with his father to Hood River, OR, last May and parasailing for the first time on the Columbia River.

"I was actually pretty good. I only fell down twice. Dad was awful. He was down more than up."

Then he starts talking about the new food truck across from Grocery Outlet. "Golly, their pulled pork sandwiches..." He smacks his lips. "And onion rings. And prime rib. And sweet potato fries. Texas BBQ isn't exactly on the diet my dad planned for me, so I've been limiting myself. Only once a day for the past week."

A gurgling laugh escapes me, and I see the flash of his teeth in the darkness. Something makes me suddenly lean against him and put my head on his shoulder. I feel him stiffen for a split second, but then his arm slides around me, and he squeezes lightly. His cheek lands in my hair.

"This will teach you to ask me to 'just talk' ever again." His fingers sketch quotation marks in the air.

"I don't think I'll ever feel like this again." The words are flat.

I hear a whoosh of air. "See? Call the paramedics to get my foot out of my mouth." His shoulders sag. "Seriously, Chel, I'm so sorry..."

I turn and put my hand over his mouth. "Shut up. Stop apologizing."

We sit in silence for about a minute. Then there's a sound.

"Geez, was that your stomach?"

"Give a guy a break! All that talking about the food truck made me hungry."

I leap to my feet. "Take me."

He clambers up as well. "Are you sure? Maybe we should go back inside..."

I stomp my foot, tottering on the emotional edge. "Take. Me. Right. Now."

He holds up his hands in surrender. "All right, *Your Highness*. We're gonna have to walk though. My great-uncle Wilhelm taught me to drive when I visited the farm during spring break, but I don't get my permit until next year."

I roll my eyes at him. "Stick in the mud. Everybody knows that driving illegally is part of growing up."

He gives me a look. "No thanks, sweetheart. I'm going to get in enough trouble for running off with you. It's not too far. Let's hike."

In twenty minutes, we're sitting on the grass outside of Grocery Outlet, and barbecue sauce is running down my face and hands as I rip meat off a rib with my teeth. I haven't eaten since yesterday morning—didn't feel hungry. But now, the prime rib is like heaven.

"Whoa, that pig's not going to run away, Chel," Bart says around a huge bite of his sandwich.

I stick out my tongue at him, and he mimes gagging. "Gross! Keep it in your mouth, little girl."

When I'm done and sit licking my fingers, he bursts out laughing.

"What?" I demand.

"You should see your face. If I've learned anything tonight, it's that ribs should DEFINITELY not be your first date food. Come here."

He dips a corner of a paper napkin in his water. I glare at him. "I don't need you to clean my face like I'm three."

"I'm not bringing you back like this. You can clean your own face, but you have to pass my inspection."

I sulkily rub the napkin over my face until he pronounces me presentable. "We better hustle, Chel. They're probably going crazy already."

The pain in my heart which had dulled to a background ache is starting to swell again, throbbing like an open wound. "I don't want to go back."

He reaches up to rub the back of his neck again. "Chel…"

I study the ground, fighting the constriction in my throat and trying to will myself back to the moment before when I was happy and the reality of Dad's death was distant and faint.

"Chel, we've got to head out. You have to go back to real life sometime."

I turn away from him, my breathing quick and shallow. "I don't want a real life without my dad."

"I know, Chel…"

"No, you don't!" I yell at him, my hands balling into fists. "You don't have a clue! Your dad is still alive! You can go parasailing with him every summer! You can talk to him anytime you like! You can hug him whenever! You can have an argument one day and know that he'll forgive you the next!"

Bart doesn't say a word, only strides forward and pulls me into his arms. For a moment, I fight him, but he doesn't let go, and eventually, I go limp against his chest, shaking with dry, heaving sobs. He strokes my hair gently, not saying a word until I finally go quiet.

"You're right. I don't have a clue," he says softly. "But we do have to go back." He takes my hand, and together we slowly walk away from the food truck.

"Okay, Cat. Okay. I'm ready." I run my hands through my hair and glance into the bathroom mirror one last time. "How do I look?"

"Gorgeous, and you know it," she grins up at me from where she's leaning against the wall, sketching something in a notebook.

"What are you drawing this time?" I peek over her shoulder just in time to see her tear Derek Allen's face off the pad and crumple it in her hand. I raise my eyebrows as she blushes.

"What?" she says defensively. "He has classic features."

My eyebrows raise higher.

"Give me a break, Chel! You've been bonkers over Bart Drossel since you were ten years old."

"I'm not bonkers over him," I snap back. It's her turn to raise her eyebrows.

"Is he or is he not the reason you've rejected eight guys in the last twelve months?"

"Okay, maybe slightly bonkers," I concede grudgingly. I study myself in the mirror for another moment. My chestnut hair falls in glossy waves around my face. My blue-green lacy top is simple but flattering. My jean capris fit me perfectly. My makeup is light, but tasteful, highlighting my narrow face and high cheekbones and bringing out the deep blue of my eyes. My only deviation from style is my earrings, which are tiny pulled pork sandwiches. Bart gave them to me the Christmas I turned thirteen, when Grandpa FINALLY allowed me to pierce my ears.

I look great. Hopefully great enough that the popular captain of the football team, student body president, and high school sweetheart will agree to go with me, a lowerclassman, to homecoming.

Cat glances up and sees me biting my lip. "Chel, if you're going to do this, you should do it already. I don't know why you're so worried. Bart has always liked you."

I grimace at her. "As a friend, Cat. As a little sister figure. As the cute little kid he's known since I was in first grade. I don't want him to like me like that, and you know it."

Cat shrugs. "I know. But you're clearly not a little kid anymore, Chel. Bart has eyes; he can see that as well as the next guy. The only way you're going to know is if you ask or else wait until he says something."

I bridle defensively. "If I wait, Bart will never say something. Like I told you, he still thinks of me as a kid. I need to show him I'm not. And he graduates this year. This is my last chance."

Cat sighs. "I didn't say anything, Chel. You know what my opinion is. We don't need to go over it again."

I open my mouth to argue, but Cat forestalls me. "You better skedaddle if you're going to talk to him. Practice lets out in two minutes."

I walk to the door, then run back to kneel on the bathroom floor and hug Cat. "Wish me luck," I mutter into her shoulder.

"You know I want the best for you, Chel," she returns, squeezing me tightly.

I hop up and stride purposefully through the bathroom door. I need to catch Bart before he leaves for the day. The Homecoming theme was announced today, and I know that as the week progresses, he'll be surrounded by girls begging him to come with them. I haven't seen him much this year outside of school. With football and his dual enrollment, he's pretty much swamped. A few weeks ago, he took me to the food truck again to try their new smoked gouda and bacon mac 'n' cheese, and then we walked along the docks and talked. It was nice, but I returned home feeling completely depressed. My crush on Bart Drossel had only deepened in the past years. With the confusing feelings he aroused in me came increased awkwardness whenever we were together. And with me, awkwardness translated into snippiness and an uptick in sarcasm and cynicism.

When I reach the football field, I catch sight of him immediately, talking to the head cheerleader, senior Sophia LaMarr. My stomach twists. Sophie is beautiful and popular among the boys. Not many girls like her, but I can't really judge her for that since I have the exact same problem. As I watch, she puts a hand on Bart's arm, trilling with laughter at something he said. He smiles down at her, shaking sweat-dampened hair out of his eyes and then walks away to collect his gym bag and backpack. I see Sophie hurrying to collect her own things and know she is hoping to walk off the field with him. How do I make sure she doesn't get her wish without making it seem like a race?

I quickly sit down near the exit to the field and put my head between my knees. I close my eyes.

*Wait for it... Wait for it...*

"Chel?"

I slowly raise my head. "Bart?" His face is inches from mine, which I totally didn't expect. He must have crouched down right after saying my name. I fight down an insane urge to lean over and kiss him.

"You okay?"

"Yeah..." I mutter, watching Sophie stalk past us with her nose in the air. The second she's out of earshot, I give him a wide grin and hop up.

"Chel." His tone changes from concerned to exasperated.

"You're better off without her fawning all over you."

The corner of his mouth twitches, and I know he's fighting a smile. "Fair. So that's why you resorted to base deception?"

I tilt my head. "A brilliant strategy, you mean."

"Whatever." He shakes his head, the corners of his mouth still twitching.

We walk in silence for a moment. My heart is pounding, and butterflies are fluttering in my gut. *Come on, Chel. Come on. Just do it.*

"So how are—"

"I was wondering—"

Our words collide in midair, and we both stop, grinning foolishly.

"You go," I say.

"It was nothing important," he says.

"Go," I insist.

"How are things with your mom and grandpa?"

I roll my eyes. "Same old, same old. Mom expects me to be her perfect little princess and is hurt because I'm not. Grandpa is trying to prepare me to be his restaurant successor while ignoring the fact that I've told him ad nauseam I'm not interested. Whatever." I shrug. "I avoid them as much as I can and console myself knowing eighteen is only three years away."

He raises one eyebrow at me and opens his mouth, then shakes his head and looks away.

"Just say it," I growl. "You think I should make more of an effort in our relationship and try to understand their point of view. Like Cat."

His eyebrow quirks again. "Cat's a smart girl."

"Was," I mumble, kicking a pinecone off the sidewalk. "Before she started thinking the sun rises and sets in Derek Allen's face."

Disgust contorts his features. "Derek Allen? That," he pauses, and I know he's holding in the names he'd really like to use, "loser jerk who's junior class president? She likes him?"

"Yep."

He shakes his head, clearly upset. "Have you talked to her? You know what he's like. And Cat's so…good. I never would have seen her falling for someone like Derek."

I throw up my hands. "I tell her how much I hate the guy pretty much every time I see her, but she just thinks I'm unreasonably prejudiced. She claims I don't like people in general."

His mouth twists, and I punch him in the arm. He mock groans and clutches at his elbow. "Oh, it hurts, it hurts," he intones, in a perfect Peter O'Toole impression.

"It's the other arm," I retort.

"The infection is spreading," he returns with dignity, and we both burst out laughing.

"So, Calvin Klein," I start, "the Homecoming Dance." He widens his eyes, combs his fingers through his hair until it frizzes around his face and gives me his most Emmett Brown face. I smirk and force myself to continue. "I was wondering if"—I lick my lips, unable to meet his gaze,—"if you wanted to be the McFly to my Lorraine?"

*That was so idiotic. Why on earth did I think it would sound clever?*

"And knock out your escort?" he asks, playing along, but when I peek at him through my lashes, I can see his smile is a little strained.

"Uh, not that part. The going to the dance together part."

He stops walking and turns to face me. His hand goes to the back of his neck—his usual stress sign. "Just to be clear…as friends, right?"

My heart plummets to my toes. I clench my jaw and look away from him. *I knew this would happen. But I can't stop now.*

I force myself to face him. *This would be a whole heck of a lot easier if he weren't so attractive. If I weren't completely crazy about him. If my heart rate didn't double every time he smiles at me.*

"No," I manage to get out. "Not as friends. I...I like you, Bart. A lot." He closes his eyes, and my heart sinks even lower. "We've been friends for a long time. And I thought maybe we could try going to the next stage. I mean," I force myself to laugh, "anyone who could like me as a friend for as long as you have probably has a significantly better chance of liking me as a girlfriend than any of the guys who think I'm hot, but don't have a clue what I'm really like. And couldn't stand me if they did have a clue."

He's silent so long I finally glance up at him through my lashes. My heart skips several beats as I stare into his green eyes. I'm tall for a woman, so he's only a few inches taller than I am and our eyes are close to level. He looks away.

"Chel, you know I like you. I always have. Okay, you pushing me off the docks might have dampened my liking a little," he gives a weak, artificial chuckle at his own pun, which quickly dies at the expression on my face. He groans and puts a hand over his eyes. Then he lowers his fingers and fixes his gaze on me. "I don't think it's a good idea for us to start dating."

My insides feel as if they've been filled with lead. "Why?"

"You're fifteen. I'm about to graduate. Chel, I'm leaving in a month to start working for my dad's fishing company in Seattle. I'll be up in Alaska most of the summer. It's just not a good idea. An eighteen-year-old dating a fifteen-year-old who's still in high school? Long distance? It's a recipe for disaster. You'll probably find someone else. You have two years of high school left. There are lots of great guys who'll be here. On the spot. Able to pursue you and make warding off your admirers their top priority."

A lump swells in my throat. "I get it, okay? I'm too young. Too babyish. Still in high school. And I'm not going to graduate with my bachelor's either like some people. I'm not good enough for you."

"Chel, that's stupid and you know it. I didn't say that."

"You might as well have done! Try just being a man and telling me you're not into me instead of making idiotic excuses! I'm not ambitious enough for you! Dad rubbed off on you, has he?"

Anger flares in his eyes. I had touched a raw nerve on purpose. "Wow, Chel. Thanks for that."

I know I'm losing him. As a friend as well as a potential boyfriend. Pain makes me reckless. "And the whole warding off my admirers thing? What's that supposed to mean? Why don't you say that you think my only thrill in life is attracting male attention? That I'd cheat on you down here while you're up in Alaska?"

"Chel, that isn't what I meant…"

"Then what do you mean?"

"I mean that you're beautiful!" He's yelling too now. "I mean that you're funny and popular and have a soft streak a mile wide for the people who are willing to dig deep enough to find it! And there will always be guys tripping over each other on their way to you. I don't think you would cheat on me, but I do think in a few months you might realize that having a long-distance boyfriend who's crazy busy isn't all it's cracked up to be. And then I'd lose you. Just like my dad lost my mom because she couldn't take his business and his being gone all the time and so she decided since she was alone half the time anyway, she might as well make it official and be free to live her life as she wished. Contrary to your opinion, my main goal in life is to NOT end up like my dad!"

I back away from him, my heart throbbing. "You're just like all the others," I whisper. "To you, I'm not worth fighting for. Or waiting for. Or going through inconvenience for. All you see is my appearance. And there are other beautiful girls, right? So, there's nothing special about me. In a few years when you're ready to settle down, there'll be another beautiful girl. A girl who won't cross you. A girl who isn't opinionated and prickly and might object to you working eighty hours a week. A girl who you don't have to make an actual effort to keep in love with you. And you'll settle for her. Because it will be simple and uncomplicated. Everything I'm not."

I turn and run, ignoring his yells to come back, hoping desperately he'll run after me. He doesn't.

"Wanna dance?" Tony grins sheepishly and gestures out at the wildly bopping couples in the center of the dance floor. He's a handsome, half-Italian guy from my chemistry class who plays on the high school soccer team. He's quiet and respectful, and all the teachers like him. When he asked me to the homecoming dance, the day after my fight with Bart, I said yes automatically. I almost wished I had waited to find some super obnoxious guy who would rub it in Bart's face that he had gotten to go with me. The next best thing was to look stunning and dance all night with Tony. I bite back a sigh. *I hate dancing.*

Giving Tony my most dazzling smile, I take his hand and allow him to lead me onto the dance floor. Shoving our way through the other couples, we find a relatively empty spot and begin to cut loose to the lousy pop song that's playing. As I wave my arms in the air, feeling like a supreme idiot, I catch sight of Bart dancing with Sophie LaMarr a few feet away. They're both laughing at Bart's stupid dance moves. He attempts an exaggerated moonwalk, looking completely ridiculous, but at the same time handsomer than ever because of his complete lack of self-consciousness.

*He took Sophie LaMarr? That little...cheerleader?* A red haze swims before my eyes followed by a stab of hurt. *Maybe I was wrong about him.*

I force my attention back to Tony. *I don't care about Bart Drossel. He can do whatever he wants. I don't care. I don't care. I don't care.*

But I can't help glancing back at him a few minutes later. Our eyes meet, and he gives me a hesitant smile and mouths, *"Next dance?"*

I return a smoldering glare for his smile and turn back to Tony with my brightest grin. *I wouldn't dance with you if you were the last person on earth, Bart Drossel.*

"Chel? You okay?" Tony must have caught the tail end of my glare.

I shake my head, as though doing so will dislodge Bart Drossel from my mind. "Great. Fine." The song winds down, and the DJ puts on a slow number. *I absolutely refuse to slow dance right now.* "Can you get us drinks?"

"Oh, sure." He heads toward the refreshment table, and as soon as his back is turned, I melt away into the crowd. I need some air.

Sitting on a bench in a shadowy corner of the school grounds, I bury my head in my hands. *Oh, why does it have to hurt so much?* I wish I believed in God like Cat. I wish there were someone who could help me bear the burden of my pain. Dad is gone. His absence is like a stone in my shoe, a niggling pain I can't forget. And now I've lost Bart. He'll never talk to me again. We'll never watch old movies and quote them at each other. We'll never visit the food truck. We'll never walk the docks watching the sun go down. I'll never feel his arms around me again, like I did the night Dad died. And I'll never love someone again like I loved him. Like I *love* him. The rational part of my brain tells me I'll probably meet someone eventually, but my soul rebels. I've given my heart to Bart over the last five years, piece by tiny piece. Will I ever get it back? Will I ever be able to forget him? All I can see in front of me is his face. His green eyes. His cleft chin. *Oh. Oh. Oh. I can't bear it. I can't.*

"Why on earth didn't you go with her?"

I freeze. Two figures are walking toward me across the grass, and I recognize the profile of the shorter one. With my heart in my mouth, I slip off the bench and into the trees behind it. Twigs crackle under my feet and I stop moving, pressed against a tree, praying they haven't seen me.

The voices draw nearer. They're heading for my bench. "I didn't think it was a good idea," Bart says slowly.

"Come on, man. She's the hottest girl in school." I recognize the voice of Fisher Davis, another member of the football team.

"Chel is a LOT more just than her looks."

Fisher laughs. "I guess you're right. She's bitchy, that one. She could slice you into ribbons with her tongue and laugh while doing it. Maybe you're right...that little friend of hers is sweet as sugar though. But I think she went with Allen."

"Yeah, I think she did. But don't use words like that, man. It's offensive."

"Whatever you say," Fisher mocks. "We can stay on her looks if you'd rather. She's...whewy!" Fisher whistles between his teeth. "I'd be willing to bear a lot of b—, sorry, cattiness for a good make out with her."

"You're disgusting," Bart says flatly. "You'd date a girl you dislike, simply for the physical part of the relationship?"

"Um, duh." I can hear the eyeroll in Fisher's voice. "I'm not a stuffed shirt like you. And besides, trying to find a girl who's sweet and sexy? It's like hunting for a unicorn."

"You just said Cat is sweet and good-looking."

"She's the only one in the school, man. Like I said, unicorn. Most of the girls are either nice enough and uglier than sin or mean and hot as hell. Now, if I had my ideal girl," a dreamy tone comes into Fisher's voice, "she'd be smoking hot, but never cross me. We'd do what I feel like all the time. And she'd be happy. No nagging, no fuss. It'd be awesome."

"If that's your ideal, Chel is certainly not the girl for you," I hear Bart give a slight chuckle.

"I guess not. I don't think she's any guy's ideal. Who wants to spend half his life arguing?"

The sound of someone calling Fisher's name drifts across the lawn, and he groans. "God," he groans. "Talk about nagging. Emma won't leave me alone for five minutes. See you later, man."

I glance around my tree and see Bart still sitting on the bench. As I watch, he gives a weird, choking sort of laugh and rubs his eyes. Then he gets slowly to his feet and follows Fisher toward the lighted doors of the school.

I sit in the darkness, ignoring the buzzing of my blackberry. Tony must be trying to find me.

I feel numb.

Bitchy.

But hot.

Bart never once contradicted what Fisher said. His ideal girl, like Fisher's, is a pretty walkover who will bring him his breakfast in bed every morning and live to gratify his desires.

*I don't think she's any guy's ideal girl.*

Fisher's words echo over and over in my head.

Eventually, I text Mom to come and get me.

For the last three weeks of school, Bart texts me almost every day asking to talk. I delete every message unanswered. We're in none of the same classes, and he has football practice every day after school, so I don't have to worry about running into him there. Twice he comes to our house and asks to see me, but when I hear his voice in the foyer, I lock my door and pretend to be sleeping when Mom knocks. One clear night, I hear rocks pattering against my window. I pull my pillow over my head.

The day after graduation, he heads for Alaska. He flies home for a visit with his mother the summer that I'm sixteen, and we have to spend one awkward evening when he and his mom come to dinner. I refuse to meet his gaze or speak to him. The next summer he's too busy to come to Port Angeles. I tell myself I'm happy. I tell myself I never want to see Bart Drossel again. I tell myself that I hope one of his boats goes down in the middle of the Pacific with him on it. I try to believe myself.

I come back to myself on the docks, cramped and shivering. My playlist has run out, and silence fills my ears. I was wrong. Remembering is rubbing salt in open wounds. Maybe the truth I really must acknowledge is that I'm never going to be free of Bart Drossel. Ever. My only consolation is that he'll never know that.

"Now the old king, seeing that his daughter did nothing but ridicule the people, making fun of all the suitors who were gathered there, became very angry, and he swore that she should have for her husband the very first beggar who came to his door."

~Grimm

# Chapter 4
## The Street Musician

"Rachel." I let the front door bang shut behind me in surprise. Grandpa is sitting on the couch in the living room, staring at me. It's past midnight. I was sure he and Mom would both be in bed.

The expression on his face causes my stomach to drop slightly. I'm not scared of Grandpa. But my soul feels like it's already received a pummeling, and I'm not anxious for a fight. Also, I've never seen him this angry.

"Sit." The word is a growl.

"I'm tired."

"Sit. Down. Rachel."

I flounce into the living room and throw myself onto the loveseat, wrapping my arms tightly around my middle. A mizzly rain was falling as I walked back from the docks, and my clothing is cold and damp. I clench my teeth to keep them from chattering. *Let's get this over with.*

"What's up?"

Grandpa stands. He's average height for a man, but his fury seems to add five or six inches. "I would like an explanation of your behavior this evening."

A spark of anger flickers inside me, and I pull myself into a more upright position. "You know, I was sort of hoping for an explanation of today myself. I thought I had made it quite clear I did not want this dinner to take place and that I refused to allow my love life to be dictated by your commercial interests."

"Unfortunately for you, Rachel, you live in my house. If I decide to invite friends to dinner, that is well within my rights. How dare you insult and ridicule guests under my roof?" His voice is rising. "You were abominably rude and offended Cooper and Grant very much, while making a spectacle of yourself with Barton Drossel! I will be lucky if Key City Fishing Company will even sell to me anymore after the way you treated the owner's only son! I knew you were selfish and self-centered, but I did not realize exactly how much until tonight! Your need to throw a colossal temper tantrum was clearly much more important than good manners, your mother and my feelings, and the family business! I am more ashamed of you than I can say!"

I leap to my feet. The spark of anger has become a raging inferno. "I'm selfish and self-centered? Wow, that's rich, Grandpa, coming from the man who planned to marry his granddaughter off to save HIS restaurant regardless of HER feelings!"

"I did not plan to 'marry you off'!" He is yelling now. "I planned to have a nice dinner and see if attraction arose between you and any of the young men, thereby satisfying a mutual coincidence of wants!"

I shriek with laughter. "Mutual coincidence of wants? What I told you I wanted was not to meet a single one of those guys! But you never listen when I'm talking, so I'm sure you missed that salient little fact!"

Grandpa turns away from me, his hands balling into fists. For a moment, there is a throbbing silence. Then he slowly sinks onto the sofa. "Rachel. I don't think you grasp how dire the situation at the restaurant is. We are barely making the interest payments on the company credit card. Every month it is a serious question whether or not we'll be able to pay our lease. I've given up my liability insurance because I can't afford it. I have to take the risk. Rachel," his voice holds a pleading note, "I have invested twenty years of my life into this restaurant. I don't think you understand what it means to me. I'm desperate. I'm watching my life crumble away from under me."

The image of two pink lines flashes across my mind, and another chunk of lead seems to drop into my stomach. "Welcome to the club, Grandpa," I mutter, sinking back onto the loveseat. For a moment there is silence. "Is Mom in bed?"

"No, she's upstairs cleaning." Some people stress eat. Mom stress cleans.

"Dad?" Mom's voice comes drifting down. *Speak of the devil.* But she sounds super weird. "Dad?" Her voice is coming nearer, and it's definitely shaking.

"Don't worry, LeAnne," Grandpa responds soothingly. "She's back."

Mom appears in the living room doorway. Her face is white as a sheet. Her wide eyes move from me to Grandpa and back.

"LeAnne? Are you all right?" Grandpa starts to get up.

"Rachel?" Mom's voice is shaking so badly she can barely speak. She holds up something small and pink. "What's this?"

My stomach drops into my toes. "Oh, God." I stare at her, feeling all the blood drain from my face.

"LeAnne? What is it?" Grandpa gets up and strides to where Mom is standing.

Her voice shaking, Mom mumbles, "I found it when I was dumping her bathroom trash can into a bigger bag..." Her voice trails off. Grandpa gazes down uncomprehendingly at the object in her hand for a moment. Then his face gets very red. In any other situation, the contrast between his face and Mom's would be ludicrous.

"No!" The word is a strangled croak. Then Grandpa rips the pregnancy test from Mom's hand and races toward me. For one terrifying moment, I'm sure he is going to start beating me up. I've never been afraid of him before. But I am now. "What is this?" Grandpa bellows, shaking the small, pink plastic stick in my face. "WHAT IS THIS?"

My heart is racing. "I'm pregnant," I whisper.

"What did you say?" Grandpa bellows.

"I'm pregnant," I say louder, forcing myself to meet his eyes.

I have never seen him look like this before. Revolted. Nauseated. He backs away from me as though afraid he will become contaminated if he stands too close.

"Whose?"

Gavin Fairchild's pale, handsome face swims before me. A different kind of terror rips through me. *If Grandpa knows, he'll force me to marry him. Somehow.* "I don't know," I lie. "It was a one-night stand." That much is true.

Grandpa's face twists grotesquely. He gulps, as though the air has suddenly become thin. When he speaks, his voice is quiet, but every word rings like a shout in my ears. "You are not having a baby. Set up an appointment tomorrow."

My mom buries her face in her hands, sobbing more uncontrollably than before. My stomach is clenching and unclenching rhythmically. I stare up into my grandpa's face. In my mind's eye, all I can see is the flickering, perfect black and white image that was Serenity at sixteen weeks gestation. "No."

Grandpa's fist comes crashing down on the end table next to him. "I will not have a granddaughter who everyone will soon know has no morals AND no knowledge of birth control living in my house! I will not allow your life to be ruined by a baby no one wants! You will never have a career as a single mother! No one worthwhile will marry you! I refuse to tacitly condone your loose and disgusting lifestyle!" His voice drops again to a low and deadly calm. "So tomorrow you will call Dr. Synet and ask how to go about safely terminating a pregnancy."

Terminating a pregnancy. I seem to feel Serenity's warm little body in my arms as she snuggles into me, hear her childish little voice. What if Cat had "terminated her pregnancy"? What if there was an aching blank in her life instead of a vibrant, beautiful little girl?

"No. I won't." I push myself to my feet. Terror licks at my resolve, but I force myself to focus on his livid face. "You might 'refuse to tacitly condone my loose and disgusting behavior,'" my fingers sketch air quotes around the words, "but I refuse to snuff out an innocent life for your or anyone else's convenience."

I try to stoke the fire of defiance inside me, but instead flickers of terror rise. *I can't have a baby. I don't know how. I can't do this alone. My life is over. What if he kicks me out?*

Grandpa's face works for a moment. Then he points to the door. "Get out."

I feel as though someone has dumped a bucket of ice water over me. "Wh-what?"

Mom clutches his arm. "Dad," she breathes, shaking her head frantically as tears pour down her face.

"I said. Get. Out." Grandpa's voice is rising as he shakes off Mom's clutching hands. "I've tolerated your rebellion for years. But not anymore. Not this."

My insides shake. "Grandpa," I can't keep a note of pleading from my voice. "Please...think...you don't mean it..."

Grandpa strides past me and flings open the front door. "Don't I?" His voice is like ice.

Mom lets out a wail. "Dad, no! Rachel, he doesn't mean it! Please, Dad, she has nowhere to go! It's the middle of the night! Think what could happen to her!"

Grandpa glances over at her, and I see his face soften slightly. But fury suddenly bursts through my terror like a geyser. *I'm not staying here another night. No way.* I stride through the door Grandpa is still holding open, not looking at either of them.

"Rachel! Honey, no!" Mom's scream rips at me, and I hear her running. She catches hold of my arm and tugs me to a stop. Tears are pouring down her cheeks as she chokes out, "He's just angry, sweetie. Don't do something rash. Think of your...condition. Come back inside. I'm sure both of you will be more rational in the morning."

I yank my arm from her grasp. "More rational?" I shout. "I am rational, Mom. Sleeping on it is NOT going to convince me that I should murder your grandchild!"

She gives a little gasp and tries to clutch my arm again, but I back away. "That's not what I meant," she whispers.

Terror and pain and fury are rolling over me in waves, and I can't keep the tumult inside. "You always side with him! Ever since Dad died! It doesn't matter that I'm your daughter. You always think he's right, no matter what he says or does! Tonight, you just stood by like a post allowing him to bully me! I'm done, Mom! I don't care! You'll never see me or the baby again. Because that's how you want it, right?"

"Rachel," Grandpa's voice has completely changed. "Rachel." He's coming down the steps toward us, and in the light from the front door, I can see that his face is gray. "Don't say that. Please. Come back inside. I shouldn't have said what I did. I reacted out of surprise and anger. Your mom is right. We should discuss it in the morning."

But I'm beyond reason. Numb to the fear and distress in both their faces. "Never," I whisper, backing away. "I'm never setting foot in your house again." And I run, covering my ears to keep from hearing the devastation I leave behind.

I don't know where I'm going. Gradually my run slows to a walk, but I don't stop. When I stop, I'll have to decide what to do. So, I walk, letting my feet take me where they will, trying desperately to push away the thoughts that batter my mind.

*I have nowhere to go.*
*No job.*
*No insurance without Grandpa.*
*I don't even have a toothbrush.*
*I can't take care of myself, let alone a child.*

My heart is hammering, pulsing to the beat of my fear. Shivers rack me, and I hug myself, realizing too late that maybe I should have at least grabbed an overnight bag from Grandpa's house. My clothing is still damp, and, although the rain has stopped, a cold breeze is blowing. I'm freezing. I need to get inside.

I pause, surveying the area. I am alone on a dim road with only a few scattered streetlights. Litter crunches underfoot. Dark alleys branch off between apartment complexes. I start to walk again, so quickly I'm almost running. Horrific images of what could happen to me flash across my mind, and I begin to run in earnest. My heart pounds to the rhythm of my feet, giving occasional jolts of terror as shadows shift in my peripheral vision. Convinced that someone is running behind me, I whip around for a moment and survey the empty street, then continue to run, realizing I mistook my own footfalls for pursuit.

*Where can I go? Where can I go? Where can I go?*

Cat's. Relief floods through me as the inspiration strikes. Cat will help me. Cat will give me a place to stay until I can figure out what to do. Cat will comfort me.

I continue to run, with purpose now, ignoring the start of a stitch in my side, heading in the direction of Cat's apartment complex.

In another block, I slow to a walk, gasping for breath. I walked to school every day in high school, but I never run. My side is killing me, and I massage the spot, gasping violently. Maybe it's my own heavy breathing, but I don't hear the music until I'm almost on top of the man playing the violin.

He screeches to a stop, bow sliding off the strings as he catches sight of me. I stop abruptly and begin to back away, my heart in my throat. Men who hang around on street corners at 1:30am in the morning are usually bad news.

"Hey." His voice sounds vaguely familiar, though I can only see his silhouette in the light of the building behind him. "Are you okay?"

"Uh…" I hesitate, trying to decide whether to run back the way I came. He steps closer, and his voice takes on a sharper edge.

"I know you. Girl whose Grandpa intends to marry her off to save this place?" He jerks his head toward the building behind him. With a jolt, I realize I'm standing outside Grandpa's restaurant. And now I know who I'm talking to.

"You're…you're the street musician… We talked the other day…" I know I'm incoherent, but it's all suddenly too much. "What are you doing out here?" I gesture to the empty street behind me. "There's nobody out and about to pay for your music. Well, except for me. And I'm afraid I can't really spare money at the moment."

"Are you okay?" he says again. "You don't sound so good."

Suddenly, I burst out laughing hysterically. "Fine," I hiccup. "Great. Peachy. Why would you think something's wrong?"

"Okay," he says soothingly, putting his violin down in its case. "I'm glad to hear things are so fantastic. Would you like me to drive you somewhere? Maybe take you home?"

I know what he's thinking, which only makes me laugh harder. What I wouldn't give to be able to have a drink. But obviously that's out of the question.

"Nah. I think I'd rather stay out here." I manage around my laughter.

He nods slowly, shoving his hands into his jeans pockets. Gradually my laughter dies away, leaving a hard, cold lump in my chest. "You never answered my question," I say.

He tilts his head in what I'm sure is supposed to be a questioning manner. Then, "Oh, what I'm doing out here?"

"Yep."

He gives a wry chuckle. "It's been a bit of a rough night. Music helps me to relax. Takes me out of myself. And this is where I'm used to going to play music."

"Couldn't you just play in your living room? It'd be warmer."

He shrugs one shoulder. "I guess. I just wanted to get out. There's something about being alone outside at night."

I shrug in return. "Whatever you say."

"Well, what are you doing out? If it's not to enjoy the quiet and solitude of the night?"

"My grandpa kicked me out."

He draws in a sharp breath. "Okay, your grandfather is starting to sound like the tyrannical father in a fairy tale. He literally kicked you out?"

I huff out a breath. "Technically, he was livid at the time and told me right before I left that I could actually stay, and we'd discuss things in the morning."

"Things?"

I hesitate. "What's your name again?"

"Clancy Jankovich."

"Clancy? Like *Man from Snowy River*?"

I can hear his smile through the darkness. "Something like that."

I roll my eyes, even though he can't see me. "Not to hurt your feelings or anything, but do you have any nicknames?"

He snorts. "Wow, aren't we the name snob. What's your name?"

"Chel."

"Chel?"

"It's short for Rachel."

"O-kay." The way he stresses the "kay" irritates me.

"Chel is cool. Clancy is pretentious."

"Tell me what you really think." He sounds half amused, half irritated.

"Hey, blame your parents. It's not my fault for noticing."

He ignores this. "All right, Chel, how come your grandpa kicked you out?"

Cold weight seems to settle in the pit of my stomach as the banter dies. I bite my lip. He's a complete stranger. Should I really be telling him anything? "We had a fight," I mutter.

His voice takes on a sardonic edge. "No kidding." There is a silence as he waits for me to continue. I hesitate, teetering on the edge of spilling my guts to him, but not quite able to take the plunge. A gust of wind swirls around us, and I tremble, my teeth clacking together.

"You want to go somewhere?" he asks. When I raise my eyebrows, he quickly backtracks. "Whoa, I did not think about how that sounded at all. Let me restart. You're obviously freezing. I know an all-night bagel shop a few blocks from here that will at least be warm."

I eye him, wishing I could see his face. For all I know, he's just playing the nice guy and actually plans to drag me into an alley and mug me. Or worse. Then, suddenly I don't care. How much worse can my life get? And I am desperate to believe he's as nice as he seems.

"What the hell," I throw my hands up. He grins and turns to gather his things. "I'm already knocked up anyway," I mutter to myself, so low I'm sure he can't hear me. But his head whips around.

"What did you just say?"

I still can't see his face, but something about his voice scares me. Maybe he's like Grandpa and regards single mothers as the scourge of society. "I'm pregnant," I say loudly and defiantly.

He's still and silent so long my teeth begin to clack together again. Immediately, he resumes securing his violin in its case. "I'm glad I didn't ask you to go out for a drink with me. Now that would have been insensitive."

I can't speak. The familiar lump is rising in my throat, but not for the usual reason. I don't know how to deal with kindness. Banter's easier.

"Yeah, I definitely would have refused to speak to you ever again if you had done that," I manage, trying to keep my tone light.

He stands up, slinging his violin case across his back. "Come on. Let's get the baby a sandwich."

I wrinkle my nose. "What kind of sandwich? This baby is a very picky eater."

His smile is evident in his voice. "Put the baby's mind at rest. This place has everything. There will be something she'll like."

"Or he."

"Or he."

We walk in silence. I cross my arms and try to unobtrusively rub some warmth into my shoulders. My clothing never dried properly from my evening on the docks.

"This shop better be close," I grind out. "Or I might freeze into a solid ice cube before we get there.

"Right here." He gestures up at a lighted sign and opens the door, holding it for me.

"You're super suave for a street musician," I remark sardonically.

He smiles slightly. "I am deeply offended. Pre-judging me because of my profession."

"Seriously though. Why are you so...sophisticated? What street musician uses 'profession' instead of 'job'?"

Bursting out laughing, he chokes and starts to cough. He hacks and hacks, finally gesturing to the board. "Just order," he manages.

Shaking my head, I turn to survey the illuminated plastic menu behind the counter. A slim girl with a pixie cut and nose stud, wearing jeans and a hoodie, ambles in from the back and observes me coolly.

"You ready to order?"

I shake my head. "Still looking."

She drums her fingers impatiently, then glances past me. Her sullen demeanor shifts completely as a wide smile breaks across her face. "Hey, Clancy! You're in late."

Finally managing to stop coughing, he comes to stand beside me, smiling back at her. "How's the late shift, Shannon?"

She shrugs one shoulder. "Bo-ring. And I'm so tired. But Hailey, the girl who normally works from ten to six asked me if I could take her shift since she needs to study for her finals. And I need money to start college next semester. Anyways," she waves an airy hand, "what's new with you?"

He smiles slightly. "Not much. I was playing late and ran into Chel here. You ready to order?"

Shannon narrows her eyes at me, then switches on her sparkling smile again as she turns to Clancy. "The usual for you? Hawaiian, cheddar instead of provolone?" *Wow. Definitely into him. And not exactly subtle.*

"I think I'm going to switch it up by trying whatever my friend has."

Pasting on a smile strongly resembling a grimace, Shannon turns to me. "All right, what can I get you?"

I glance at Clancy. The pressure is definitely on now that he's having whatever I'm having. "Uh, how about the Turkey Supreme?"

Shannon taps on her computer screen. "Two Turkey Supremes. Anything else?"

Clancy turns to me and raises his eyebrows. "Drink? Chips? Cookie?"

"I'll take a Sprite."

"Just water for me. I guess that's it."

"Okay, your total comes to $22.68."

Clancy pulls a battered leather wallet out of his back pocket. I fumble in my pocket and pull out a ten-dollar bill, what's left from last month's allowance, and hold it out to him.

"This should cover me."

"My treat," he says firmly.

"No, seriously," I protest, but he turns his back on me and lays three ten-dollar bills down on the counter.

"Keep the change." *A seven-dollar tip? No wonder she likes him.*

Ignoring Shannon's gushing thanks, he turns and leads the way to a booth in the very back corner of the restaurant. I slide into the side facing the door and examine the space around me. This place sure has character. Records and kitschy musical instruments dangle from the walls and ceiling. Brightly colored Fauvist pictures of Elvis and Madonna mingled with black and white photographs of John Lennon and Bob Dylan.

"So," Clancy says.

I turn back to him, waiting. His face is pale from the cold, and the tattoo across his cheekbone stands out in sharper relief. As I watch, he slides a hairband from his wrist and uses it to pull his many braids into a knot at the base of his neck.

"What are you going to do?"

The question throws me for a complete loop. I had expected him to ask me how I got pregnant or about the scene with my grandpa. I had been bracing myself to tell him it was none of his business, and I didn't want to talk about it. So the straight-forward, practical question he actually asked leaves me reeling.

"Um..." I start, having no idea how I am going to finish the sentence. "I..."

"Do you have a job?" he cuts across me.

"A part-time gig singing on Friday nights at O'Hara's," I mutter.

He raises his eyebrows. "I hadn't realized I was speaking to a fellow musician. That explains some things."

"What things?" I shoot back defensively.

He grins. "Geez, chill out. It wasn't an insult. It explains why you seemed so interested in my music. And why you always tipped a poor street musician so lavishly."

"You're better than any other street musician I've ever heard. And I normally don't even like violin."

He puts a hand to his chest in mock outrage. "Be careful what you say. My violin is my baby."

I hold up my hands in surrender, just as Shannon strides over with a tray. Wasting another dazzling smile on Clancy who is digging in his pockets for something, she carefully sets the tray down in front of us.

"Anything else I can get you?"

"No thanks. It looks great," I answer, giving her a tentative smile, as Clancy continues to be absorbed in the contents of his pockets. My only answer is a glare before she turns and stalks off.

Clancy finally raises his eyes. I lean toward him. "Okay, what is the deal with you and her?"

A dull red flush creeps up his neck as he smooths out a crumpled piece of paper he got out of his pocket. "To be honest, I didn't realize there was any 'deal' before tonight."

I huff out a laugh. "Come on. You're saying that you only just realized she is totally into you? How often do you come here?"

He lowers his voice, casting a glance toward the counter. "Once or twice a week after playing. But seriously, she's not normally like this. She was always friendly, but there wasn't any of this smiling, syrupy voice stuff."

I smirk and unwrap one sandwich, pushing the other toward him. "You shouldn't tip her so much. Any girl would be in love with a guy who tips thirty percent."

He toasts me with his half-unwrapped sandwich. "Nice mental math." Shaking his head, he continues to unwrap his bagel. "Maybe I should tone it down. I just like to tip a lot at places like this. The wages are horrible. But I don't want her getting any ideas about me."

*He is so likable it's unreal.* He lowers his gaze to take a large bite of his sandwich, and I notice with a weird little bump of my heart that his eyelashes are long, thick, and dark with a slight upward curl at the tips. *Why do guys always have the longest eyelashes? Bart did too.* My heart gives another bump, a hard painful one. "I think she might have thought you were the competition and that was why she needed to up the charm."

I take in my wrinkled, slightly damp party dress with the ratty black hoodie I grabbed as I ran out the door. My makeup is probably smudged from being out in the rain, and my hair is a frizzled, half-dry mess. "Right this second, I don't exactly look like stiff competition. More like a charity case you found under a bridge."

He grins and then bows his head slightly, with his eyes closed, hands clasped over his sandwich. I recognize the gesture. "Are you a Christian?" I ask, the second his head comes up.

He nods. "A really new one. I didn't grow up in a Christian home, but I have a friend who kept badgering me to come to church with him. I went a few months ago and the pastor talked about how Christianity is the only belief system where we can't work ourselves to God. Every other religion claims that if we work hard enough, God will accept us. And that's how humans tend to think. If you get a job, you get paid. If you study hard, you get good grades. If you work overtime, you get a promotion. But Christianity claims God did the work and offers acceptance and grace to us as a gift. That's so counterintuitive to how the world works it seems unlikely that humans would have invented it. I think it's the real deal."

He bites into his sandwich and speaks around the mouthful. "What about you?"

This is a conversation I don't want to have. I quickly bite into my own sandwich. "What about me?"

He waves a hand. "What do you believe? Do you have a religious affiliation?"

I chew to avoid answering, but he continues to regard me. "If you must know, I believe God is real, but that most Christians—not all, but most—are hypocritical, arrogant and judgmental. And God Himself couldn't care less about what happens here on earth. People claim He loves us, but I've never seen any evidence of it."

"Hey, there's a lot of beauty for the fact that He doesn't care about us."

I grit my teeth. "That's like saying that because Picasso painted beautiful paintings, he loved his wife. Which he didn't as evidenced by numerous affairs."

He opens his mouth, but I raise my hand. "I really don't care to talk about this, okay? Believe me, I've heard it all before. My dad loved Jesus. And he died a grisly death—a combination of testicular cancer, chemotherapy, and radiation. My best friend is a Christian. She has a beautiful little three-year-old girl whom her family, who also claim to be Christians, have never seen because they disowned her when she got pregnant out of wedlock. So, I don't need to be witnessed to. I know all about Christianity, and I'm not convinced."

I see he is struggling not to continue arguing, so I quickly change the subject. "Do you have a job other than being a street musician?"

"Yep. I work in the fishing industry."

"Here in Port Angeles?"

"All over. Fishing isn't exactly a sedentary industry."

A random thought comes, and I choke on a laugh.

"What?" he asks quizzically.

"Hey, I could marry you. My grandpa is set on me marrying someone in the fishing industry. And I wouldn't be a single mother anymore either." The thought of what Grandpa would say if I showed up with Clancy and said that I'd had a change of heart and decided to marry into the fishing industry after all, makes me burst into hysterical laughter. A concerned furrow appears between Clancy's brows, but I can't stop. I know I'm acting like a lunatic, but I lay my head down on the table and shriek with laughter, tears beginning to roll my cheeks.

"Chel," a man's voice says softly, and I raise my head, expecting for one mad moment to see Bart's green eyes looking into mine, but it's Clancy's brown ones regarding me with so much compassion and, weirdly, pain that I break down completely.

"Grandpa told me to 'schedule an appointment' for Monday. To get an abortion. And in the moment of defying him, I felt like a champion for this baby's life. But now? I'm not so sure. I have no job. I have no insurance. I don't even like kids. I'm going to be a horrible mom. And I'm going to bring this kid into a horrible life. We'll never have enough money. We're in the middle of a recession, and I probably won't even be able to get a job. No job means no money, means no place to live. Should I even bring a baby into the world when the only home they'll have is with a homeless single mom?" I lay my forehead on the table for a moment and then look up at him again. "I can't just take this child's life. I can't. But I don't even know whether that's just selfishness on my part. Maybe I just can't bear the thought of this baby haunting me every day for the rest of my life even though they would be happier not ever being born."

"Chel. Stop." Clancy's eyes are blazing as his hand clasps my wrist. I gaze at him in shock. He's so different from the laid-back, humorous guy I've been sitting with this whole time. "Stop talking like that. Stop thinking like that. How on earth could taking this baby's life before they've had a chance to live it make anything better? You're doing the right thing."

"But I don't have anywhere to live," I say. "I won't be able to get a job. I don't have any money saved..."

"You said your grandpa was angry," Clancy starts slowly, releasing my wrist, but I shake my head before he can finish.

"I'm not going back. Live with someone who would even suggest killing his own great-grandchild? No."

"Any place might be better for a child than living on the streets."

"No," I say flatly. "I'm not going back. I'll find some way to make money. And I'll find somewhere to live. Somehow." An image flashes into my mind of a slender, bleach-blonde woman in a skimpy dress and high heels standing on a street corner, trolling for business. I shudder involuntarily, pushing the thought away. My one experience of...that...was enough to convince me I don't ever want to do it again.

"What about the baby's father?"

Gavin's face appears in my mind with the usual sickening surge of cold. I shake my head again. "I—it was a one-night stand. And he's—–I don't know what I was thinking. But I hope I never see him again. He doesn't even know I'm pregnant, and I'm planning to keep it that way."

Clancy starts to rub the back of his neck and then quickly withdraws his hand to scratch his chin under his beard instead. He is silent for a long time, and I peer out of the window, knowing I should get up and head for Cat's, but for some reason this table in this little bagel shop feels like an oasis, a shelter from the turmoil of the outside world.

"I accept."

My head jerks around, and I blink at Clancy. "Excuse me?"

The corner of his mouth twitches. "You said you should marry me. I accept your proposal."

"I'm sorry... What?"

He's definitely smiling now. "I'm not sure I want a deaf woman for a wife, but I guess I'll have to risk it."

A hand seems to squeeze my heart. "Wow, this is really hilarious, Clancy. Thanks for making light of a horrendous situation."

He reaches across the table as if to take my hand, but I jerk it away. "I'm not kidding, Chel. Let's get married."

"What is wrong with you?" I leap to my feet, furious and oddly devastated. *I actually liked him.*

He stands too, blocking my way to the exit. "Chel, will you sit down and listen to me?"

"No! Get out of my way! You're either crazy or dying to get me into your bed!"

My shouting brings Shannon sprinting. "Um, what is going on?"

"Nothing." Clancy's hand lands on my shoulder, and I let him steer me back onto the bench. "We were just having a discussion, and it got a little out of hand."

Fuming, I wait for Shannon to head into the back, still casting suspicious looks at us. I had forgotten Shannon was here, and I definitely can't have her listening in. The second she's gone, I get up again.

To my surprise, Clancy doesn't move to stop me. He just says, "Chel, please." I stride toward the door. "Chel." I turn back and see him standing by the table, one hand stretched toward me. I'm ludicrously reminded of a tragic prince in some romantic movie. "Please hear me out."

I hesitate. He bought me dinner. He listened to me. He didn't press me when I shut down his attempt to talk about God. He tipped Shannon exorbitantly without wanting anything from her.

Maybe he doesn't want anything from me either. What harm can it do to hear him out? I walk slowly back to the table and slide into my side.

"Okay, I'm listening," I say stiffly.

"Think about it, Chel. I have an apartment. I have insurance through my job. I can support you until you can get a real job yourself. If we're married, you can stay home with the baby once he or she is born instead of paying through the nose for daycare."

"What do you get out of this?" I shoot at him. "Because if your idea is to get a free bedroom partner, forget it! If you come near me, I'll make you wish you hadn't."

"Wow. Is that really the kind of guy you think I am?" His voice is calm, but I can tell he's furious.

"I don't know what kind of guy you are! I only met you tonight. And what kind of guy suggests getting married to a girl he's only just met?"

His anger fades, and I can see laughter sparkle in his eyes. "Every prince in every fairy tale ever."

My own anger ebbs before his lightheartedness. He's like no one I've ever met before. "That's only because fairy tale princesses are idiotic enough to swoon into their arms."

He leans toward me, elbows on the table. "Chel, I know you think I'm crazy. But let me clarify a few things about what our marriage would be like before you make your decision. Firstly, I swear I will never touch you against your will. Secondly, I would expect this relationship to be a partnership in which you would be expected to pull your weight, by getting a job, helping around the house, etc. The same expectation applies to me. And finally, when this baby comes, I will be a father to him or her. I am offering a home to this baby as much as I am offering it to you."

I stare at him. "You are crazy." He holds my gaze for a moment and then shrugs and starts to get up. I grab his arm. "What if I told you I'm in love with someone else?"

"Are you?"

"Yes. He doesn't care about me, but I don't think I'm ever going to feel about anyone like I do about him. So if you're hoping some sort of romance is eventually going to develop between us, I'm telling you now, it's not going to happen."

"Okay."

"What do you mean, 'okay'? Doesn't this change things?"

"Do you mean, do I take back my offer? No."

I continue to scrutinize him, completely nonplussed. He reaches down to clear our trash onto the tray and takes it over to the garbage can. I watch in silence as he returns and stands with his hands thrust into his pockets, watching me. "I think I'm going to head out," he says awkwardly. "Do you need me to walk you somewhere?"

I shake my head, still unable to speak. He nods slowly. The silence stretches between us. Finally, he says, "Goodbye," and walks away. His hand is on the door when my voice comes back.

"What do you get out of it?"

He turns to look back at me. "I'm not sure," he says slowly. "An adventure, I guess."

He starts to push the door open. And I make up my mind. "Wait!"

I jump out of the booth. When I reach him, I stop and focus on his face. This is completely insane, and I know it. But I don't care. Or maybe like him, I'm hoping for an adventure. "I'm in," I say. "Now don't I get a ring or something?"

"The priest was called in and she had to marry the beggar at once. After that had happened, the king said, 'It is not proper for you, a beggar's wife to stay in my palace any longer. All you can do now is go away with your husband.'"

~Grimm

# Chapter 5

## Confessions and Confrontations

"Chel, are you out of your mind?!" I'm slumped on Cat's couch, in a half doze. Prying my sagging eyelids open, I force my eyes to concentrate on her. I'm so tired. I'm not sure I have enough life in me to have this conversation, but I also know I have to give her some sort of explanation.

"What gives you that idea?" I mumble. Cat glares at me from where she's sitting in the ragged La-Z-Boy she bought at a garage sale last summer and opens her mouth. Then she shuts it again and closes her eyes. I think she might be praying.

When she speaks again, her voice is much gentler. "I guess the first question is, how did you get pregnant?"

"Hey, I never thought I'd be having the bees and birds talk with you," I quip, but I know it's a lousy joke, and she doesn't crack a smile. I force myself into a more upright position. It's suddenly very hard to look her in the face.

"It was on my birthday," I mutter. "You know Grandpa and Mom forced me to have that big party? I knew it would be awful and, guess what, it was awful."

"Did something happen?" Cat says softly. I glance up at her for a moment and then return to my perusal of a pinkish stain in her carpet—a souvenir of Serenity's struggle against pink-eye medication.

"Nah. Nothing crazy." Memory surges, and I hear again polite, stilted conversation and my own awkward attempts to be social. I remember the strained smiles at my strange jokes and my own weirdly high-pitched laughter. That night wasn't like earlier this evening—I hadn't been trying to alienate anyone. I had actually tried to be likable, tried to endear myself to Grandpa's guests. Maybe that's why my abysmal failure hurt so badly. My ears were full of my own awkwardness and then my overcompensating gregariousness. I knew what Grandpa's guests whispered about me behind my back. "Strange." "Cynical." "Socially awkward." "Weird sense of humor." "Poor LeAnne, how did she get a daughter like her?" "At least she's pretty." I hated them for their words. But not nearly as much as I hated myself for the justice of them.

"It was the usual," I finally say. "I hate parties. I was awkward. The guests didn't like me but had to pretend they did. I wanted to scream after five minutes but had to endure four hours of it." I scratch my ear and force myself to continue with the story. "After everyone went home, I pretended to go up to bed, but actually snuck out to O'Hara's. I needed a drink."

I don't look up, but I know Cat has stiffened. We agree on next to nothing when it comes to alcohol. I've been drinking since I started singing at the gastropub. The owner likes having me sing, so he turns a blind eye when the bartenders slip me beers between numbers. Cat, who firmly believes in refraining from underage drinking, was shocked and horrified when I casually mentioned how much I liked pear martinis. She also objects to getting drunk—"drinking to excess," as she calls it—whereas I think there's nothing wrong with getting buzzed if you aren't an alcoholic and aren't driving.

She says nothing, however, and I plow on, eyes fixed resolutely at the carpet. "The only thing I wanted was to get so hammered that I could forget the whole damn—sorry, Cat—darn night. And how much I hated myself and my own inability to manage basic social interactions. So, I sat down at the bar and started ordering shots of vodka."

I stop abruptly as I feel her hand on my knee. She must have slipped across the carpet while I was talking, because she's leaning against the couch beside me. Our eyes meet, and hers are full of a pain I don't understand. But she still doesn't say anything.

My throat clogs up. I love her. I love her kindness and her gentle spirit. I love that I never feel judged by her, even though I know she disagrees with the choices I make. I love that she knows when to say something to me and when not to.

I swallow. "I'm a happy drunk. I get WAY more friendly than usual when I'm buzzed. So after about my fourth shot, I was starting to feel better. And then, this guy sat down next to me." I swallow again. "I knew what he was after, Cat. He was handsome and smooth and had already paid for my drinks. I wasn't so drunk I didn't know what he wanted. I did." I hang my head, my hair falling in black curtains to hide my shame. Cat's fingers tighten on my knee, an expression of mute sympathy. I force myself to keep going. To remember. "I wish I could say it was all the vodka. That if I'd been sober, I would have—I don't know—told him to get lost?" I choke on a dry sob. "But I don't think I would have. I don't know, Cat. I just...I just... It just felt like nothing mattered. And I thought, well, everybody says it's just pleasure. And I guess I just was bent on drowning in pleasure that night." I look up at her through my lashes, feeling dead inside as I remember. "I'm not like you, Cat. I don't think it's wrong to sleep with someone you love even if you're not married. But even I think one-night stands are...disgusting. No commitment. No responsibility. Just using the other person. But he was charming. And handsome. And the guy I'm head over heels for couldn't care less about me." I know I'm becoming incoherent, but I don't know how to express these things, and I wouldn't try to with anyone except her. "So, when he asked me to dance with him, I did. And when he asked if I wanted to come back to his place, I said I did."

I can't go on, and I know that she knows what happened next. Laughter bubbles up inside me, bitter and insane. "If you ever want to feel completely worthless, go out and hook up with random strangers, Cat. Success guaranteed."

"Oh, Chel." Her voice is choked with tears. She pulls herself up onto the couch and gets her arms around me.

Talking has brought all the memories of that night back, and darkness seems to engulf my soul. People always say you can't get innocence back. And you can't. Some stains don't wash out.

"I feel damaged," I say into her shoulder. "Dirty. Like I'll never be clean again."

I don't expect her to respond, because after all, what is there to say? But she speaks softly, words I don't recognize. "If you, O Lord, should mark iniquities, O Lord, who could stand? But with you there is forgiveness, that you may be feared."

I don't answer. But the words are ice on the burns of my heart, relieving the searing pain.

She holds me for a long time. Finally, she says quietly, "What are you going to do about the baby?"

I bite my lips. "I'm going to keep him. Her? I don't know...I guess I should probably go to the crisis pregnancy center, right?" I grip her hand and give her a weak smile. "You'll be there for me this time."

She squeezes my hand back, hard. "You know it. Are you going to go with an OB? Or a midwife?"

"Definitely an OB. No way am I having a baby at home. And"—I raise my eyes to her face,—"Clancy told me he has insurance. Clancy." I shake my head. "What kind of name is that?"

Cat gives a crooked smile. "Kind of awesome. If you like *Man from Snowy River*. Which I do. But, Chel," her voice sobers, "you do realize this guy could be telling you anything. Anything. You say he's a street musician, and, yet, he has insurance? How?"

"He's just a street musician by night. He has a regular job during the day."

"Doing what?"

"He's in the fishing industry."

"In the fishing industry?" Cat wrinkles her nose in suspicion. "That's helpfully vague. Chel, has it occurred to you that he's just looking for someone to have sex with whenever he wants? You're gorgeous and clearly in a rocky position. He's just trying to take advantage of you."

"I don't think he is, Cat."

"Chel! You're normally the cynical one, and I'm Miss Naivete. I don't like swapping spots!" She grabs my face and forces me to look at her. "Chel, listen. Listen! Think about the baby. He could...he could abuse the baby. He could be an alcoholic. He could be selling drugs out of his basement—"

"He doesn't have a basement. He lives in an apartment."

"Chel, I mean it."

I hang my head. "I know, Cat." Silence stretches between us for a moment. "If he's awful, I'll get a divorce."

"Do you know how much that costs?"

"I'll leave him then! Cat, I think he's a good guy. He says he just became a Christian."

"Because he thought that was what you wanted to hear?"

"No. I told him I pretty much hate God. Cat, what is my other option? Live in some trashy neighborhood for the rest of my life? Always be below the poverty line? Work my butt off to barely put food in my kid's mouth?"

"In other words, my life."

My shoulders sag. She doesn't sound offended, just resigned and mildly amused, but I can't contradict her. I would hate to have her life.

"I'm going to marry him, Cat."

"Why, Chel?"

I gaze out of her window at the darkness that is beginning to fade to gray. Morning is coming. "Because he's the exact opposite of the kind of guy my grandpa would like me to marry. Because he plays music. Because Bart Drossel is never going to sweep me off my feet. Because he might give my kid a better life. Because it will be a change from the boring, people-pleasing life I've had ever since Dad died." I study her face. "Are any of those good reasons?"

She shakes her head, but only says, "When are you getting married?"

"In three days. That's the waiting period in Washington. Clancy and I are going to the courthouse to get the license later today. And I need to stop by Grandpa's house to get my birth certificate. Cat, can I stay with you for a couple of nights?"

She nods, "Of course. Are you going to tell your mom and grandpa?"

"No."

"Chel, you should at least call them. They're probably worried sick."

"I don't care."

"You should." She pulls herself back up onto the couch next to me. "Chel, you're your mom's only child. How do you think I'd feel if

Serenity ran off when she was eighteen, and I didn't know whether she was dead or alive?"

I glower at her, but she meets my eyes with a steely look. "Fine," I snap eventually, throwing myself backward on the couch. "Whatever. I'll call them tomorrow. Then they'll know I'm not dead. But that's the last time I'm going to voluntarily contact them."

Cat seems to know this is the best she's going to get out of me. Standing up, she pulls a blanket off the back of the couch and drapes it over me. "Don't let the bed bugs bite."

I'm jerked out of sleep by a pounding on the apartment door. Bolting upright on the couch, I clutch the blankets around me, staring around. Watery sunlight is streaming through the window, and Cat is standing frozen at her kitchen counter, her gaze locked on the apartment door, while coffee grounds trickle unheeded from the open bag in her hands onto the countertop.

A faint wail of "Mommy!" from the bedroom at the end of the hall seems to pull Cat out of her temporary paralysis. She strides across to the door and peers through the peephole. "Chel, it's your grandpa. And your mom."

Grandpa pounds on the door again. Serenity wails louder. For one wild moment, I contemplate suggesting we pretend no one is home. Then I push the blanket off me and clamber to my feet. Smoothing the skirts of my crushed, battered party dress, I walk slowly past Cat and grasp the door handle.

"I'll get it," I say wryly.

"I need to go get Serenity. Do you need me to come back out here?"

I shrug one shoulder. "Probably better not. This is going to be a nasty scene. I don't want Serenity scarred for life."

She nods and heads down the hall. The banging has just started again when I wrench the door open. "Well, good morning."

Grandpa freezes, his fist still raised. He seems shocked to see me. "Rachel," he rasps out and then grabs me in a bone-crushing hug.

Since this was the very last thing I expected to happen, I don't have a clue how to respond. Mom is standing behind Grandpa, her face paper white. And the look in her eyes is the same as the morning that Dad died. As I watch, tears pour silently down her cheeks.

"Mom," I whisper.

Her face crumples, and she sobs. Grandpa releases me, and I walk slowly toward her and put one hand on her shoulder, unsure what else to do. She stumbles forward, burying her face in my shoulder, and I awkwardly put both arms around her.

"Chel," she chokes. "Honey, w-we were s-so worried. W-when you didn't c-come home!" The last words are a wail.

Embarrassed, I survey the closed apartment doors around the landing. "Let's get you inside, Mom," I mutter, pulling her gently into the apartment after me and shutting the door. I steer her onto the couch and gesture to Grandpa to take the La-Z-Boy. I remain standing.

There is a long, awkward silence broken only by Mom's hiccuping sobs. Finally, Grandpa and I start speaking at the same time.

"Chel, I'm so sorry—"

"Guys, I'm getting—"

We both stop.

"I'm sorry—"

"You go—"

I gesture at Grandpa and move to shove my hands in my pockets. Realizing I don't have any, I twist my fingers in the folds of my skirt. Grandpa clears his throat and speaks huskily.

"Rachel, I am so sorry for what happened last night. I spoke in haste and anger. I don't wish you to get an abortion. I have always viewed abortion as wrong and only suggested it last night because I was so upset by the suddenness of it all. There are other options. You could give the baby up for adoption." He pauses, then waves his hand as though to clear the air. "That's not the point. Rachel, the point is I am sorry. I would like us to start over. I want you to come home."

I twist my fingers harder and slide my focus to my mom. She gulps. "Rachel, please come home. Please, dear."

Their words touch me. But one instance of them acting rightly can't undo the past seven years.

I square my shoulders. "Thanks, but I'm actually getting married in a few days."

As a news bombshell, it is more than satisfactory. Mom lets out a choked little scream, and Grandpa jumps so hard his leg hits the coffee table, causing an old mug of coffee standing near the edge to teeter off, spilling its contents all over the carpet.

Grandpa doesn't notice. "What!"

I run into the kitchen and begin banging open drawers searching for a towel. I speak over my shoulder. "Clancy and I are going to the courthouse today to get a marriage license, and we're getting married on"—I quickly count on my fingers,—"Sunday, Monday, Tuesday. On Tuesday."

Re-entering the living room, I kneel down and clean up the spill. I expect yelling, but there is silence all the time I am on the ground. When I finally stand up, Grandpa's face is gray, and his eyes are popping slightly. He opens his mouth, but only a garbled sound comes out. Mom jumps up and lunges toward him, shaking his shoulder. "Dad! DAD! Are you all right? Answer me! Dad!"

Grandpa impatiently pushes her hands away. "LeAnne, I'm fine," he growls. "Sit down."

"I thought you were having a stroke," Mom whimpers, sinking back onto the couch.

"Not yet," Grandpa grinds out. Then he rounds on me. "Is this the baby's father?"

I force myself to sound nonchalant, although my stomach is beginning to tremble at the idea of explaining the situation to them. "No."

"Who the hell is he?"

At that moment, there is a rap on the door. I dart over and squint through the peephole. "Speak of the devil," I say and pull open the door. Clancy grins at me, his hands shoved deep into the pockets of his dark-blue jeans. The tattoo beneath his eye scrunches when he smiles and his tiny braids are twisted together in one long, neat braid down his back instead of his customary messy bun. His beard is cropped close and doesn't look scraggly. He's wearing a belt and a striped, gray button-up tucked into his pants. With a shock, I realize how handsome he is. But then an unbidden image of Bart at the party last night rises before my eyes, with his dark hair curling around his face and his bright green eyes laughing behind his big glasses and the deep cleft in his chin. Clancy can't touch him. I swallow and pull the door open wider. "Come on in."

"Morning, sunshine," he says as he slides past me. Then he notices my grandpa and mom. "Oh, I'm sorry," he says, his tone becoming much more formal, as he strides forward with an outstretched hand. "I'm Clancy Jankovich."

Grandpa studies the hand and then flicks his eyes up to his face. He scans Clancy's tattoo, his hair, the diamond studs in his ears. His lip curls. "You're marrying this...this..." He can't seem to think of a word bad enough to describe Clancy. "This?" he finishes, waving his hand at the young man before him.

I watch Clancy. He's looking away from me, but I see the corner of his mouth twitch slightly. Is he fighting a smile? Yet I feel anger rising. "Yes," I say loudly, slipping my hand into his.

Clancy glances at me, eyes widening for a moment, his fingers loose around mine. Then he turns back to face my grandpa, and I can only see his profile as his fingers tighten around mine. Warmth shoots up my arm, and my skin tingles. Why do I feel this way? It scares me. And I don't like being scared.

I'd rather snatch my hand away, but that would kind of defeat the gesture I was trying to make to Grandpa. So, I just raise my chin and meet Grandpa's eyes, not saying anything. A muscle jerks convulsively in Grandpa's cheek. He opens his mouth. He shuts it again. When he finally speaks, his words are surprisingly measured.

"I'm afraid I still don't understand who exactly this"—he waves a hand at Clancy—"is."

*How am I going to explain this without sounding like a complete lunatic?* But Clancy forestalls me. "I'm a street musician," he says.

My stomach plummets. Could he have explained himself worse? So much for not sounding like a lunatic. Then suddenly, I'm choking back laughter. He couldn't have said anything about himself that would enrage Grandpa more if he was trying to enrage him. Suddenly I scrutinize Clancy's profile. *Was he?*

Grandpa's imposed calm is cracking. "You..." he stutters. "You're...a...what?"

"A street musician. I play my violin on street corners, and people put money in my case. Recently, I've been playing outside your restaurant, Mr. King. That is where your granddaughter and I met."

Mr. King? Laughter is bubbling up inside me, fighting to come out. Clancy's pleasant smile and calm, deep voice contrast so sharply with Grandpa's red face and furious stuttering that it's ludicrous.

Clancy's manner is infuriatingly sweet. I really think he's enjoying this.

"And how, may I ask, are you planning to support my granddaughter on the few measly dollars that are put into your case every week?"

Clancy shrugs one shoulder. "Busking is actually surprisingly lucrative, Mr. King. But"—he smirks slightly at the incredulous expression on Grandpa's face—"I also have a day job."

"Doing what?"

"I work in the fishing industry."

"A non-answer if ever I heard one. I repeat, doing what?"

"This and that."

Grandpa's face twists with anger. He stares at Clancy, and Clancy stares coolly back, his face a calm and pleasant mask. Grandpa looks away first, his gaze shifting to me. "Rachel," he says, fighting to control the shaking in his voice. "Please. Listen to reason. Come home with your mother and me."

Clancy tilts his head slightly to look down at me. He is still wearing his cool, pleasant smile, but there is a flicker in his brown eyes. His fingers tighten slightly on mine. Warmth spreads up my arm again, and, for one mad moment, I almost wrench myself away and run to my mother and grandfather, not because he's a stranger, but because I want him to stay a stranger. But I've come too far.

"No, Grandpa," I say softly. "I'm going to live with my husband."

His face twists again. "Then don't ever come near our home again," he says. My stomach clenches. He strides to the door and then pivots, his hand on the knob. "You had everything going for you. You're beautiful. You're intelligent. You're talented. You have a family that loves you. You have always had everything you could need or want. And what do you do with all of this? You become pregnant in a one-night stand. You refuse help from family and friends. And you marry the first doped-up street musician you meet. But you can't have your cake and eat it too, Rachel. Not one more penny will you get from me or your mother. If you want to 'live with your husband', do! But don't come near us."

My heart is pounding in my ears, and my throat is so thick I can't speak, but I find I don't have to.

"That's enough," Clancy says softly, stepping toward my grandpa.

My grandpa glares at him with such hatred, I'm surprised fire doesn't shoot from his eyes. "Stay out of this," he snarls.

"No," Clancy says. "I think you should leave now."

Grandpa gives him one last scowl and yanks at the door. It doesn't open, since I, on autopilot, dead-bolted it behind Clancy. Grandpa rattles the handle for about a minute and then, finally realizing what is wrong, turns the deadbolt and heaves the door open.

"Come, LeAnne," he says.

I turn toward my mom, who is standing frozen next to the sofa, tears pouring down her cheeks. "Chel," she whispers, pleadingly.

"LeAnne!" Grandpa barks.

She continues to stand, her eyes darting between her child and her father. In that moment, I want to beg her to come and visit me. I yearn to tell her that I don't want to lose her, that I don't wish my child to grow up without a grandma, but the words won't come. So, I tear my gaze from her ashen face and fix it resolutely on the carpet, my eyes burning and my throat so tight it is difficult to breathe.

Seconds pass like eternity. Then I hear my mom release a choking sob followed by the sound of her feet running from the room after my grandfather. The door slams.

Clancy releases my hand abruptly. Still staring at the carpet, I hear him stride into the kitchen and begin opening drawers. Surprised, I look up.

"Aha," he says and pulls a purple Sharpie from Cat's miscellaneous drawer. Grabbing one of the bills from the mail pile he scrawls across the back and then races to the window. I see him press the envelope against the glass.

Completely nonplussed, I stare at his back, my throat gradually loosening. When I finally feel able to speak without sounding like a frog with a head cold, I say, "What are you doing?"

He doesn't respond, just stands at the window with his envelope pressed against the glass, peering down into the parking lot.

"What are you *doing*?" I snap, tenuous emotions beginning to fray.

Finally, he leaves the window and faces me. "Giving your mom your new address." He holds up the envelope. His writing is illegible, but I recognize the format.

I roll my eyes. "Nice thought, but number one, she'll never come. She would never defy my grandpa."

"I think you might be selling her short."

Being interrupted only makes me madder. "Number two," I say loudly, "your writing is completely illegible so there is no way in hell she is now any wiser about where I'm going to live than she was before."

He presses his lips together. "Number one," he says, mimicking me in a carefully measured voice, "I happen to know my writing is legible since everyone at my work can read it. Number two, I don't particularly appreciate your choice of language."

I glare at him, completely incensed. "Oh, really? Well, just because I'm going to marry you doesn't give you any right to dictate what comes out of my mouth."

He presses his lips together again, and I expect him to lash back at me, but he takes a deep breath and says slowly, "No, it doesn't. But don't you think being a mom should maybe influence what comes out of your mouth?"

A sound makes me turn. Cat has come out of the back bedroom and is standing there holding Serenity's hand. She raises her eyebrows ever so slightly, and I know she heard what Clancy just said. And agrees. *Great, now they're banded together against me.*

Serenity breaks the tension by dropping her mother's hand and running up to grab my knees. "Chellie! What are you doing here?"

I stoop and lift her into my arms. "I stayed the night, Serry-Berry."

"You didn't say ni-night when Mama put me in my bed."."

"Nope. I came later."

"Wanna see ducky?" She's showed me her worn-to-shreds-by-love ducky every time I've come over for the past month. But I can't say no to her. "Sure, cutie." As we turn to go, I glance at Clancy who mouths, "*Chellie?*" at me. But even as I firmly turn my back on him and stalk toward Serenity's room, I realize the expression in his eyes was much softer than mockery.

I sit, winding my fingers together, on a bench in the back of the courtroom. Today is my wedding day. The knots in my stomach tighten as I remember childish dreams of what my wedding would be. For some reason, I always envisioned getting married in a vineyard, with fairy lights strung between the trees. I pictured a wedding dress—not one of the enormous, bedazzled, princessy kind—but a simple thing with a flowy chiffon skirt and lacy, off-the-shoulder sleeves. I saw a fancy catered dinner with just a few guests, the people dearest to me in the world. My first slow dance would be beneath the twinkling lights with my skirt whispering around my ankles in the dusk and soft jazz music from a band beneath the trees. And when the party was over, I wanted to slip away in the dusk holding hands with... My insides twist, and for one wild moment, I consider jumping up and running out of the courtroom. Then I set my teeth together so hard they click together. I will not back out now.

I observe the man sitting beside me. He's dressed in his nice jeans and striped, gray shirt again, and his hair is pulled back in a half ponytail with braids dangling down his back. I don't like the hairdo on him, but I can't really complain. He doesn't look like a groom, but I don't look like a bride either. When she was convinced I was going to go through with this, Cat begged me to go out and at least buy a second-hand wedding dress. But if I can't have the wedding I'd always dreamed of, I don't need some cheap knock-off version. This isn't a real wedding. I don't love the man sitting next to me. So, I'm wearing black jeans, a tea rose top with three-quarter sleeves, and black pumps—all of which were in the bags of my clothes that my Grandpa left on the front porch the day after I told him I was going to marry Clancy. And the sooner this is over, and I can move into Clancy's apartment and file taxes with him and try to forget I ever had another life, the better.

"Clancy and Rachel King?" the officiant calls.

"How come he didn't say your last name?" I hiss at Clancy. He gives a half shrug and motions for me to get up. Annoyed by his bossiness, I hop up at exactly the same moment he stands. My hip brushes his, and I feel hot blood pouring into my face. Even as I jerk away, I can't help glancing back. His face is a mask of stoicism. There isn't a hint of happiness there. I march up the aisle, catching my high heel once and nearly falling. *What did I expect? That he'd be overjoyed?*

Clancy catches up to me as I reach the officiant. To avoid meeting his eyes, I peek over my shoulder at the nearly deserted courtroom. Cat gives me a tight-lipped smile from where she sits on a bench three rows back. Serenity is leaning against her, fidgeting with the bow her mother had tied around her blonde ponytail. As I watch, Cat catches hold of her fingers to keep her from pulling the hairdo out. On the other side of the courtroom sits a young man in a suit jacket who keeps checking his cell phone. I don't know him, but I'm guessing he's Clancy's witness.

"Rachel?" the officiant says, and I know from his tone that he already said something, and I missed it.

"Yeah?"

"Please take a seat."

Clancy reaches for the back of my chair, but I get there first. Today, I just can't take his gentlemanliness. Not when he gives the impression he's at his mother's funeral instead of at his own wedding. I plunk down, and Clancy sits as well. I can tell he's watching me, but I refuse to meet his eyes.

The officiant, a short, balding man with crow's feet around his eyes, reaches into the breast pocket of his suit and takes out a pair of reading glasses, then pulls our file toward him.

"Clancy, Rachel, my name is Matthew Arnold. I'll be officiating your ceremony today, but I'd like to get to know you a little bit before we actually get started. How did you two meet?"

Before Clancy can say a word, I'm on my feet. "Could we cut the crap? I appreciate the excellent customer service, but all three of us know you couldn't care less about how we met, so let's just skip the small talk and get to the vows part."

My words are followed by a ringing silence. I didn't know how much louder silence sounds in a courtroom. As the seconds tick by, I want to apologize, but I'm sure if I open my mouth, I'll just make everything worse. How is it possible that I am completely incapable of basic human interaction?

After what feels like an eternity, Clancy's fingers close around my wrist, and he pulls me back down next to him. "Easy, honey," he says softly. Then he turns to the wide-eyed clerk with a twinkle, "I'm sure you've never seen a bride *this* ready to be married, Matthew."

Matthew gives a weak laugh and shakes his head. "Well, shall we get on with it then?"

I can't remember a single word of the ceremony. A pounding migraine is beginning behind my eyes and nausea, whether from the headache or the pregnancy, is pulsing in my stomach.

*I can't throw up or pass out before I get married. I can't go through this whole nightmare again.*

Somehow, I must manage to get my *yes's* in at the right moments, because eventually Cat and the cellphone guy make their way down to the front to sign the marriage certificate. The cellphone guy scans the paper, gives Clancy a broad grin, and scribbles his name and the date on the first line. As Cat reaches for the pen and pulls the marriage certificate toward her, my breakfast rises toward my windpipe. My hand clamps down on her arm, and she glances toward me, eyes widening as she scribbles her signature haphazardly across the second witness line.

"Chel? Are you okay?" she mouths, and I shake my head desperately, terrified of what will happen if I open my mouth.

"Chel?" Clancy pushes the marriage certificate toward me, his eyes fixed on my face. I scrawl a loopy "RECK" on the Bride line without looking. On principle, I never read documents that require my signature: there's too much print. Clancy applied for the license, and I just went with him to pick it up.

I'm swallowing convulsively now, trying desperately to settle my stomach. "Chel?" Clancy's voice is full of concern, and as my vision blurs at the edges, I wish desperately that he could have had a nasal, squeaky voice. Then my brain would have a harder time pretending he sounds anything like Barton Drossel.

"I think that does it," Matthew Arnold's voice breaks in as he sweeps his papers together. "Congratulations, you two—"

*Nope. Nope. It's not staying down. Gotta go. Gotta go!*

I stagger to my feet and run. Voices clamor behind me, all alarm and concern, but I have to find a bathroom before I...before I...

My hands collide with the swinging doors, and I am out in the hall, the black spots at the edges of my vision swarming dangerously close together. If I don't sit down, I'm going to be sprawling on the courtroom hall in the next ten seconds. But if I don't find a bathroom...

My stomach heaves, and I catch desperately at the wall as the contents of my stomach empty onto the floor. Panting and swallowing against the sour taste coating my tongue, I slide slowly down the wall, careful to avoid planting my butt in the pool of vomit.

"Chel! Oh, Chel."

"Ew! Mommy, what is that?"

"Oh my...I suppose I should...find the janitor..."

The voices swirl around me, but I'm afraid if I open my eyes the light will cause the migraine to spike. Then a hand touches my cheek, cool and big and oddly comforting.

"Don't worry." My eyelids inch open enough to see Clancy kneeling beside me. His breath grazes my cheek as he leans close and whispers, "I doubt anyone was too attached to this carpet."

I glimpse the truly horrendous purple and orange paisley-pattern beneath us and purse my lips against a smile before allowing my eyelids to drift closed again.

"The king's daughter knew nothing about lighting fires or cooking, and the beggar had to lend a hand himself to get anything done at all."

~Grimm

# Chapter 6
## Mrs. Jankovich

When we finally make our way outside, the gray skies hang low, like they always do here. Cat reaches out and pulls me into a wordless hug, and I lean my still-throbbing head against her shoulder, waiting for the Tylenol she gave me inside to take effect. Clancy is standing a few feet away, hands pushed deep into his pockets, talking softly to the cell phone guy. I still don't know his name. After a moment, he claps Clancy on the shoulder and strides away. But instead of turning back to Cat and me, my new husband gazes off into the distance, his posture rigid.

"Would you rather just go home?" Cat murmurs in my ear. "I was going to offer to take you out, but if you're still feeling crummy..."

My eyes find Clancy again and I wonder, with increasing irritation, what is causing the vacillations in his mood. During the ceremony, he was cold and remote, but after the whole barfing-in-the-courtroom-hall incident, he was the perfect paragon of a concerned husband. Now he's back to ice personified.

"That's okay. Let's go out," I say, glaring at my fake husband's back. *The last thing I want right now is to be alone with him.*

"If you're sure," Cat says quietly, her perceptive eyes flitting between Clancy and me. "Anywhere you like. My treat."

"Oooh, oooh, oooh!" Serenity begins jumping up and down. "Frugals, Mommy!"

"Honey, I was talking to Chel. Today is her big day, and she gets to decide."

Serenity grabs my hand and continues to jump, pulling on my fingers. "Say, Frugals, Chel! Pleaaassseee!"

"Serenity," Cat says sternly, detaching her from my hand. "Let Chel decide."

I eye Clancy's poker-straight back again. *What is with him? Is it too much to expect some attention from my* husband *on our* wedding *day? Especially since I'm clearly not in the best shape?*

I toss my hair out of my face. There's enough of a breeze now that strands of my hair have come loose from the bobby pins I put in this morning. "Sure," I say. "Frugals sounds great." Cat raises her eyebrows slightly and motions with her head toward Clancy. I shake my head and speak to Serenity.

"What are you going to get, Smalls?"

She wrinkles her nose. "The little cheesy things."

"Huh?"

"You know! The little cheese balls."

When I still look baffled, she turns to her mother, quivering with annoyance. "Mommy!"

I turn and see Cat standing next to Clancy. As I watch, she puts a hand on his arm and says softly, "Is it all right with you if I take you and Chel out, Clancy? I don't want to butt in if you had other plans." She gives a small smile. "And I know Frugals wouldn't be everyone's ideal wedding fare."

He smiles down at her. My heart gives a hard little lurch. *Oh. He does know how to smile. At some people.* "Frugals sounds fantastic," he says. "Thanks for offering, Cat."

Serenity catches hold of her mother's coat sleeve. "Mommy!"

"Baby, don't interrupt. I am talking to Clancy. If you want to say something, put your hand on my arm, and I will say, 'Yes, Serenity?' and then you may talk."

She turns back to Clancy, while Serenity vibrating with impatience, clutches at her forearm. "Yes, Serenity?"

"Mommy, what's the little cheesy things at Frugals?"

"The cheese curds?"

Serenity whirls to face me. "Curds! I couldn't 'member!"

"Frugals is only a few blocks away," Clancy says, gesturing down the street. He grins at Serenity. "I'll race you."

She scrunches up her nose quizzically, then glances at her mother, who smiles. "He's a friend, honey. It's fine."

"Do I get a head start?" Serenity demands of Clancy.

He pretends to waffle. "You look pretty fast. I almost think I should get a head start."

"No! You're older!"

"Really? How old are you?"

She holds up two fingers. "How old are you?"

He flashes both hands at her twice and then holds up one finger. She scowls. "I don't know how many that is. But it's more than me."

A grin breaks over his face. "Fair enough. I'll give you ten seconds."

As she races off, I see his lips moving, counting. Then he takes off after her. Cat tucks her hand into my arm, and we walk slowly behind. Cat tries to engage me in conversation, but my monosyllabic answers quickly convince her I'm not in the mood.

He's twenty-one. Like Bart. And I'm going to Frugals on my wedding day because my new husband didn't even think to book a nice restaurant.

Clancy pushes the door to the apartment open. It creaks. We haven't spoken a word since we left Cat and Serenity outside Frugals. I was inside yesterday, when Cat and I came to drop off my stuff, but we were in a hurry since Cat needed to get Serenity from daycare, so I didn't really get a chance to look around. Now, as I shrug out of my coat, I survey my new home. A tiny entryway, consisting of a square of laminate and three coat hooks set into the wall, opens directly into the living room. There are three pieces of furniture to break the monotony of the tan carpet—a hideous olive-green sectional backed into a corner, an oak coffee table, and a reddish bookcase which clashes horribly with the couch.

I hang up my coat and follow Clancy, who is walking around flicking on lights. Peering into the kitchen, which is half separated from the living room by a bar, I spot a fridge, the oldest oven I have ever seen, and a sink with a dirty plate and fork at the bottom. A towel with a pile of dry dishes sits next to the sink.

I turn back into the living room and see Clancy has plunked down on the sofa. He glances up and meets my eyes.

"Home sweet home," he says shortly.

"Everything I ever dreamed of," I retort, my voice so sharp, it surprises even me.

He folds his lips tightly together and looks away. I know he's swallowing all the things he'd like to say to me, but I can't swallow the things I want to say to him. And I don't intend to.

"Yes," I continue, leaning on the faux countertop. "As a little girl, my greatest ambition was to marry a man who wouldn't buy me an engagement ring. I hoped on my wedding day I would go out for fast food. God forbid, my husband would actually take me to a sit-down restaurant. I dreamed I would come back to a tiny apartment with mismatched furniture and no dishwasher." My voice is rising. "I expected my husband wouldn't buy me flowers. Who wants roses for their wedding? And my dearest wish was that on my wedding day, not only would I permanently stain the carpet of the courthouse, but the groom would IGNORE me and spend his time playing with the three-year-old daughter of my best friend!"

He is breathing heavily, gazing at me. The tattoo under his eye somehow makes his anger more formidable, and for one fleeting moment, I wonder if I should be afraid of him. But when he answers me, his voice is level. "You're the one who wouldn't look at me, Chel."

Fury surges inside me, exacerbated by the fact that I know he is right. I couldn't look at him, because every time I did, the fact that he wasn't Bart Drossel hit me again like a slap across the face. But I can't tell him that. So, I lash at him, like a wounded animal.

"Not many women would care to!"

Clancy stiffens. Then he says in the same level voice—which only increases my urge to scream at him—"This conversation is going nowhere. It's late. I'm going to bed."

He stands up, saying as he starts to walk down the hall. "The bed is yours. I'll take the sectional."

"You coward," I say to his retreating back. "Can't even stay and fight it out."

He stops. After a very long moment, he turns to face me. "Okay," he says. His voice is still soft, but it is no longer level. His next words are shaking with anger. "You want me to talk? I'll talk." He steps toward me. "You say this wedding was such a disappointment to you, but guess what, Chel? I had dreams too." His voice is rising now, and we are facing each other across the counter. "I never planned to get married in front of a judge in a courthouse—I wanted to get married in a church, before God. I told you I would prefer a church wedding, but you said no, and we went with what you wanted. I hoped to get married to a woman who had dressed up for me, and you couldn't even be bothered to wear a dress. And, Chel, believe it or not, I envisioned getting married to a woman who would spend our wedding night in my bed!"

Heat rushes up my face, and I open my mouth, but he forestalls me. "Yeah, I know what you're going to say. That I'm exactly as sex crazed as every other male in the species. Save it, Chel."

He starts to turn away and then turns back. "Is that so much to hope for? That I'd marry a woman who would be excited to marry me? And one who wouldn't yell at the judge in the middle of the ceremony?"

I can't speak. His words slice through me. He's right. Why would anyone want someone like me? Difficult. Prickly. Mean. Impossible. No one's dream girl.

I stare down at the countertop, my eyes tracing patterns, my throat too tight for speech. *Go away. Go away. Go away.* I chant over and over in my head.

Silence hangs in the air for so long I finally lift my head. He's still standing there, his head bent, one hand over his eyes. Seeming to sense my gaze, he lowers his hand. His eyes are not angry anymore, just bleak and sad.

"Chel," he starts, "I should…"

But I push past him, heading down the hall. At the bedroom door, I turn. "You're right," I say, unable to look him in the eye. "I've been a nightmare. Sorry." Then I run into the bedroom, slamming the door, and throw myself onto the bed, fully dressed. I bury my face in one of the pillows and try desperately to cry. If tears will come, maybe they'll wash away the ache inside me. But they don't come, and eventually I flip onto my back and lie there, staring into the darkness, pain throbbing inside, until my eyes drift close.

I wake to the sound of someone talking. The red glowing letters on the clock by the bed read 2:37. Who on earth is Clancy talking to? He doesn't have a TV. My mouth full of the sour taste of unbrushed teeth, I tiptoe to the door and ease it open. I can distinguish words now, but they don't make any sense.

"God, I'm sorry..."
"I know I should..."
"...haven't loved her..."
"...need to tell..."
"So hard...she's...you know..."
"...so scared...lose...again..."
"...not thinking straight..."
"Should have gotten flowers..."
"Help me."

I slip into the hall and inch along the wall to a spot where I can see into the living room. Clancy's sitting on the couch, shirtless and wearing pajama bottoms. My heart trips as my eyes take in the lean curves of his muscular frame. I glance quickly away, then back, because I want to know what he's doing. He's sitting bent over something spread on his knees, his hair pulled into a messy bun at the base of his neck. And he's wearing glasses. He begins speaking again, and I realize there must be a book in his lap, but I don't recognize the words.

"Therefore, I am now going to allure her; I will lead her into the wilderness and speak tenderly to her. There I will give her back her vineyards and will make the valley of Achor a door of hope. There she will respond as in the days of her youth, as in the day she came up out of Egypt. 'In that day,' declares the Lord, 'you will call me 'my husband'; you will no longer call me 'my master'."

The Lord? Is he reading the Bible? But what on earth is he reading? I've never heard anything of the sort in church before.

He pauses, and I flatten myself against the wall, praying he won't notice me. A moment later his voice picks up the cadence of reading again, and I slip back down the hall to the bedroom.

Inside, I take off my black jeans and climb into bed, under the covers this time. Through the door, I can still hear the murmuring of his voice, and it's a strangely comforting sound. Is he really awake at 2am, praying, because of our fight? And what does he need to tell me? I close my eyes, struggling to articulate, even to myself exactly what I'm feeling right now. Thoughts slip randomly through my brain, tangling and untangling as sleep creeps ever closer.

*I wouldn't want to tell me anything either.*
*Not when I was so shrewish.*
*But I can't be the wife he wants...*
*Was this all a mistake?*

A crashing wave of exhaustion pours over me, and my last conscious thought before I drift off is *I'll be nicer to him tomorrow.*

Day one of married life. So much for being nicer to Clancy. When I wake up and stumble out into the living room, he's gone. A blanket is crumpled in the corner of the sectional and a shiny leather book is sitting on the coffee table next to an empty coffee mug with a brown ring in the bottom. Coffee. I stagger into the kitchen, rubbing my eyes. There's a coffeemaker sitting on the counter, but it's empty. *Unbelievable. He didn't think to leave anything for me?*

How hard can making a pot of coffee be? I begin rummaging around in Clancy's cupboards. At last, I find the beans and coffee filters. I open the top of the coffee maker and put a filter with a quarter full of beans in the basket. I'm not sure what the ratio of water to beans should be, so I just guess and hit the on button.

My stomach heaves a little bit, and I glance at the clock on the oven. It's after 9:00. Cat told me that eating right after you wake up really helped her morning sickness with Serenity, so I searched for food. There's a plate covering another plate sitting on the counter, and I lift the top plate to see a weird soggy mash of eggs with a bunch of random vegetables. *Ew. Leftovers on the counter. This guy needs a wife.*

I scrape the plate into the trash and put both plates into the sink, feeling virtuous. But the scent of the garbage can makes me gag, and I quickly yank open cupboard doors. There's almost nothing there. I find a roll of four Ritz crackers and take one to nibble on as I hunt for something more substantial. Checking the fridge yields nothing better. There are a few bell peppers, an onion, and a bag of baby carrots in the vegetable drawer. Other than those, there's a box of butter, a partially used carton of eggs, and a pint of whipping cream.

*Geez.*

I guess I'm going out with the ten bucks that is all the money I have to my name. I head to the bathroom to freshen up and throw up my Ritz cracker as soon as I try to brush my teeth. This is turning out to be such a winner of a day.

When I'm finally walking downtown, eating a Starbucks breakfast sandwich and nursing a peppermint hot chocolate, I realize I have no idea what I'm going to do with myself today. At home, Grandpa or Mom usually have plans they expect me to participate in. I go to the gym most mornings, but for the past few weeks, I've been feeling exhausted and nauseous and like exercise is the last thing I want to do. The pregnancy! I stop in the middle of the sidewalk, and someone swears at me before swerving around.

*Oh my God, I totally forgot.*

How far along am I now? I start walking again slowly, attempting to do the math in my head. I got pregnant the night of my birthday: July 12th. But you count from the first day of your last period, right? So June 30th... And today is August 26th, so a little over eight weeks. Two months.

I need to start getting prenatal care, right? Now I have something to do today. I'll stop by the crisis pregnancy center and set up an initial appointment.

"Chel?"

I jerk awake and jump backward on the sofa with a little scream. Clancy's face is inches from mine.

"Damn it, you nearly gave me heart failure," I say as I struggle to sit up. "What time is it?"

"A little after five." Clancy gets up and walks into the kitchen. I hear the refrigerator door open. A pleasant scent lingers in the air behind him, and I realize for the first time that I didn't take a shower after walking all over Port Angeles. I'm wearing my oldest sweats and a T-shirt with a stain on the bust. *Wow.*

"How was your breakfast?" Clancy's face appears around the refrigerator door, and he's wearing this goofy grin.

"Um…" I frown at him, confused. "Good?"

His smile falters, and his face disappears back into the refrigerator. *What on earth?*

"Um," I say to break the awkward silence, "I went to the crisis pregnancy center today."

He shuts the refrigerator door and walks back into the living room, taking a seat on the floor across the coffee table from me.

"Yeah? How was it?"

"Good."

A smile tips the corner of his mouth sardonically. "You're a bit monosyllabic tonight, sweetheart."

"Don't call me that."

His smile widens. "Hey, we're married. How else should a husband address his wife?"

I open my mouth to say something cutting about what kind of "marriage" he and I really have, and then I shut it again. In my mind's eye, I see him huddled on the couch with a Bible in his lap at two in the morning, mumbling broken prayers, and the words stick in my throat. Instead, I say,

"You *can* sit on the sofa if you'd like"

He smiles again, but a different kind of smile, and slowly pulls himself up near me. "When's the baby due?"

"I don't know for sure yet. Today was just a consultation thingy, and they set up a preliminary ultrasound for next week. I made sure it was in the evening so Cat and Serenity can come with me."

Something shutters behind his eyes. There is a moment of silence, and then he gets up and heads back into the kitchen. "What do you want for dinner?"

*What is with him?*

"What are my options?"

"Currently, eggs."

"Um... How about orange chicken instead?"

He pops his head around the wall again. "You know how to make orange chicken?"

His tone annoys me. "No, but Zhang's does."

He chuckles. "I see how it is. The baby wants orange chicken, does she?"

I pull myself to my feet, scowling at him. "No, I want orange chicken. And why do you keep calling the baby a she? I think it's a boy."

He shrugs noncommittally and puts on his shoes.

"What are you doing?"

"Going to get you and Junior some orange chicken."

"Ever heard of delivery?"

"Ever heard of gratitude?"

He raises his head and looks me directly in the eyes. I glare at him, then throw up my hands. "Fine! Thank you. I'm eternally grateful."

His mouth quirks. "Want to come?"

The fact that he asked me causes a ball of warmth to spread inside my chest. "Sure. But I need to get ready."

Number of minutes it takes me to get ready: thirteen. Number of times he threatens to leave without me: two. Number of times he groans about women: five.

Number of times I smile into the mirror: five.

I wake up with darkness pressing around me. Rolling over to blink at the clock, I see it's 2:37 again. *Okay, that is freaky. And why am I awake?*

Suddenly, I shoot up in bed. *Oh my God. Oh my God. Oh my God.*

Pushing the covers off my legs, I hop out of bed and race into the living room. In the grayish light filtering through Clancy's curtains, I can see the dark hump of his back curled up on the couch.

"Clancy!" I hiss, reaching down to shake his shoulder.

He gives a moan and tries to push my hand away.

"Clancy!"

He rolls over, and I see one of his eyes crack open. "Chel," he mumbles. "Wa's wrong? You okay?"

Then his eyes fly open, and he pushes into a sitting position, grabbing my hand. "Chel! Are you okay? Is it the baby?"

"Geez, no! I just needed to know: did you make breakfast for me yesterday morning?"

Clancy releases my hand and falls backward onto the couch with a hand over his eyes. "Oh. My. Gosh."

"Did you?"

"Yeah. Yeah, I made you breakfast."

"That weird egg veggie mixture?"

He chokes out a laugh. "It's called skillet."

"Uh, I didn't realize what it was. I threw it away."

He starts laughing so hard I think he's going to fall off the sofa. "You did?" he manages to get out.

"Yes. I'm really sorry."

He still hasn't stopped laughing. "Don't sweat it."

Finally, his laughter fades. Silence stretches between us, me standing next to the coffee table, him propped on his elbow on the couch. I notice that he's shirtless again, and my stomach flips.

"I just wanted to say thanks."

"And you thought three in the morning would have the maximum weight?"

Realization hits me, and I slap myself in the forehead. "I'm sorry! I just...I only just realized... Geez, what is wrong with me..."

"Chel." His voice breaks through my ramblings.

"Yes?"

"You're welcome." Something about the way he says it makes me devoutly grateful it's dark. I don't want to see what's in his eyes. Without another word, I turn and head back to bed.

Day four of married life. 6:01 blinks at me from the bedside clock as my stomach gives an unignorable heave. I throw myself out of bed and barrel through my door and into the bathroom, barely making it to the toilet. As I clutch the edges of the bowl, panting slightly, the fact that the bathroom is full of steam suddenly dawns on me. Slowly turning my head, I see, with a thrill of horror, a towel-clad hip inches from my face. With a squawk, I scramble to my feet and stagger out of the bathroom, my eyes meeting Clancy's stunned gaze for an instant in the mirror, before I slam the door behind me.

A light tap sounds on the bedroom door five minutes later. I pull the covers off my head and regard the door for a moment, seriously considering pretending to be asleep. However, since falling asleep that quickly seems a little far-fetched, I say, in as unconcerned a voice as I can muster, "Come in."

The door creaks, and Clancy—now clothed—leans against the door jamb, eyeing me. He doesn't immediately say anything, and my defensive hackles rise. "What? Failing to knock isn't a crime."

"No," he says slowly, "I just thought...you might have seen..."

I stare at him. "I'm pregnant," I say, the words tumbling out before I can stop them. "I've seen shirtless guys before."

His face crumples, and I feel sick, though it's not the kind of nausea that would be helped by throwing up. "God, I'm sorry," I mutter, my eyes sliding away from the black line under his eye, where his tattoo has scrunched into a dark blob. "Wait." My eyes come back to his face, and the memory of that same face reflected in the foggy bathroom mirror smacks against my consciousness. "Your tattoo," I say slowly and watch his shoulders slump. "You didn't have one a minute ago. In the bathroom."

"No," he says quietly, his eyes lifting to meet mine.

"Why are you wearing a fake tattoo?" I demand.

"I..." he swallows. "I guess I didn't have the guts to go out and get a real one."

We stare at each other for a long moment. "That's ridiculous," I say finally. "Do you think it makes you look cool or something?"

He gnaws his bottom lip for an instant. "I guess it's more of a facade," he says, his words halting. "Something to keep people from really seeing my face. A kind of...disguise."

Something about his tone is strange, as though his words are the hint to a riddle, and he expects me to blurt out the answer at any moment. "That's even worse." I know how harsh I sound, but it's six in the morning for Pete's sake. Why would he act like I should know something when I don't have a clue what he's on about? I grit my teeth in frustration. "It's basically a lie, which makes me feel like a fool for not knowing. I hate it."

He doesn't say anything. Irritation swells, and I'm about to flip over onto my side and pull the covers over my head again when he says, "What if someone lied to you because they cared about you?"

*Why can't he just apologize for lying about the stupid tattoo instead of asking irrelevant questions?*

"Lying isn't caring," I snap, pushing down into bed so my head isn't propped uncomfortably against the headboard anymore. "It doesn't matter what the reason is."

There is another pause, and I close my eyes, hoping that he'll leave me alone so that I can go back to sleep.

"Do you want me to stop wearing them?" I open my eyes. His shoulders are slumped, and his gaze is fixed on the floor.

"The tattoos?"

"I have a whole pack under the sink."

For a minute, I scrutinize him. He hasn't apologized. But the look on his face might be apology enough. "Finish out the pack," I say. "They aren't atrocious on you." Then I roll over and pull the blankets over my head.

Day twelve of married life. When Clancy says, "Chel, we need to talk," as soon as he walks in the door, his tone reminds me of how my grandpa addressed me whenever I was in trouble.

"Yeah?" I lay aside the copy of *What to Expect When You're Expecting* that they gave me at the pregnancy center last week. It's surprisingly interesting. Honestly, the whole appointment was pretty amazing. The counselor told me all about their resource room and their parenting classes where you could earn points to "buy" more expensive items like Pack-n-Plays or car seats. She also showed me the racks of baby clothes that were free for anyone who needed them. For some reason the sight of all the tiny onesies and pajamas and dresses made my throat close up. But the best part was definitely the ultrasound. My baby was bouncing around all over the place. It was impossible to see details, but I could make out the head, a tiny round belly, and stubs for arms and legs. The nurse printed out pictures for me to take home, and when I arrived back at the apartment, bubbling after my appointment, I offered Clancy one. I expected him to be excited for me, but he didn't ask a single question about the appointment, simply took the picture and went back to the book he was reading about Andrew Carnegie. His indifference had hurt

Number of minutes it takes me to get ready: thirteen. Number of times he threatens to leave without me: two. Number of times he groans about women: five.

Number of times I smile into the mirror: five.

I wake up with darkness pressing around me. Rolling over to blink at the clock, I see it's 2:37 again. *Okay, that is freaky. And why am I awake?*

Suddenly, I shoot up in bed. *Oh my God. Oh my God. Oh my God.*

Pushing the covers off my legs, I hop out of bed and race into the living room. In the grayish light filtering through Clancy's curtains, I can see the dark hump of his back curled up on the couch.

"Clancy!" I hiss, reaching down to shake his shoulder.

He gives a moan and tries to push my hand away.

"Clancy!"

He rolls over, and I see one of his eyes crack open. "Chel," he mumbles. "Wa's wrong? You okay?"

Then his eyes fly open, and he pushes into a sitting position, grabbing my hand. "Chel! Are you okay? Is it the baby?"

"Geez, no! I just needed to know: did you make breakfast for me yesterday morning?"

Clancy releases my hand and falls backward onto the couch with a hand over his eyes. "Oh. My. Gosh."

"Did you?"

"Yeah. Yeah, I made you breakfast."

"That weird egg veggie mixture?"

He chokes out a laugh. "It's called skillet."

"Uh, I didn't realize what it was. I threw it away."

He starts laughing so hard I think he's going to fall off the sofa. "You did?" he manages to get out.

"Yes. I'm really sorry."

He still hasn't stopped laughing. "Don't sweat it."

Finally, his laughter fades. Silence stretches between us, me standing next to the coffee table, him propped on his elbow on the couch. I notice that he's shirtless again, and my stomach flips.

"I just wanted to say thanks."

"And you thought three in the morning would have the maximum weight?"

Realization hits me, and I slap myself in the forehead. "I'm sorry! I just...I only just realized... Geez, what is wrong with me..."

"Chel." His voice breaks through my ramblings.

"Yes?"

"You're welcome." Something about the way he says it makes me devoutly grateful it's dark. I don't want to see what's in his eyes. Without another word, I turn and head back to bed.

Day four of married life. 6:01 blinks at me from the bedside clock as my stomach gives an unignorable heave. I throw myself out of bed and barrel through my door and into the bathroom, barely making it to the toilet. As I clutch the edges of the bowl, panting slightly, the fact that the bathroom is full of steam suddenly dawns on me. Slowly turning my head, I see, with a thrill of horror, a towel-clad hip inches from my face. With a squawk, I scramble to my feet and stagger out of the bathroom, my eyes meeting Clancy's stunned gaze for an instant in the mirror, before I slam the door behind me.

A light tap sounds on the bedroom door five minutes later. I pull the covers off my head and regard the door for a moment, seriously considering pretending to be asleep. However, since falling asleep that quickly seems a little far-fetched, I say, in as unconcerned a voice as I can muster, "Come in."

The door creaks, and Clancy—now clothed—leans against the door jamb, eyeing me. He doesn't immediately say anything, and my defensive hackles rise. "What? Failing to knock isn't a crime."

me so much I hadn't spoken more than a handful of words to him in the last five days.

Putting down four plastic bags of groceries, he pulls off his shoes and comes slowly into the living room. I wait for him to say something, but he just stands next to the coffee table shifting from foot to foot and rubbing the back of his neck. After a minute I say,

"You said we needed to talk. So...talk."

He raises his eyebrows at me, clearly annoyed, but I hate beating around the bush, especially if the topic is unpleasant, so I just stare coolly back at him.

Finally, he says slowly, "Well, when we got married and, you, you know, moved in, I kind of thought you were planning to help out."

I continue to stare at him. "Help out?"

He gives a short laugh. "I don't own house elves, Chel. And I work full time. Grocery shopping, dish washing, bathroom cleaning, dinner prep, etc. don't happen automatically."

For a second, I'm offended. Then, I force myself to be reasonable. He's letting me live here, rent free. I guess I should've offered to help before, but it didn't occur to me. Mom loves housework. I never had to do anything at home; everything just happened.

"Okay," I say slowly. "So what should I help out with?"

He looks taken aback. I guess he was expecting pushback. Feeling suddenly smug because I've shocked him with my compliance, I smile.

He grins back at me, and it is clear he knows exactly what I'm thinking. Warmth spreads through my chest and down my arms, tingling in my fingertips. He's wearing a white T-shirt that stretches tight across his chest and the tattoo under his eye crinkles up when he smiles. My stomach flips, and I glance away.

"So what do you want me to do?"

The brusqueness in my voice causes the smile to slide from his face. His voice is cold when he answers. "I wasn't expecting you to do everything, of course. So, I made a Division of Labor chart."

I hear the "shh" of a paper landing on the coffee table. Still avoiding his eyes, I pick it up and study it.

Grocery shopping - Chel (Monday)

Trash - Clancy (as needed)
Dishes - Chel (MWF), Clancy (TRS)
Dinner - Clancy (MWF), Chel (TRS)
Vacuum apartment - Chel (Friday)
Clean bathroom - Clancy (Friday)
Laundry - Chel (Monday), Clancy (Thursday)

Finally, I peer up at him. "I don't think this is fair."

His lips tighten for a moment, but his voice is level when he speaks. "How so?"

"You work full time, and I don't work at all, but you still took half the housework."

Surprise flashes across his face, and then he smiles. I love his dimples. "You're a twerp," he says, grabbing at the paper. I hold on, just to be annoying, and his fingers collide with mine. Our eyes meet. I jerk my hand away, my heart thudding dully against my ribs.

"We done talking?"

"Yeah, I guess so," he says, turning away and crumpling the Division of Labor chart in his fist.

Day thirteen of married life.

I. Hate. Housework.

And I'm lousy at it. The first day of the Division of Labor implementation is Wednesday, so Clancy cooks, and I wash the dishes. To start with, he makes this delicious barbecued chicken with caramelized onions and quinoa on the side. *What guy knows how to cook like that? And way to be a show-off.*

By the time I'm done washing ALL the dishes it took to cook dinner, my fingers are rough and wrinkled. Then, when we're clearing our plates into the sink for me to wash them, Clancy gives a yell like a scalded cat.

"Chel!"

I literally drop my plate, which cracks into four pieces on the kitchen floor. "What the hell?"

"You didn't dry the cast iron pan! It'll rust!"

"Geez, Clancy! You just made me break my plate! Don't shout like that!"

"It'll ruin it, Chel!"

"Stop yelling at me!"

He doesn't answer as he grabs paper towels and carefully wipes out the bottom of the cast iron pan. Fuming, I stalk around rummaging for a broom. Finally, I snarl at him, "Where's your freaking broom?"

"Didn't I tell you I don't appreciate that kind of language?" he snaps.

I stomp down the hall and slam the bedroom door so hard the walls rattle. Flinging myself backward onto the bed, I scowl at the ceiling, furious and humiliated. He can cook a three-course meal, and I can't even wash a pot right.

Outside I can hear him moving around, probably cleaning up my mess. Then there's a hailing sound accompanied by the yummy smell of popcorn. About ten minutes later, I hear a knock on the door. Getting up, I walk slowly over and pull it open. "What?"

He's standing in the door with a bowl full of fluffy white kernels in his arms. "I totally overreacted," he says awkwardly. "I'm sorry."

His apology makes me feel worse. "Well, I'm a trash roommate," I mumble.

"Yeah, but not because you can't wash dishes."

"Huh?"

"You never hang out with me. I feel like I live with a ghost. A really cranky one. Come on, it's movie night."

"You don't even have a TV."

"Haven't you ever heard of watching movies on a laptop?"

"Yeah, Bart—a friend of mine—used to do that." My insides twist painfully. I don't want to think about Bart. But I also don't want to not think about him. Especially not with Clancy standing there, handsome and thoughtful and capable and not Bart.

His head tips quizzically as his brown eyes study me. "Who's Bart?"

I grit my teeth. "No one."

His eyebrows rise. "More than a friend then?"

"Less! Much less. We haven't spoken in years. Okay, I spoke to him the night we met, and it was awful. So, not talking is fine. I prefer it that way."

"Why haven't you spoken in years?"

"Why do you care?"

His eyes flicker away and then back, his fingers drumming absently against the side of the popcorn bowl in his hands. "I guess I just wonder what would make you mad enough at someone to completely cut them out of your life."

A fist of combined grief and guilt squeezes my heart. "He deserved it," I say, my stiff lips struggling to form words. "He..." *Broke my heart.*

"He what?" Clancy's eyes are too intense, and this conversation is clawing at scars that even after all this time are still pink and fresh.

"I don't want to talk about it, okay? It doesn't matter. Not anymore." Clancy opens his mouth, but before he can get a word out, I say curtly, "What are we watching?"

I can see him debating whether or not to go along with the subject change. After a moment, he says quietly, still studying me, "How about *Casablanca?*"

*What. The. Hell. Did thinking about Barton Drossel somehow conjure up one of his favorite black and white movies out of thin air?*

"No way."

"O-kay. What do you want to watch?"

"Something from this century. What do you have?"

After a lot of bickering, we settle on *National Treasure*. We sit down on opposite corners of the sectional and start watching. Ben has just announced to his dad that Abigail was carrying his child when I feel something hit my cheek.

*What?*

I glance down and see a piece of popcorn sitting beside me on the sofa. Looking over at Clancy, I see him focused on the TV screen. Deciding to ignore him and the popcorn, I return my attention to the movie.

After the 43rd piece of popcorn hits me, I snap. "Stop it!"

He hits pause on the remote. "This is a good part; I don't want to miss it. Stop what?"

I glare at him. "You know what, Clancy."

His eyes are wide and innocent. "I thought you might like some popcorn."

"Well, as a matter of fact, I do, but normally the polite thing to do is pass the bowl."

"Or you could move a little closer, and we could share."

I cross my arms. "No thanks."

"Scared?" In the blue light of the TV screen, his eyes are mocking.

"Of you? Don't make me laugh."

"Then come on. I won't bite."

He has me cornered, and he knows it. With a huff I move to the middle of the couch, leaving a healthy foot of distance between us, but he scoots over, closing the gap and drops the popcorn bowl into my lap. His hip brushes mine. My heart jumps into my throat. *I can't move or he'll laugh at me. That's the only reason I'm staying this close to him.*

I don't remember the rest of the movie except that we keep glancing at each other and missing the other's eyes. And then, right when they're about to go into the tunnel and Abigail kisses Ben, our eyes catch and hold.

He smiles, and the dimples pop into his cheeks. And I just reach up and trace the groove, feeling the sandpaper of his skin. My thumb brushes his lip, and my heart stops. Then, I jump up, the empty popcorn bowl clattering to the floor.

"I—I'm tired," I gasp out. "This—the movie—the popcorn was…really great. I— Good night."

He's on his feet too, staring at me, his breathing fast and shallow. "Good night," he says, his voice heavy with something that makes butterflies explode in my stomach.

"Good night," I say again and stumble down the hall to the bedroom. But instead of sleeping, I lie in the darkness, trying not to remember the feeling of his skin beneath my fingers and the sound of his deep laugh and the warmth of his hip against mine and the huskiness of his voice when he said goodnight. *What is wrong with me? I've loved Bart*

*Drossel my entire life. Clancy Jankovich is NOT my type. I am not falling for him. I must just have gone temporarily insane. Nothing has changed. We're roommates. Roommates, Chel. Tomorrow we'll act like this never happened.*

Day fourteen of married life. So much for tomorrow. At ten o'clock my cell phone rings, and the caller ID says Clancy Jankovich. My heart does a weird thumpy thing.

"What's up?"

"Hello to you too."

I roll my eyes at the ceiling. "I'm sure you didn't just call me to say hello."

"Oh yeah? Sometimes husbands do that."

My heart does the weird thumpy thing again. *Did he really?* Next moment, my bubble bursts. "But you're right. I called to say that I'm going to be out of town for the next ten days."

"What?"

"Going to miss me?" he says lightly.

For a moment I can't speak. Then I pull the phone from my ear and press the red circle with the phone inside it. I stand in the kitchen, staring at the pile of breakfast dishes in the sink. My pancakes were charred because I forgot to grease the pan.

He doesn't think to tell me he's leaving town until the day of. Why do I keep expecting him to act like we're really married? I have to stop it.

Day sixteen of married life. My phone rings while I'm at Cat's apartment. I view the name on the screen and hit the ignore button. This makes fourteen times now Clancy has called me since I hung up on him on

Thursday. Serenity is making "dinner" for me in a corner of the living room, brightly colored plastic food scattered around her. Cat glances up at me from where she's sitting on the floor, scribbling down a shopping list.

"You can take that, you know."

"I don't need to."

Cat looks at me again, more sharply this time. "Who's calling you, Chel?"

"Clancy."

Cat's eyes narrow. "How many times has he called you?"

"Today? Four times."

"What do you mean today? Did you guys have a fight?"

"Nope."

"Chel, that's obviously a lie."

"It's not a lie. We didn't fight because I hung up on him after he told me on Thursday that he was skipping town for ten days."

"What? Chel, you told me he was gone on a business trip."

"He is. He just didn't think to tell me he was leaving until the morning of. Because this marriage is a sham."

Cat moans and drops her forehead onto the coffee table in exasperation. "Chel! For all you know, his boss could have told him that morning he needed to go! Or else he forgot because you guys have only been married for two weeks! And you'll never know because you haven't answered any of his four calls!"

"Fourteen calls."

"Rachel Elizabeth Corinne King! What is wrong with you?"

"Ra-Chellie Lizbeff Crinn King," Serenity echoes from the corner and then cackles with laughter. "That's funny."

Her laugh is so crazy I can't help laughing too in spite of myself. But I force myself back to sobriety as Cat continues to regard me sternly. "Or he might have known for weeks and didn't tell me until the day of because it just wasn't a priority for him."

"Chel. Call him." I bite my lip. Cat puts her notebook down and scoots across the floor toward me. "Chel, if you think Derek ever called me after we had a fight, you've got another think coming. He always waited for me to call him and patch things up. You shouldn't treat Clancy like this. If I ever found a guy who would call me fourteen times to try to fix a fight, I'd think I'd struck gold."

I blow out my breath. "Fine."

I walk into the hall and press Clancy's name in my Missed Calls, then lift the phone to my ear. After three rings, Clancy picks up.

"Hi," I say in a small voice. Suddenly, my annoyance over the past few days seems stupidly petty and childish.

"Well, look who finally decided to call." His voice is brittle.

I have no idea what to say. I hear him blow out his breath. "Why did you call, Chel?"

I swallow. "Why didn't you tell me you were leaving until the day of?"

He makes an incredulous sound. "Is that what this was all about? Geez, because the way my job works, I sometimes get told at a moment's notice I'm leaving. That's what happened on Thursday."

"Oh. That's what Cat said might have happened."

"Cat's a smart girl."

The words and tone make my heart stand still. I swallow convulsively. For an instant, the words, "Did you ever know Barton Drossel?" hover on my lips. But then I remember trying to talk about Bart the night before Clancy left. I'm tired of probing old wounds.

"I know." I mean the words to sound light and affectionate, but somehow they come out taut and snippy instead.

There is a moment of silence before he says, "How come I couldn't get ahold of you for three days, Chel?"

His tone annoys me. "I'm not your employee," I retort.

"No," he says, clearly struggling to keep his voice even, "you're my *wife*."

The word touches a raw nerve. "In name only, Clancy! Why do you have to keep throwing that at me? I don't even know what you do for a job! We don't sleep in the same bed!"

"We could, Chel!" He's yelling now. "It's not my choice that we live at arms' length!"

"I knew that was what you wanted!" I yell back. "Why else would you allow some strange girl to move in with you if not to eventually sleep with her?"

"I've never even tried to touch you! As I remember, all the touching came from you, sweetheart!"

I'm so angry I can't speak for a moment. The words, when they come, are breathy with emotion. "I lost my head for a second, all right? Don't worry, it won't happen again, *sweetheart*."

"Chel." He's no longer yelling. "That's not what I meant."

"Well, it is what I mean! I'm your roommate, Clancy! I'll help with the housework. I'll start looking for a job so that I can chip in for rent! But I'm not your wife. And if that's what you're hoping for, you should kick me out right now."

The silence which follows is long and throbbing. "All right," Clancy says finally. "Get a job. I'll expect your share of the rent on the first of every month. 425 bucks." The phone clicks.

"Then the man said, 'Wife, we cannot go on any longer eating and drinking here and earning nothing. You had better spin.' She sat down and tried to spin, but the hard thread soon cut into her soft fingers until they bled."

~Grimm

# Chapter 7
## Failure

Turns out getting a job in the middle of a recession is next to impossible. After Clancy hung up, Cat helped me draft a resume—with next to nothing on it—her lips pursed the entire time. Then she told me to go to the library and use one of their computers to search job postings. If I came up empty, I should call the Chamber of Commerce and ask them about job openings. And if that failed, I should start pounding the pavement.

Clancy's coming back in four days. And I *have* to have a job by the time he gets back. But there were only four job postings online, and they all required either a bachelor's degree or experience or both. I called the Chamber, and they said they hadn't had any job postings from their members in about a month. Yesterday, I went to every restaurant downtown and asked about job openings. No one was hiring. No one has the money.

I lift my feet onto the coffee table and moan slightly as the raw, red skin on the back of my heel slides against the edge of the table. I thought it would be a good idea to dress professionally when asking about job openings, so I wore a gray pencil skirt and navy blouse with black pumps. Not. Smart.

There's a knock on the apartment door. My heart rate speeds up. Clancy can't be back yet. What if it's a stranger? Should I open the door?

Gingerly sliding my feet off the coffee table, I tiptoe to the door and peer through the peephole. My breath catches in my throat, and I slowly slide back the deadbolt and open the door.

"Mom."

Her face is pinched and pale and there are shadows under her eyes. When she sees me, her eyes brim with tears that she quickly dashes away.

"Rachel," she says, her voice thinner and higher than usual. "I mean, Chel. May I come in?"

Silently, I stand aside to let her pass, and she slips past me, the wrapped boxes she's carrying brushing against the doorframe. Scanning the room, she slides out of her brown heels and places the presents on the counter. I can see her taking in the mismatched furniture, the dust on top of the bookcase, and the pile of dishes in the sink. Thank God she can't see into the refrigerator.

"This is...nice."

My lips twist sardonically. "Have a seat, Mom." She perches on the edge of the sectional, and I sit down on the other end, folding my legs beneath me.

There is a pause, and then she says, "How are you?"

"Fine."

She persists. "How are you feeling with the pregnancy?"

"Exhausted. And nauseous. And my heels hurt." She glances quizzically at me, and I smile slightly. "I guess that's less from the pregnancy and more from walking around in high heels all of yesterday." She still appears puzzled. "I'm looking for a job. But there aren't any."

Her lips form an O, and I can see a crease forming between her eyes. Angst building inside, I wait for her to suggest I come home. But she surprises me. "I believe Western Supply is seeking someone to work in their clothing department. Bart mentioned something about it the last time he was over."

My insides turn to lead. "Oh, has he been in town?"

"He's actually living in the area again. I think he commutes to Seattle now or else works remotely."

Bart is back in the area. And I'm married to a street musician who expects me to earn my keep.

I feel my nails biting into my palms. Miniature semicircles of pain, mirroring the agony pinpricking my heart. Mom's voice breaks into my consciousness. "And how is your...husband?" she stumbles slightly over the word. "Clancy?"

I try to force my lips to form the word *fine*, but the sounds are frozen inside me. In my mind's eye, I see him.

Curled on the couch with his violin in his hands, coaxing melody from the strings.

Wearing his denim Grill Master apron, bent over the stove, heavenly smells rising around him.

Lying on the sectional, one arm flung over his head, mouth open in a snore, completely relaxed in sleep.

Cleaning the toilet, nose pinched with one hand, scrubbing brush in the other after one particularly bad day of morning sickness.

Crouched over the Bible in his lap, muttering broken prayers to his God for me.

Smiling down at me, dimples creating creases in the lines of his face, so close I could have kissed him, the night before he left.

I try again to speak, but all that comes out is a strangled sort of moan. In an instant, Mom is beside me with her arms around me, and for once I don't mind as she strokes my hair and holds me close, my head nestled under her chin. My chest is tight, and my throat is aching, but still the tears won't come.

"Is...is he abusing you, honey?"

My head jerks up. "No, Mom!"

"Then...what's wrong?"

What's wrong? That he's good. And kind. And funny. And attractive. That I think he could maybe love me if I would let him. That I can't let him. That I hate myself for pushing him away. That I'm not over Bart. But at the same time, that I think I'm falling for Clancy.

"Everything is just...complicated," I finally get out.

"And everything always feels worse when you're pregnant," she says softly, giving me a squeeze. "Lots of hormones." I gulp out a laugh, and she squeezes me again. There's a pause, and if we had a different kind of relationship, I think we might have started apologizing for the past. But neither of us feels comfortable enough around the other to do that, so eventually, she pulls away, fussily straightening her coat. "I just wanted to come by and see how you were doing," she says briskly, dabbing quickly at her eyes again, as she gets up.

I get up too and stand next to the door as she wriggles into her high heels. "I wanted to bring by a few things too," she says, awkwardly gesturing to the gifts on the counter. "A wedding present. And something for the little one."

My throat constricts again. "Thank you."

She nods and opens the door, stepping out onto the landing. As she begins to descend the stairs, I finally find my voice. "Come again."

She turns and gives me a small smile. Then she is gone.

Picking up the boxes from the counter, I lug them over to the couch. After studying them for a moment, I tear open the perfect paper. There's a spinning spice rack. And a car seat. Practical gifts. Mom gifts. I love them.

I don't know how long I sit there, staring at my presents, but finally, I pull myself off the couch and go to the bedroom to put on my pencil skirt and navy blouse again. I need to go interview for a job at Western Supply.

Either I make a great impression, or Western Supply is desperate (I'm choosing to go with the former), because after a quick glance at my resume and chat with the manager, they tell me I have the job.

Day one of being a Clothing Salesperson. I hate customers. Today, I was shadowing a twenty-something young woman named Jillian. The first customer of the day was a mom with two little boys. While the younger one raced through the sales racks, shrieking at random intervals, the mom and the older one pulled out a box of red Nikes, and the child attempted to force his feet into them.

"They're too small," he whined.

"Do you have these in a size four?" the mom asked.

"We will check for you, ma'am," Jillian responded smoothly. "Chel, could you run back and check what we have for children's Nikes in storage?"

I wended my way back to our storage area, which I had been shown in the hour before opening and checked in the Nike children's section for the red shoes. It took a while, but finally I found the red shoes and ascertained that we only had them in children's two, three, six, and seven.

"No size four, I'm afraid," I reported. "We only have sizes two, three, six, and seven for that particular shoe."

The mother scowled at me as though this was my fault and then cooed to the child, "Sweetie, is there another color you like?"

"No! I want red!"

"Poppet, they don't have them in your size. How about orange?"

Sulkily, the child gazed at the orange Nike his mother held out. "Fine."

"Chel, could you run back and get a size four?" Jillian asked, her quick eyes skimming the shelves.

Plastering a smile onto my face, I trudged back to the storage area. The Band-Aids I had put over the blisters on my heels were slipping, and I could feel my shoes beginning to chafe. When I returned with the box, the mother snatched it from me without a thank you and flipped it over to view the price.

"You're charging $69.99 for a pair of children's shoes! This is criminal!" She flung the box down. "We're going to Payless Footwear. Come on, Mikey! Justin, come here!" Her younger son raced away from her, laughing evilly. "Justin! I'm going to count to three! One, two...! Justin, come here this minute! Mommy is getting very angry! Honey-bunny, we'll stop at McDonald's on the way if you come now."

When they finally left, Jillian grimaced at me. "Welcome to customer service. Can you take these back to the back?"

Then a man came in and tried to return a pair of slacks without the receipt. When we told him we needed the receipt in order to be able to process returns, he demanded to speak to our manager. When the manager came and told him the exact same thing we had just said, he smiled and went away.

A young woman tried to talk down the price on a pair of yoga pants. When we told her prices were fixed and we could not barter, she flounced out after telling us she wouldn't be shopping here ever again. "She comes in every other week," Jillian muttered to me, rolling her eyes.

When I finally get home and collapse onto the sofa, I calculate in my head. I'm getting paid $8.07 an hour. I worked eight hours today. I'm going to get a measly $64.56 as compensation for slowly going crazy.

Day three of being a Clothing Salesperson. "We need to restock the lingerie racks before we go home today," Jillian tells me at 4pm. "A new shipment just came in. I really need to get off on time because my husband can't pick up our son from daycare today, so I'm going to just have you open the boxes and bring piles of stuff out to me, and I'll do the actual restocking. I'll show you how another day."

She hands me a box opener, and I head to the back. My feet are still killing me. Three days on my feet means my blisters have gotten re-ripped open every single day.

"And this, kids, is why you should stay in school," I mutter to myself in a singsong voice, slashing viciously at the top of a box. The cutter slips and gashes across the palm of my other hand.

"Ow! Crap!" Blood bubbles along the cut in my hand. Swearing under my breath, and cradling my hand, I run to the bathroom and stick my hand under the faucet. I have no idea where a First Aid kit is. Jillian has been edgy all day, and she'll be mad if I make her late to pick up her son. I go into one of the stalls and pull off a long length of toilet paper. I wrap my hand until I can't see blood seeping through the paper anymore and tuck in the ends.

Then I run back to storage, finish cutting open the box, pull out a pile of cream-colored panties and carry them out to Jillian. "God, where have you been?" she snaps, grabbing the clothes from me and hurrying away without waiting for an answer.

My hand continues to sting as I open boxes and carry the contents to Jillian. I'm on the last three boxes when I hear her yell. I race out and see her holding up a lacy champagne pink negligee.

"Chel, what is this??"

My heart plummets to my navel as she points to a rust-colored streak on the skirt of the nightgown. I glance down at my hand, and my heart lands in my shoes. Blood has soaked through the toilet paper, and I didn't notice. I clear my throat.

"I, um, I cut myself with the box opener, and I guess, I must have..."

Jillian gives an inarticulate yell of frustration and runs back through the shelves, rifling through the things she just restocked.

"This!" she snarls, flinging a pair of panties down on top of the negligee. "And this!" A light-green pajama top follows. By the time she's done, a sizable pile of lingerie I've marked with my blood is lying on the floor, and my heart is back up in my throat.

"Listen," I say, "I'm really sorry..."

Jillian ignores me and pulls out her walkie-talkie. "Could I get Michael in the lingerie section, please?" she says in a voice of deadly calm.

"It was an accident," I try, but she just glares. In a moment, the manager is with us. Jillian points at me.

"Your newest employee," she says in a shaking voice, "has just ruined over $500 worth of merchandise!"

When I get home, I realize there's no food in the apartment. I forgot to go shopping this week since I started at Western Supply. It doesn't really matter though. I'm not hungry. With shaking hands, I fill Clancy's tea kettle and turn on the stove. Then I sink onto the couch and stare into space.

Has anyone else in the history of the world managed to get fired on their third day on the job?

The kettle whistles, and I climb slowly to my feet and pour hot water into a chipped mug. I add a tea bag and limp back to the sofa, clutching the steaming mug in both hands. For some reason my teeth have started chattering, even though I'm not really cold.

After being a complete jerk to Clancy, I won't even be able to pay him this month's rent.

I focus on the wall in front of me, my eyes burning. Cat is a single mom, but she's managed to hold down a job for four years. She can at least support her own child. I won't even be able to do that. Who's going to hire me now after I've been fired?

The darkness in the apartment presses around me. I only turned on the kitchen light, and one of the two lightbulbs is dead. Setting my cup down on the coffee table, I press the heels of my hands into my eyes. I'm a disaster. I'm eighteen years old, and what I have to show for my life so far is unrequited love, an unwanted pregnancy, a fake marriage, severed relationships with my only living relatives, and a lost job. My life is completely pointless. Of no use to anyone.

Feeling the blackness of despair enfolding me, I grope for my phone. Scrolling through my contacts, I click on Cat's name. I need someone right now. The phone rings. And rings. And rings.

*Pick up, Cat. Please.*

The phone rings again. Then Cat's voice sounds in my ear. "Hi, you've reached Catalina. I can't get to the phone right now, but—" I click the red circle and fling the phone onto the couch next to me.

"God…" I don't know what makes me say it. Maybe because there's no one else. "Please, if you're there…" I don't even know how to finish my sentence. "I need help," I mumble. "I need something. God, I'm at the end of my rope. I'm a failure. I don't even know what I need. But, Lord, I need help."

Clancy's shiny leather Bible sits on the coffee table like always, and on a whim, I reach over and flip it open, rifling through until a verse catches my eye.

"Peace I leave with you; my peace I give you. I do not give to you as the world gives. Do not let your hearts be troubled and do not be afraid."

My throat closes, and I lean my throbbing forehead against my hands. I need peace. But sometimes I think I was born fighting with life. Maybe I'm incapable of accepting peace. Even if God could give it to me.

I pull the Bible back toward me. *Show me something, God. Please. Something from you.* Opening the Bible near the beginning, a header jumps out. Jacob Wrestles with God. The words seep into my soul.

*But Jacob replied, "I will not let you go unless you bless me."*
*The man asked him, "What is your name?"*
*"Jacob," he answered.*
*Then the man said, "Your name will no longer be Jacob, but Israel, because you have struggled with God and with humans and have overcome."*
*Jacob said, "Please tell me your name."*
*But he replied, "Why do you ask my name?" Then he blessed him there.*
*So Jacob called the place Peniel, saying, "It is because I saw God face-to-face, and yet my life was spared."*

Allowing the cover to fall closed, I slip the Bible onto the coffee table and lay back on the sofa, shutting my burning eyes. And I don't have peace. But Jacob's words beat over and over in my mind.

*I will not let you go unless you bless me.*
*I will not let you go unless you bless me.*
*God.*
*I will NOT let You go unless You bless me.*

I awake to the sound of crackling and the smell of burning. Struggling to my feet, I stagger into the kitchenette. All vestiges of sleep evaporate. The stove top is on fire. A strangled scream erupts from my lips. Springing to the sink, I wrench the water on and am just about to throw a cupful on the flames when something in my brain clicks. Isn't it a bad idea to put water on an electric flame?

*What then?*
*Think. Think. Think! THINK!*
*Oxygen. Cut off the oxygen supply?*

Yanking open a cupboard, I send saucepans jangling onto the floor as I scrabble for our biggest metal pot. Then I slam it down over the blazing burner. Darkness fills the apartment. The burning smell seems to intensify now that the flames are gone. As I stand shaking in the blackness, with my heart pounding against my ribs, my only thought is, *Really, God?*

Then the apartment door rattles and slowly opens.

"Now I was at our king's palace and asked if they couldn't use a kitchen maid. They promised me to take you. In return, you will get free food."

~Grimm

# Chapter 8
## Getting Acquainted

I can't help it. I shriek like a banshee, sure that on top of everything else I'm about to be murdered because I forgot to lock the apartment door.

"Chel!!" The light flips on, and I'm looking into Clancy's wide, terrified eyes as he slams the apartment door behind him and lets a backpack fall to the ground. In two steps, he's in front of me, hands gripping my biceps so hard it hurts. "Are you okay? What's wrong?"

"I-I'm fine. I just—" My heart rate slows, and I glare at him. "Except you scared the crap out of me! What the hell did you come barging in like that for?"

He drops my arms, his eyes hardening. "I'm sorry. I'll knock next time before coming into *my* apartment."

"You're not supposed to come back until tomorrow!"

His lips tighten for a moment, and then he turns away and scoops up his backpack. Guilt pricks my conscience. "Where are you going?"

"To unpack," he says shortly and strides away down the hall.

For a moment I stand still, and then I reach slowly out and turn off the burner, leaving the pot sitting over it. My heart begins to pump a slow, ominous march in my chest as I take in the charred circle on the ceiling above the stove.

I hear the shower turn on and walk slowly down the hall to the bedroom. Sinking onto the bed, I stare at the wall. As soon as he gets out of the shower, I need to tell Clancy that not only did I just throw away his damage deposit, but I don't have a job anymore, so I can't even pay him back.

I don't know how much time passes before the door opens, and Clancy walks in humming tunelessly and heads straight for the dresser, not noticing me on the bed.

"Clancy?"

"G-aaaah! Chel!" He whirls, clutching at the towel around his waist. Breathing heavily, he puts a hand to his face. When he speaks again, his tone is one of forced calm. "Yes?"

I look away, because the sight of his smooth skin still speckled with drops of water from the shower does funny things to my insides.

"I-I..." I start and glance at him again, trying to formulate words. His face is scrunched in confusion, and I remember the feeling of stubble beneath my fingertips and the softness of his lips.

Sliding off the bed, I make a beeline for the door. "Can we have this conversation when you're dressed?"

His eyebrows raise, and I hate myself for the blush I can feel spreading from my neck all the way to my hairline. The look in his brown eyes is making me feel hot all over. "Sure," he drawls, and I pull the door open and dive into the hallway.

A minute later, he emerges, wearing sweats and pulling a white T-shirt over his head. For some reason, the pot that I'm compulsively scrubbing slips through my fingers at that exact moment, clattering against the sink and sending up a wave of soapy water to drench the bottom of my T-shirt. I can feel my cheeks burning again as I turn to face him. He's sitting in the middle of the sectional with his arms spread across the back and his feet on the coffee table, his eyes fixed on me.

Something is wrong with my breathing as I slowly dry my hands on a dish towel and lean against the counter, avoiding his gaze. I wait for him to say something, but the silence stretches and finally I look up at him. He's still staring at me, and my heart jumps into my mouth.

"Can you stop looking at me like that?"

"Like what?" he says softly, getting up slowly from the sofa. My heart begins banging against my ribs so hard it sounds like a bass drum in my ears.

"What are you doing?" I hate how shrill my voice sounds.

"Coming over to talk," he responds, stopping on the other side of the bar and leaning against it, arms crossed, eyes still fixed on my face.

He's only a couple of feet away, but thank God, the bar is between us. I gaze down at my own hands, clenched on the countertop and force myself to speak.

"I left the burner on, and it caught fire, Clancy. So there's a burn mark on the ceiling. Which means you lose your damage deposit. Not to mention how it looks. And I forgot about the burner because I was in such a funk over losing my new job. Which means that I don't have any money to pay rent, let alone repay your damage deposit." My eyes start burning, like they always do when the tears are trying to come. "I'll pay you back though," I say to my hands. "I'll get another job. Somehow. Maybe I'll take a leaf out of your book. Sing on street corners."

He's silent for so long that I mumble, "Say something."

What happens next completely floors me. He takes my face in his hands and lifts my chin so that we're looking into each other's eyes. My breath catches in my throat as he leans toward me, stopping so close that I can smell the minty scent of Aim on his breath. "Gosh, I've missed you," he whispers and kisses me on the lips.

When we break apart, I can't speak. I just stare at him, my blood thundering, my chest aflame. His face flushes, and his shoulders slump. "I'm sorry," he mutters. "I told you I wouldn't touch you. I just—I don't know what I was thinking..." I stride around the counter and grab the front of his T-shirt, and he stops talking.

"Kiss me, Clancy," I say, and I see a smile curve his lips at the reference before his arms come around me and his mouth finds mine.

I can't think, and I don't want to. It's just him. His hands on my waist. My fingers in the soft hair at the base of his neck. His kisses lighting a fire inside me as my body presses into his.

For a moment he pulls away from me, his breathing shallow and rapid, his eyes raking my face. "Are you sure?"

"There's a reason I didn't promise not to touch you," I say, pushing onto my tiptoes and allowing my lips to graze his neck.

"There's a reason I slept on the couch," he responds, scooping me off my feet and striding down the hall.

Hours later, he pulls me into the curve of his body, his breath warm against my ear. "You're gorgeous."

A thrill shoots through me, and I turn my head slightly, rubbing my temple against the stubble of his chin. I don't know what to say. I've never been good at sweet nothings.

His hand caresses my belly which is barely starting to curve. "How's the baby?"

"Good, I guess." My stomach drops. His words make me remember another time. Another place. Another man. Sickness washes over me, and I turn my head away from him. *Am I not his first, just like he isn't mine?*

"Chel?" He props himself up on his elbow, gently turning my chin to look into my eyes. His fingers trace my face. "What's wrong?"

I close my eyes, unable to meet his gaze, shame burning inside me. I want to get up, to run, to hide from him, because he's good and pure and whole, everything I'm not. The burning is beginning in my eyes, but this time I feel something I haven't felt in seven years—liquid, seeping through my lashes and rolling in a long, slow rivulet down my cheek.

His thumb scrapes my eyelashes as he brushes the tear away. "Sweetheart…" He's said that word to me before, but not like this, and more tears come, pouring down my face until I'm sobbing, burying my face in the pillow, crying out the pent-up pain of years. He holds me, stroking my hair.

*God, I'm sorry. Lord, what have I done? I'm so broken. I blamed you for Dad's death. I said you weren't good, but if you're not, then why am I here with this man who is so good to me? With this man who will be a good father to this child? I don't know how he loves me. I've been nothing but horrible to him. I've sneered and sniped at him. I've broken his stuff. I've allowed him to provide for me without a word of thanks. And, God, I've run away from you for years. I've probably broken every commandment you ever gave. I've hurled anger and hatred at you. How could you still WANT me?*

And Cat's words come back to me, the ones she spoke the night I told her what I had done.

*"With you there is forgiveness that you may be feared."*

*Forgive me, Lord. Jesus, I'm the prodigal daughter, aren't I? But I want to come back. Please let me come back.*

And for perhaps the first time in my whole restless, at-war-with-the-world life, I feel peace.

"Come to church with me." Clancy leans on the counter, a coffee mug clasped in his fingers, studying me as I sit curled in a corner of the sectional with his Bible open on my knees, devouring the words I've closed my heart to for seven years. Last night, I told him I was giving my life to God again. I had begged him to forgive me for everything, my face buried in the pillow as my muffled voice told the barebones story of my one-night stand. He forgave me, holding me close to kiss away the tears still pouring down my face. But the one glance I risked at his face told me my words were a knife in his heart. His pain hurt worse than anything. I had ugly cried myself to sleep.

"No."

"Wow. Maybe Acts 2 should be next on your reading list."

I rifle through the tabs of his Bible, looking for the Acts one. "That's a while out. I only started this morning."

"Are you reading cover to cover?"

"Um, duh. How else do you read a book?"

He throws up his hands. "Hey, everybody told me I should start in the Gospels. They said Leviticus is a little rough for a new Christian."

I raise my eyebrows at him. "Wimp."

"Show-off."

Leaving his mug on the counter, he plops onto the couch next to me and wraps one arm around me, drawing me into his side. Pushing aside a strand of hair, he lightly kisses my temple. Tingles run through me, and I feel a blush rising up my face.

"I'm trying to concentrate," I say, not looking at him because I don't want him to see how much he makes me feel.

"Oh yeah?" he whispers, blowing into my ear so that I shy away from him, giggling involuntarily.

"What do you want?" I demand, rubbing my ear to eliminate the tickles he's created.

"I want to know why you won't come to church with me."

I drop my eyes, my fingers skimming the golden edges of his Bible's pages. "When my dad died of cancer, there were a lot of church people who said a lot of things. 'He's in a better place.' 'God works all things for good.' 'It was all in the Lord's plan.' 'Rejoice in the Lord always.' I didn't believe that then. And I don't believe it now. I don't think God wants an eleven-year-old girl to watch her dad going through that kind of pain. Maybe it's the devil. Maybe it's the fact that the world is broken. But I don't think it's what God desires. And I didn't need a lot of people whose families were well and healthy telling me that kind of crap. I want to know God again. But I don't need church. Or the people in it."

I expect him to argue with me. But after a moment, all he says is, "You're right about it being crap for healthy people to try to tell someone who's hurting that kind of stuff." He kisses my temple again and gets up. "I'll see you when I get back."

When he arrives home, Clancy makes me go for a walk with him. "It's good for the baby," he says, and I can tell this is going to be his trump card for the next six months. We drive downtown and walk along the docks. Memories of times with Bart intrude, and I push them away. But they continue to prick at my heart, and guilt rises. I'm falling for Clancy.

I know I am. Do I love him yet? I'm not sure. But I know that's where I'm headed at breakneck speed. I need to forget Bart Drossel. But my whole childhood was Bart. I don't know how to forget him. And I think there's a part of me that doesn't want to.

"You're awfully quiet," Clancy says.

I give him a tight-lipped smile. "Sorry. I don't have anything to say."

He raises his eyebrows. "What's bothering you?"

"I didn't say anything was."

"I'm not an idiot, Chel."

"I didn't say that either."

He huffs out a sigh of exasperation. "Are we headed back into the roommate zone? I kind of thought last night had changed things."

I know I should be different now, but anger still rises. "My soul is still my own, Clancy. No amount of having me read about how great the early church is will make me go with you, and no amount of pestering is going to pry windows in my soul!"

"I'm not trying to pry windows in your soul!" He gazes out at the Straits, rubbing the back of his neck. "All I mean is that I really want to be married to you. I want us to talk. I want you to tell me if something's bothering you."

"Like you talk to me?" I don't know where the words are coming from, but they continue to spill out. "I hardly know anything about you. Do you have any family? Friends? Where do you work? What do you do? You haven't told me a single personal thing about yourself, Clancy! And you suddenly expect me to just start spilling my guts?"

"You never asked me."

"Okay, I'm asking now!"

We've stopped walking, and I turn to face him, my hair whipping around my face in the wind flowing off the Straits. His mouth twists slightly as he says, "That's a little broad. How about you condense your curiosity into twenty questions? And then, you tell me what's bothering you."

"I don't want to talk about it."

He throws up his hands. "Then we don't have a deal."

I gaze into the gray waters of the Straits. "You don't want to know what's bothering me, Clancy."

"Try me."

"You can't just forget what people tell you, Clancy." I turn and look straight into his eyes. "And I'm telling you that if I tell you this, you're going to wish I hadn't."

His brown eyes flicker for a moment, then harden. "Chel, I'm a big boy." Voice softening, he steps toward me, putting both hands on my waist and drawing me forward. "I don't want my wife to have to carry burdens alone."

I want to take his face in my hands and kiss him until we both forget that this conversation ever happened. But I force myself to step away.

"I get twenty questions first. Birthday?" He doesn't answer immediately, and I poke him in the side. "Is that a hard question?"

"May 7th."

*He has the same birthday as Bart. What are the odds?*

I swallow. "How old are you?"

"Twenty-one."

*Oh, I knew that. Waste of a question.*

"Where do your parents live?"

"They're divorced," he says shortly. "My mom lives here. My dad in Seattle."

"Why haven't I met your mom?"

Again, he pauses, and my stomach drops. "You don't think she'd like me?"

"Why do you always jump to the worst conclusions, Chel?" His voice is tired.

"Um, that seems like the only logical conclusion! Since your mom lives in town, but you haven't introduced me to her."

He breathes deeply, eyes drifting closed for a moment. "You'll see my mom soon. I was just waiting for...the right time."

A snarky comeback rises to my lips, but I choke it back. After what I had to tell him last night, harping on his poor choices seems like a very bad idea. "Do you have any siblings?"

"No."

"Where did you go to school?"

"Mostly Seattle. Some here."

I wrinkle my nose. "I don't remember meeting you."

"I didn't have braids then. Or a fake tattoo. Or a beard. And I wore glasses." He's staring at me, that look in his eyes again. The one where he's just dropped a huge hint to a riddle, and he's expecting me to shout out the answer at any moment.

"Most teenagers don't have beards, Clancy."

His shoulders slump slightly. "No kidding."

*Is he really hurt that I don't remember him?*

"Where do you work?"

"American Seafoods." My heart lurches. Bart's company.

"What do you do?"

"I work in HR."

*Bart is his boss.*

I can feel heat rising up my face and look out over the Straits. A cool wind brushes at my cheeks, cooling them. "Favorite movie?"

"I don't have just one."

"Name a couple then."

"*National Treasure. Catch Me If You Can.*"

"Best friend?"

"My roommate, of course." He gives me a sly smile.

"Not funny. Who is it really?"

"His name is Drew Jennings. We work together at American Seafoods. He lives in Seattle."

"Is he married too?"

"Nope. He has a steady girlfriend though."

"Favorite food?"

"Calamari."

I make a face. "What question am I on?"

"Thirteen. Counting that one."

"What? That does not count!"

He smirks. "'What?' is a question too."

I scowl at him. "Favorite animal?"

"I'm not an animal person. Anything edible."

"Favorite artist?"

"Jackson Pollack."

"I meant musical artist."

"Still counts as two questions," he says smirking. "David Oistrakh."

"Who?"

"He's a classical violinist."

I shrug. "Favorite song with lyrics?"

He grimaces. "You know that's too hard to narrow to one."

"One of your favorites then."

"'Wonderful Tonight' by Eric Clapton."

"You like blondes, then?"

His lips twist as he fights a smile. "I take it you've listened to it a few times yourself."

"Answer the question, Clancy."

His smirk widens. "'I like blondes. Chubby ones.'"

"Gosh, you think you're smart. Are you into chick flicks too?"

"Not in general. *While You Were Sleeping* is a classic. You've got one more question, love."

"Only because you completely cheated with the counting. Fine…" I think for a moment. "Life's ambition?"

"'To rid the world of evil and market my own range of hair care potions,'" he says without cracking a smile.

"Oh my Go—gosh. What are you—a walking library?" He's smiling again, and I'm pretty sure he noticed my swearing correction. "What's your real answer?"

"Wow, I'm offended. Way to diss my life's ambition."

"Clancy."

He raises his eyebrows at me, and I know he's not going to answer. "Your turn. Tell me what's up."

How on earth am I supposed to put something this complicated into words? I study the cracked wooden planks beneath my feet to avoid looking at him. "You know Bart Drossel? Your boss?"

His eyes widen and then narrow. "Yeah…"

"I've known him since I was six years old. I was in love with him for most of high school."

"Are you still in love with him?" Clancy's voice is strange, almost as though he can't get enough air into his lungs.

I stare between the cracks of the dock at the gray, surging water. At this moment, I want to lie to him. I want to say that Bart Drossel doesn't mean anything to me anymore. My gut twists as I remember our conversation last night. I'm ripping him apart. Oh, why did he fall for me? I just hurt him. Over and over again. And that's starting to rip me apart too. "Most days I don't think so," I say softly, the words the best I can honestly give him.

"Most days you don't think so?" His voice cracks, and I can't look into his face.

"I told you you wouldn't like it," I say into the gray water. The ensuing silence is so long that I finally glance up at him. His eyes are fixed on the horizon, but I can see something sparkling in the corner. As I watch, he lifts his hand and dashes it across his face. My heart drops. "I'm sorry," I whisper.

"What for?" he asks, still staring out across the water.

"For...not being the kind of girl you deserve, I guess."

I feel his fingers wrap around mine. "You are the kind of girl I want though," he says, eyes still fixed on the blue mist across the Straits. My throat clogs. The words I always wished Bart would say. Coming out of Clancy's mouth. We stand in silence for a long time before heading back to the apartment.

I'm lying on the sofa in a stupor when he comes out of the bedroom after dinner carrying his violin.

"Where are you going?" I mumble.

"Down to the restaurant." One corner of his mouth lifts. "Like I told you the night we met, music helps me relax."

I nod sleepily. "K." When he leans down to kiss me, I grab his T-shirt. "When you get back, can you help me look for another job? I seriously want to pay you back for the fire damage."

"Would me telling you not to worry about it make any difference?"

"No."

"Didn't think so. Yeah, I'll help you."

A few minutes later, or that's how it feels, the sound of the apartment door opening jerks me awake.

"Have a good nap?" Clancy asks.

I sit up, rubbing my eyes. "I'm still exhausted. How the heck can growing a human make you this tired?"

"I think growing a human is the crucial part of that sentence," Clancy answers, heading for the fridge and pulling out a beer. Popping off the cap, he flops onto the couch next to me. I gaze longingly at the bottle in his hand as he takes a swig. "I found you a job," he says as he swallows.

"What?! Where?"

"The Morning Catch. They're looking for hosts."

# Chapter 9
## New Jobs and Familiar Faces

"No."

"Chel, come on. They pay hosts ten bucks an hour plus tips. You're not going to find a retail job that pays better. And"—he looks at me sternly over his bottle,—"it'll give you a chance to work things out with your grandpa."

"I don't want to work things out with him! How is he hiring anyway? I thought The Morning Catch was on the rocks."

"I heard something about American Seafoods cutting a deal with him last week."

I stare at him. "Wow, you kept that quiet."

"We weren't speaking last week. Oh, I mean, *you* weren't picking up my calls last week."

"You're still bitter about that."

Setting his bottle on the coffee table, he tangles one hand in my hair and pulls my face toward him. "Definitely bitter," he whispers as his lips find mine.

"There is no way my grandpa is going to hire me," I say as we break apart and I cuddle into his side.

"Actually, he told me you can start tomorrow."

I jerk away from him. "Wha-at??"

"Oh, did I forget to mention I met him coming out? And he asked how you were doing. I told him you were looking for a job, and one thing led to another."

I scramble off the couch, jostling his arm causing beer to slop all over his front. "Chel!"

"What is wrong with you!!"

"I might ask you the same thing!" he retorts, striding into the kitchen and ripping off a wad of paper towels. "You ask me to help find you a job and then yell at me when I find you a great one."

"I'm yelling at you because you had the gall to tell my grandpa, whom you know I hate, that I would work at his restaurant, which I also hate!"

"Geez, Chel, I'm sorry! It's not a binding contract. I can easily go down tomorrow night and tell him that I talked to you, and you're actually not interested."

"You'll do nothing of the kind! I'll take it from here. And I'll thank you to stay out of my relationship with my family!"

"Okay!" he lifts his hands, the soggy paper towels still clamped in his fist. "Okay."

Shooting one last glare at him, I storm down the hall and fling myself into bed.

Hours later, I wake up when I feel him slip into bed and put his arms around me. "I'm sorry," he whispers in my ear. "I shouldn't have interfered."

I turn in the circle of his arms and tuck my head under his chin. "I think I'm going to take the job," I say slowly. "Like you said, I won't get a better paying job anywhere. And after I've repaid the damage deposit, I want to start saving money."

His body stiffens. "Save money for what?"

"A first month's security deposit."

"What? Chel, I said I was sorry..."

I stop his flow of words with a kiss. "I'm kidding! I just wanted to see what your reaction would be. I want the money for college. With the baby, I know I won't be able to go full-time, but I'm hoping to start taking classes toward a music performance degree."

"You're a brat," he mutters, kissing me again, hard. "But I think that's a great idea."

Sitting on the polished leather entry benches of the Morning Catch, I am definitely having second thoughts. For one thing, the smells drifting from the kitchen are making me feel like I'm about to lose my breakfast. For another thing, I'm remembering how much I hate customer service. And, most importantly, the reality that my grandpa is going to be my boss is starting to really sink in.

"Rachel?" A girl in a turquoise button-down and gray slacks approaches me. She looks about my age, with light-brown hair pulled into a loose French braid and large blue eyes outlined heavily with eyeliner. Her voice is bored and supercilious, and it couldn't be more plain that she drew the short straw in having to train the newbie. "I'm supposed to show you the ropes. Come on."

I get up and follow her as she leads me through the restaurant, gesturing spiritlessly to the kitchen, the host stand, the dance floor, and the dish pit.

"What's your name?" I ask hesitantly as she pauses to open a door marked Employees Only. She raises her eyebrows at me as though it's a stupid question and finally says,

"Camila."

"I usually go by Chel," I say in as friendly a voice as I can manage. She casts me one icy look over her shoulder and then pushes open the door saying,

"Pick a shirt and pants or a skirt in your size. They'll come out of your first paycheck. Find me at the host stand when you're through. The restaurant opens for lunch in half an hour."

Heart sinking, I survey the piles of uniforms. What size should I take? I'll probably outgrow whatever I take in a month—I've already gained seven pounds. And what is with Camila?

When I join her at the host stand ten minutes later, dressed in my new medium-sized shirt and elastic skirt, both of which are on the large side, she snaps, "Pull your hair out of your face. Nobody wants hairs in their bouillabaisse."

Thanking God silently that I happen to have a hairband on my wrist, I pull my hair up into a ponytail, biting my tongue to keep from demanding what her problem is. "Here's the seating chart." She thrusts a laminated sheet under my nose. "You better have it memorized by the end of the night, or you'll never last. Today's servers are Aria, Chenille, Gavin, Ross, and Susanne. Aria is in section A, Chenille in section B, Gavin…" Her voice washes over me as I frantically scan the chart, trying to match the position of tables to the little squares on the diagram. Butterflies are beginning in my stomach, and I'm feeling sicker by the minute. What was I thinking? I'm going to get fired from this job too.

"We have five reservations for tonight. You can find them recorded in this book. Date and time on the side. Always double check a person's first and last name *and* phone number to make sure the reservation is legitimate." She's talking like "reservation fraud" is rampant.

Suddenly, Camila looks up and smiles so widely that I am sure her face is going to hurt for days afterwards. "Hi Gavin," she purrs.

I turn to see whomever she is talking to and feel my insides freeze. Gavin Fairchild is leaning on the host stand. As his eyes meet mine, they widen ever so slightly, and then a slow smile spreads across his face.

"Chel. How nice to see you again," he says softly.

Camila's smile slides off her face like melting butter off a piece of toast. "You two know each other?" she asks jealously.

"Chel and I are old friends," Gavin replies, before I can force my frozen tongue to move.

"I thought you worked for your dad. And had your own advertising business." The implied question about what he is doing here is clear, and Camila stares at me, clearly shocked by my rudeness.

"My father and I had a falling out a few months ago," Gavin says easily. "Turns out working with family has its pitfalls. As you're probably already aware." He gives me a small smile. "Unfortunately, recessions are also not kind to small-time photographers. But I've wanted to go in a different direction for a while now. I'm waiting to hear back on some applications, and The Morning Catch is a delightful place to work in the meantime." He shrugs. "Enough about me. How are things for you?"

Why should I be scared of him? He can't hurt me. I force myself to smile composedly. "Just peachy," I say. "I actually got married a few months ago."

The friendly look in his eyes shifts to something much more dangerous. Like a snake coiling itself up to strike. The next moment, shutters fall, and the snake is gone. "Congratulations," he says smoothly. "We should definitely go out for a drink to celebrate your marriage."

*There is no way I am ever going anywhere with you again.* "Oh, sorry," I say carelessly, "but I'm pregnant. No more drinking for me until April."

Again, the flicker in his eyes. "Double congratulations," Gavin says. "So, you must be, what, three months along?"

"Something like that," I say carefully. *Why does he care?*

"Oh look," Camila breaks in at this point, "customers!" She points through the revolving glass doors at the elegantly dressed couple entering. "Rachel, take them to section A, will you? And make sure to let Aria know."

The rest of the night passes in a blur. I get snapped at by several of the servers for not seating them enough or for seating them too much or for not letting them know after seating a table. Gavin never snaps at me. He just smiles and compliments me on how quickly I'm learning. His smiles make my insides writhe as though all his snake friends have taken up residence in my stomach.

My brain is so overloaded with restaurant procedures and takeout orders and servers' advice that I can't process what his being here means. But his presence hovers in the back of my mind like a fog creeping on the edge of my peripheral vision, waiting to sweep in the moment I have respite to think.

By the time the last customer leaves a little after midnight, fear is lapping persistently at the edges of my brain. As I sit with Camila, wrapping silverware for the next day, my mind churns. Should I tell Clancy? But tell him what? That I'm freaked out because the father of my baby is working at the same restaurant as I am? I remember the look in Clancy's eyes two nights ago when I told him about my one-night stand. My heart twists. What good will it do to tell him? Gavin can't do anything to me, can he? And anyway, it's not like he raped me or something. What happened is my fault as much as his. It's not technically his fault that the sight of him makes me want to vomit.

What if I tell Clancy and he wants me to quit? I already have a LOUSY employment record. What if I tell him and he starts to wonder whether I would sleep with Gavin again given the chance? What if the knowledge that I'm working with a guy that I had a one-night stand with plants seeds of doubt in our relationship, which is just starting to blossom?

I feel someone place a hand on the back of my chair, fingers brushing against my shoulder. I jerk away reflexively as Gavin says, "I think your ride's here, Chel."

I glance down at my phone, which is sitting next to the half-full box of rolled silverware just in time to see the screen light up with a message from Clancy.

I'm outside

Then:

Can't wait to see you <3

Feeling Gavin's eyes, I flip the phone over and say curtly, "Thanks, but I need to finish up."

"I'm done with mine," he says. "I can help Camila."

"No, thank you," I snap. Then, as Camila's eyes widen, I soften my tone. "I really need the practice so that I can speed this process up."

"Suit yourself," Gavin says lightly and walks away. A weight seems to lift from my chest as he leaves.

It's a little after one in the morning when I climb into the car. Clancy closes the biography of Bill Gates he was reading and smiles at me as I settle into the passenger seat.

"How was the first day?"

My chest constricts. I can't lie to him. "It was all right," I say as brightly as I can, not quite meeting his eyes. "Just hard. Super long. My feet are killing me, and my brain feels like mush from trying to remember five hundred instructions at one time. And I guess I should have realized, but I didn't, that 'closing time' for a restaurant isn't actually when you get to go home."

He grimaces in agreement. "You must be exhausted. Did you get anything to eat?"

I grimace in turn. "I could have gotten a free meal because I had a full shift, but everything on the menu made me want to barf."

He rolls his eyes at me. "You do realize that most people would love to get a free meal from the Morning Catch? They cost about thirty bucks a piece." Still shaking his head, he turns onto a side street and pulls up to the curb.

"What are you doing? Aren't we going home?"

He gestures out the window. "I thought I'd grab my wife something to eat first. I called in an order since I thought The Morning Catch's menu might not have anything to tempt you."

A ball of warmth expands in my chest as he hops out of the car and heads into the all-night bagel shop we ate at the night we met. But beneath the glow, heaviness fills my gut. I'm doing the right thing in not telling him. Gavin hasn't done anything to me. I'll just stay out of his way, and everything will be fine. Right?

*Whoosh, thump, thump, thump, whoosh, whoosh, thump.* I can't help the smile that spreads across my face as I listen to the baby's heartbeat. My baby. I'm eighteen weeks, three days, and this is my third appointment with the OB, Dr. Robinson. I like her. She's a tall, thick-set woman with dark-brown hair streaked liberally with gray. Everything about her exudes calm and control. Somehow, she makes me feel like everything's going to be okay.

"That's a heart rate in the 140s," Dr. Robinson says, removing the doppler from my abdomen and using a towel to wipe off the warm, sticky gel. "Conventional wisdom would say there's a little boy in there. In any case, everything sounds good."

I sit up on the paper-covered table, and she slides back down into her swivel chair, making a note on a clipboard. She flips a few pages and then pauses. "At your first appointment, I have a note here saying you would have classed your stress level as high." She shoots a piercing glance at me over her clipboard. "Would you say that is still the case?"

I shift slightly on the table, feeling the paper rustle beneath me. When I told her at my ten-week appointment that my stress levels were high, I hadn't spoken to Clancy in four days. I was struggling to perform the most basic household tasks. I was spending every morning leaning over the toilet. I hated God and was busy running from him. Right now, all those things have changed. Clancy is out of town again, but he calls me every night, and he's coming home tomorrow. The very thought makes my heart do a happy dance. My housework still isn't exceptional, but I can make basic meals, our cast iron is rust free, and I now know to check laundry tags before washing things on hot. The morning sickness has been gone for a while, and I feel better than I have all pregnancy. I am seeking God again and devouring chapter after chapter of the Bible every evening. And despite all this, my answer to the stress question still hasn't changed.

A month and a half of working at The Morning Catch has been enough to convince me I dislike hosting intensely. Half the time it is mind-numbingly boring, and the other half I'm getting yelled at. On top of that, I see Grandpa almost every day, but he acts as though we are complete strangers. And somehow, Gavin and I seem to have the exact same schedule. He's polite. He's friendly. Too friendly. His presence gives me a sick feeling of dread, and I can't seem to block out the dark, twisted images of that night whenever he is near. A gulf seems to be opening between Clancy and me, even as I fall harder for him every day. Outwardly, nothing has changed. But the truth about Gavin, which I am withholding from him, hovers between us like a dark mist, obscuring the closeness we briefly had. And, God, who for one glorious week, felt so near to me, seems to have gone behind a curtain as well.

"I guess I'm still pretty stressed," I mumble, staring into my lap. "I just started a new job. And there's some…personal stuff."

There is silence for a moment, and then she says in a tone much softer than her usual direct manner, "There is help available, Chel. Stress can be very detrimental during pregnancy, and if there is anything I or anyone else can do to help alleviate your stress, we would be more than happy to."

I continue to gaze into my lap, my eyes prickling. She says there's help. But I don't even know what kind of help I need. Finally, I force myself to look up.

"Thank you," I say. "But I think I'll be fine."

"So are you excited for your man to be home?" Cat asks me that night. She's curled up in a corner of her couch, hands wrapped around a steaming mug of chai. I'm sitting in the La-Z-Boy, also clutching a mug. I usually come to Cat's at least one night a week to hang out after Serenity is in bed. Clancy has come with me a handful of times, and each time I feel Cat's attitude toward him warm up a few degrees.

Her question makes me fix my eyes on the golden-brown liquid in my cup. I seem incapable of making eye contact these days. Is yes a truthful answer? I miss him so much it hurts. But in these days that he's been gone, I've been able to sit alone in the apartment at night and stare at the walls, quaking inside because I know I'll have to go to The Morning Catch tomorrow and see Gavin again. I haven't had to tell myself over and over every day that I'm not lying. I'm just not telling him everything.

"Yes," I mutter, still feigning interest in my cup. I can feel Cat's eyes on me. *Why do I have no poker face?*

"Chel," she says slowly. "You don't honestly expect me to believe that answer, do you?"

Finally, I wrench my eyes away from the sodden tea bag still floating in my cup and meet her gaze. "The baby's father," I blurt out. "He works at The Morning Catch. And I haven't told Clancy."

With the words, a tiny bit of the pressure on my insides seems to ease. I needed to tell someone. Cat's eyes widen. "Why not, Chel?" she asks slowly.

"He'll want me to quit," I say, running my thumbnail up and down the inside of my mug handle. "Or he'll think there's still something going on with Gavin and me."

"Should you quit? Is this guy dangerous?"

"Not that I know of. And...that night...he didn't rape me, Cat. It was a two-way street."

"I still don't understand why you haven't told Clancy. If anything is going to make him think something is going on, Chel, it will be him finding out you kept this information from him."

My thumb's speed increases. Down, up, down, up, down, up. "I don't want to lose this job," I say into my mug. "My employment record is awful. After being fired from my first job, if I quit my second after a month and a half, I'll never get hired again. And," I look up at Cat defiantly, "I don't want Gavin to think he has that kind of power over me. Just because he works somewhere doesn't mean I can't work there too."

"No, it doesn't," Cat says slowly. "But it might not be prudent. Chel, you said this guy has money. He could take you to court and sue for parental rights. He could take the baby away from you if he wins."

I hadn't thought about that at all. "He has no idea the baby is his," I say shakily.

"He might suspect, given the circumstances," Cat says grimly. "You got married very quickly. And if he knows exactly how far along in your pregnancy you are and when you and Clancy got married, he can figure out by basic math that the baby was conceived before you got married and somewhere around the time that you two..." she trails away uncomfortably. "If he wants to make trouble, he can claim the baby is his and demand a paternity test. And, Chel, you know as well as I do what the results of that test will be. Maybe you should quit. Get away from him."

"Cat, I can't get away from him now," I say bleakly. "He knows I'm pregnant. You're right, he was asking me questions about when Clancy and I got married and how far along I am. Even if I quit at The Morning Catch, he knows my grandpa. Port Angeles is a small town. He can find me."

Cat's face twists in horror. "He was asking questions about when you guys got married and how far along you are? Chel, this isn't good."

I set my mug down on the coffee table with a clink and bury my head in my hands. "He terrifies me," I say through my fingers. "It's nothing he says or does. He just feels…dark. I hate going to work because I know I'll have to see him."

Cat leans toward me, wrapping slim fingers around one of my wrists and squeezing. "You have to tell Clancy," she says urgently.

I lift my head. "Why? He can't do anything about it."

"Because if he's about to be involved in a custody battle, he deserves to know!"

My stomach slides another few notches. "He hasn't said anything about the pregnancy in the last few weeks," I argue feebly. "I'm probably just overreacting. Like I said, it's just a feeling."

Cat hasn't released my wrists. Now she drops to her knees in front of me so our faces are level. "Chel, please listen to me," she begs. "You say Gavin is rich and well connected. That is what courts care about! If you get involved in a custody battle, everything might boil down to the fact that he can send the child to a better school than you and Clancy can and buy him or her more fancy clothes and pay for music lessons and sports that you two could never afford! I think you should quit. Maybe out of sight out of mind will help. No job is worth losing your baby, Chel. And you need to tell Clancy."

I stare into her eyes and see my friend who gave up her education, her family, and any chance at a decent job so she would not be separated from her child. "You're right," I say, and I slide off the La-Z-Boy to the ground, wrapping my arms around her. "You're right."

"It happened that the wedding of the king's eldest son was to be celebrated, so the poor woman went up and stood near the door of the hall to look on. Then suddenly the king's son entered, clothed in velvet and silk, with gold chains around his neck. When he saw the beautiful woman standing by the door, he took her by the hand and wanted to dance with her. But she refused and took fright, for she saw that he was King Thrushbeard, the suitor whom she had rejected with scorn."

~Grimm

# Chapter 10
## News

Clancy's coming back today. The thought sends my blood shooting through my veins in hot bursts, a mixture of joy and anxiety. I'm going to have to tell him about Gavin.

There is a knock on the apartment door, and I drop my spatula on the counter next to the stovetop where I'm cooking pancakes. I did remember to grease the pan this time. Hurrying to the door, I peer through the peephole and feel a jolt of pleasure. Mom is standing outside.

She's come three more times since that first time, and our relationship is gradually undergoing a metamorphosis. She never stays long, and we don't talk about deep things, but she comes. And that means the world to me.

Pulling open the door, I stand aside to let her enter. "Hi, Mom."

"Hello," she says, smiling slightly and holds out a small potted rubber tree.

"Mom, you don't have to bring me a present every time you come."

Her face falls a little, and I reach quickly for the plant. "Not that I don't love it. But you don't want your daughter getting spoiled, do you?"

A slight smile curls the corners of her mouth, more mischievous than anything I've ever seen from her, and she mumbles something under her breath.

"Excuse me. Did you just say, 'It's too late on that front'?" Shaking my head in mock indignation, I carefully place the plant in the center of the coffee table and gesture for her to sit down. "Would you like some pancakes—oh no!" The scent of burning has just reached my nostrils, and I tear into the kitchen to see the pan smoking as the uncooked side of my pancake bubbles like crazy. "Aghhh," I moan, as I flip the pancake to see a blackened top. "Dang it."

I hear a clucking sound behind me and turn to see Mom eyeing my wrecked cooking efforts over my shoulder. Resisting the urge to roll my eyes and biting my tongue to keep from saying something cutting, I turn back to the stove and begin scraping out the charred pan. After a moment, Mom says, "I hear you're doing well at your new job."

Surprised, I turn to look at her. "You hear I'm doing well? From whom?"

She shrugs, a faint pink flush rising on her cheeks. "That's what your grandpa says."

I turn back to the frying pan. "Glad to hear he talks about me," I mumble. "It's not like he ever talks to me."

"Give him time, Chel. He'll come round. Maybe sooner than you think." There's something weird about her voice.

My hands clench so hard on the measuring cup I'm using to ladle more batter into the pan that it jerks, and a dollop lands on the counter. I fight to keep my voice steady as I say, "I don't think time is what is going to heal our relationship, Mom."

She must hear the suppressed anger in my voice because she says hurriedly, "How was your last appointment?"

"Good. Dr. Robinson says the baby is doing well. I'm excited for my ultrasound next week."

"Oh, yes," she says, animation rising in her voice. "Let me know whether it's a boy or a girl so I know what things to get."

Amused, I glance over my shoulder at her. "You did hear what I said about not having to bring presents all the time, didn't you?"

"But I'm a grandma now," she protests. Our eyes meet, and an unexpected lump rises in my throat. When I can speak, I say lightly, "All right, just remember that the apartment is small. I don't want Clancy to have to move out so that we can fit all the baby stuff."

An odd, furtive look crosses her face as she says, "I don't think you need worry."

"What is going on with you, Mom?"

Her eyes widen, and the flush on her cheeks deepens. "What? Nothing. What are you talking about?"

"Mom. You look like you always looked the month before my birthday. What are you not telling me?"

"Nothing!" she protests again, hurrying into the living room to sit on the couch, her face still a bright magenta.

"Mom..."

"Grandpa's having a proposal at the restaurant," she blurts out. "Someone booked the entire place. He wants it to be perfect, so I've been helping out with logistics. I've been really busy the last few weeks."

Shooting her a final suspicious glance, I decide that my best chance of finding out what is going on is just to let her talk. Mom can't keep a secret to save her life. "Okay," I say. "Who's getting married?"

She hesitates for a fraction of an instant before saying, "Bart Drossel."

There's a funny ringing in my ears. It feels as though my heart has stopped beating. From a long way away, my own voice comes, asking, "When is the proposal?"

"On November 18th." Two weeks.

"I didn't know he was dating anyone."

"Apparently everything happened really fast. That's part of the reason there's so much work to be done. Bart is pulling out all the stops. It's going to be beautiful. Any girl's dream." She peers into my face. "Chel, honey, are you all right?"

Again, my far-away voice sounds in my ears. "I'm fine."

Mom pats my hand, and I resist the urge to jerk away from her. "I'm sure it's disappointing that he didn't tell you himself when you two were such friends growing up, but I think you'll at least get to see it. You're on the schedule to work that night."

I'm giving in my two weeks on Monday. That means my last day of work will be the twentieth. I breathe deeply, trying to get oxygen to my numb brain. I wish Mom would leave. I need to be alone. I need to think.

But she talks on, telling me that Bart is bringing in a live jazz band, that he ordered seven courses with all of his fiancée's favorite foods, that he has requested that the entire restaurant be decorated with ivory roses and candles and fairy lights.

Her words wash over me, and there is no pain yet, just a sense of complete unreality. *Leave. Leave. Leave. Please, Mom. Leave.*

Finally, after what feels like an eternity, she stands up. "I really should head out," she says brightly. "But it was good to see you, dear." I force my lips to stammer a reply and watch as she pulls on her ankle boots. She carefully zips each one. She pulls on her coat. She begins to button it. She misses a loop and unbuttons it. She begins buttoning again, going more slowly this time to avoid a mistake. She buttons all eighteen buttons. She hugs me. Then, at long last, the door swings shut.

I sink onto the couch and put my head in my hands. Bart is getting engaged. I didn't even think to ask whom he is planning on marrying. My heartbeat has come back, thudding dully against my ribs, like a drum inside my chest. I force myself to breathe deeply, dragging lungful after lungful of air into my body. Gradually, the ringing in my ears goes away. My frozen mind slowly grinds back into action.

It doesn't matter. I love Clancy. I've never yet said those words to him, but I know they are true. I haven't thought about Bart in months now. I haven't had a real conversation with him in years. It doesn't matter that he's getting engaged. Not to me, anyway.

But then I see him in my mind's eye kneeling on the shining floors of my grandfather's restaurant holding out a ring to a beautiful girl in a sparkly dress, and I see myself, standing in the shadows in my too-big hostess uniform, watching them, just like I watched him once, dancing with Sophia LaMarr at the homecoming dance. And tears come, though I try desperately to choke them back.

I love Clancy. I love Clancy. I love Clancy.

What is wrong with me? I've tried to get rid of my feelings for Bart Drossel. I have tried.

And I have gotten rid of them. I don't obsess about him anymore.

But still. I know that *Casablanca* is his favorite movie. I know that he always felt like he was disappointing his father. I know that he would rather go to a food truck than any sit-down restaurant anywhere. I know that he dreams of going to Polynesia and scuba diving in the turquoise waves. I know the expression on his face before he laughs.

And it isn't so much that I'm still in love with him. It's that I'm sure no girl in a sparkly dress will ever know him like I do. A part of me will be sure until the day I die that I was meant for him. And he for me.

*God, what do I do?* Because we'll never be together. I have Clancy. Bart has...someone. But I feel tied to him. And I don't know how to cut myself free.

"Chel?" For just a moment, as I hover in the mists between sleep and waking, I think it is Bart's voice and that I am going to open my eyes on my childhood bedroom and see him bending over me, asking if I want to watch a movie or go down to the docks or take a walk downtown.

But it's Clancy bending over me, lips brushing my forehead, my nose, my lips. "Hey, sleepyhead," he whispers. "Look what I brought you." And he pulls from behind his back a bouquet of white roses.

For a moment, I stare at them. Then I burst out crying.

Poor Clancy. It takes five solid minutes of bawling before I become coherent enough to try to tell him what is wrong. He sits next to me, the roses lying forgotten on the coffee table, rubbing my back, his face scrunched in lines of bewilderment.

Finally, words start to come. "I'm sorry...It's just...my mom told me today—hiccup—Bart Drossel is getting m-married and"—I break out into fresh sobs as I feel his hand pause in its rotations on my back—"and I l-love you...it just hurts and...he's going to have ivory roses at the proposal..." I bury my face in my hands, crying too hard to continue.

I feel his arms come around me and squeeze. I turn my head into his chest and sob and gulp, trying to calm down. When I finally look up at him through the painful, swollen slits that my eyes have become, wiping my nose with the back of my hand, I don't understand the expression on his face. It's the look of someone on the edge of a high dive, debating whether to take the plunge. But he doesn't say anything, just leans down and kisses me softly on the lips.

I feel tears coming again and bury my head in his chest. My heart aches so badly I wish I could rip it out. I wish he would say something, but maybe there isn't anything to say.

Later, as I lean against him, my tears spent, he says softly, "There's somewhere I want to take you. How quickly can you get ready?"

I sniff. "Where are you taking me?"

"It's a surprise."

"How on earth am I supposed to know what to get ready for, then?"

His eyes take in my stained sweats and oversized T-shirt, which is actually his. "Just lose the homeless look."

The coffee shop is cozy and dimly lit. Bookshelves line the walls, and a long scrubbed wooden table provides a focal point in the center of the room. Smaller tables hug the edges. The smell of coffee and pastries wafts around us as we squeeze our way toward the counter. The place is packed.

Chatter buzzes as we add ourselves to the end of the line that snakes into a back room. I give Clancy a questioning glance, and he smirks back at me.

"You're not going to tell me why we're here, are you?" I say.

"Nope."

I shake my head at him before studying the people around us. A harassed-looking couple are trying to keep their four rambunctious children seated on the benches around the big table. In a corner, a young woman, probably a college student, hunches forward over her laptop, eyes scanning the screen as she absently sips from the round white mug in her hand. An old man and woman share a piece of cheesecake at a small round table near us. As I watch, he feeds her a bite off his own fork and then leans close to peck her lips. My chest constricts, and I glance up at Clancy to see that he's noticed them too.

Something makes me reach out and slip my arm around his waist. The look he gives me as he pulls me close and plants a kiss on my forehead makes me want to start bawling again. And I might have too, if at that moment, the music hadn't started.

Somehow in my people watching, I totally missed the fact that the space next to the big front windows is filled with wiring, speakers, a keyboard, a drum set, and music stands. Now a middle-aged man with big glasses is strumming a guitar, while another middle-aged man harmonizes to his vocals and plays the keyboard, and a young woman with long blonde hair and a nose ring sits behind the drum set.

They're playing "Fire and Rain."

The music seeps into the cracks in my soul, and I barely notice Clancy ordering behind me. It's only when the song stops, and clapping breaks out around me that I discover we're sitting at a small round table near the musicians, and there are two steaming white mugs and a piece of cheesecake resting between us.

Everything weaves together. The classic old songs that I love. Clancy's fingers covering mine on the table. The smooth texture of cheesecake in my mouth. The rich, dark smell of coffee. The swelling of music that causes everyone in the coffeeshop to join in on the chorus of "Uptown Girl."

Too soon, the man with the big glasses is saying, "Thanks, everyone, for coming. This is going to be our last number for the night."

I see the corner of Clancy's mouth jerk as the intro begins. And as the sound of Eric Clapton's "Wonderful Tonight" surrounds me, I wonder if there could be a more perfect song to end this evening. My eyes catch Clancy's, and as the music drifts away, I mouth, "Thank you."

When I wake up the next morning, sheets tangling around my bare legs as I push my hair out of my eyes, Clancy is gone. Pulling myself upright in bed, I yawn and study the clock face. The numbers 9:36 register.

Realization hits me. I didn't tell Clancy about Gavin. And I'm supposed to go into work in just over an hour.

On the walk to the restaurant, I pray over and over and over that Gavin won't be there. But he's the first person I see as I walk through doors. And the smile he gives me causes my insides to twist into a pretzel.

*God, why?*

Forcing myself to act nonchalant, I stroll to the host stand and greet Mikayla, another newbie. She's quiet and very sweet. I like her. She reminds me of Cat.

"We've got six servers today," she says in her soft voice. "Justine in A, Michael in B, Aria in C, Jayden in D, and Gavin and Camila are taking E and F together since this is the second day of him training her."

"Oh, I didn't realize she'd stopped hosting."

"Well, since today is Gavin's last day—"

I drop the handful of quarters I'm counting. Most of them clatter back into the drawer, but a few dance away over the tiled floor.

"I'll get them," Mikayla says, scurrying after the change. "I bet it's getting hard for you to bend down."

My heart is thundering in my ears. I try to keep my voice even. "Did you say today is Gavin's last day?"

"Sadly, it is," says a smooth voice behind me.

My heart has moved from my ears to clogging my throat. I turn slowly to meet Gavin's dark eyes. His gaze is too intense. "I told the rest of the staff on Saturday," he says. "I received an HR position at American Seafoods and will be moving to Seattle at the end of the month."

My heart lands back in my chest as relief washes over me in waves. "Congratulations," I say blandly. "Sounds like a great opportunity."

He smiles. "Thank you. We should eat together tonight. I haven't had a chance to catch up with you since you started, and now I'm leaving."

Dread pricks my heart. "Oh, I never take the comp meal," I say. "I'm not a fan of seafood."

"Honestly, neither am I. But the goat cheese and spinach mac and cheese is to die for. And I'm sure you're starving at the end of your shifts. Eating for two and all that."

"I don't think—" I begin, then break off with a gasp as his hand closes around my wrist. Hard. Mikayla has drifted away to talk to the manager about having Saturday off.

"I would *really* like you to have dinner with me," he says softly. His eyes are like chips of obsidian.

"Let go of me," I say, fighting to keep my voice from shaking.

His fingers tighten for just a second, and pain shoots up my arm. Then he releases me. "I'll see you after work," he says. I open my mouth, but he leans swiftly toward me. I jerk reflexively away from him, but I can still hear every one of his whispered words. "Or else I might have to have a chat with your grandfather about the paternity of his great-grandchild."

He straightens. "I'm going to miss you, Chel," he says, brushing his fingertips along my forearm before striding away.

The rest of the day passes in a haze of fear.

*What do I do?*

I make stupid mistakes.

*He knows.*

The servers snarl at me.

*God, help me!*

By the time the shift ends, my heart feels worn out from the constant thumping. I sink into a booth in sight, but out of earshot of the table where most of the employees have congregated. Unwrapping my knife and fork, I scoop up a mouthful of the mac and cheese. It tastes like sawdust, and I have a hard time swallowing.

Gavin slides in across from me, putting down an identical round white dish, filled with creamy noodles. He doesn't say anything for a moment but slowly unwraps his silverware and forks up a few noodles. Chewing slowly and deliberately, he surveys me.

"This is delicious," he says.

Glaring at him, I drop my fork into my noodles and shove them across the table. "You can have mine as well, then."

A cat-like smile twists his handsome face. "Did you add arsenic?"

"What do you want?"

"So businesslike," he muses, lifting his napkin to dab a speck of spinach from the corner of his mouth.

"What do you want, Gavin?" My voice is shaking now, but not from fear.

He cocks his head, eyes hardening. "What I want is to know why you blocked my number after our night together. And why, when you discovered you were pregnant with my child, instead of reaching out to me, you eloped with a street musician."

"The answer to the first question is that I never wanted to see you again," I snap without thinking.

The look on his face chills my heart. It is ugly. Swallowing hard, I force my tone to become neutral. "And I don't know what you're talking about. Your child? The baby is Clancy's. We've been together for about a year. The night I met you at the bar? We'd had a fight. I was upset and stupid. But we made it up, and he's thrilled to be a father."

With a sinking heart, I watch his lips curl into a mirthless smile. "How do you know the baby is Clancy's?" he says softly. "Had a paternity test, love?"

I clench my hands on my knees beneath the table so he won't see them shaking. "I don't need a paternity test," I respond coolly. "The night I was with you wasn't the right time of the month."

*Please, God, forgive all the lying. I have to save my baby. I have to.*

Gavin leans back against the dark leather of the booth, tracing his lips absently with a long, slender finger. "If you're so sure, then you have nothing to lose if I request a paternity test," he says softly.

My fingernails are biting into my knees. "And what do you gain by requesting such a thing?"

"The chance to be a father, of course."

"You don't want to be a father, Gavin," I say, unable to fully eliminate the contempt that drips off the words.

His lips twist again, into a parody of a smile, and he leans across the table toward me, stopping so close I can feel the warmth of his breath on my face. I press backward into my seat, feeling the leather give slightly, but the gesture is reflexive and useless. I know I can't get away from him.

"But there are things I do want," he whispers, lifting one finger and tracing it slowly down my cheek. I slap his hand away.

"Don't you dare touch me or I'll scream," I say, glancing toward the rowdy table of servers. "Tell me what you're after."

He draws back slightly, eyes boring into mine. "I'm told the salary at American Seafoods is very adequate," he says musingly. "But the cost of living in Seattle is high. And I like to live in a certain...style...if you know what I mean."

"How much do you want?" I cut across him brittlely.

"Are you always so...brusque?" he inquires, running a finger around the rim of his glass. "No, wait, I seem to remember that alcohol does take the edge off."

My blood is thundering in my ears, but I grit my teeth and study my congealing plate of macaroni, waiting for him to tire of baiting me and get to the point. Silence stretches between us for a moment, and then he says, "Fathers normally pay child support, don't they? But in this case, I think we should turn that on its head. After all, I think I'll need some 'emotional support' to help me get through losing my only child. Why don't we call it $250 a month until the brat's eighteenth birthday?"

$250 a month.

12 months in a year.

18 years.

I sit stock-still, my mind moving zeros. Finally, I say, my voice sounding as if it is coming from very far away, "Fifty-four thousand dollars."

"Impressive mental math," he says coolly, and in my mind, I can hear Clancy saying those same words on the night we met.

My heart is thudding against my breastbone as I force myself to say, "So, you're saying that if I pay $250 a month until the baby reaches majority, you will stay out of our lives."

"I couldn't have put it more succinctly myself."

I swallow. "But how do I know that you'll hold up your end of the deal? How do I know that a few years in, you won't show back up and try to up the price? Or file a lawsuit and try to get custody?"

The smile is back on his face, and I wonder how I could ever have thought him handsome. "Now that is the question, isn't it?"

Insides writhing, I attempt to sound in control. "I want some sort of written assurance that you are going to uphold your end of this."

He laughs softly. "This, my dear, is what you would call bribery, which is illegal under any court of law. So, it doesn't matter what I sign. If you try to take me to court with some little paper that says I will stay out of your and my kid's lives if you pay me, you will be indicting yourself of a crime, making it all the more likely that the court system will decide the child would be better off with its law-abiding father."

*God, please. Help me. Help me!*

"I'm sure it isn't considered law-abiding to accept a bribe either," I say.

He toasts me with his empty water glass, "Touche. But that doesn't change the fact that nothing to do with bribery would hold up in a court of law."

In the silence that follows, my mind churns and reels, trying desperately to come up with any solution that will protect my baby. But the blanks in my mind only multiply, and my panic surges higher and higher. Glancing desperately around me, I realize, with a fresh jolt of terror, that the table across from us has emptied. I can still hear people in the kitchens, but we are alone in the main area of the restaurant.

I surge to my feet, grabbing my barely touched plate. "I need time to consider your offer," I grind out.

He stands too, blocking my way to the kitchens. "How much time?"

"The baby isn't due until April," I say. "We can't even fight a custody battle until then."

"But a paternity test can be performed at any time," he returns, eyes hardening. "And I wouldn't like you to get any ideas about running off with the baby. How about we say you'll let me know in two weeks? And you can start paying next month."

"The baby isn't born yet!" I explode. "You said this is supposed to be like child support. No father pays child support for an unborn child!"

"But don't you 'pro-lifers' think life begins at conception? I seem to remember hearing your grandfather ranting on the phone one day back in August about how his granddaughter called him a 'murderer' for suggesting she get an abortion. And, if life begins at conception, and you are—let's say, five months along—that means you actually owe me $1250 next month."

This is what it's going to be like for the next two decades. He will suck me dry, emotionally, financially, and in every other way he can. I will be powerless against him, because I have to stand between him and my child, even if I am destroyed in the process.

Wordlessly, I stride around him. I can hear his footsteps trailing me as I stalk through the kitchens and drop off my plate in the dish pit, calling out terse good nights to the people I pass. My phone buzzes, and I pull it out as I push through the restaurant's revolving doors and out into the cold night. It's Clancy.

Where are you at?

I can see his truck, idling in the third parking spot from the doors, the same place he always parks when he picks me up from work. I am just slipping my phone into my back pocket when I hear a shout behind me.

"Chel!"

I turn to see Gavin exiting the restaurant, his breath creating a white cloud in the frosty air.

"What?" I snap.

He closes the space between us in two long strides. "Back there you asked what I wanted," he says, standing much too close.

"And you told me!" The anger that has been simmering inside is beginning to boil. "Fifty-four thousand dollars!"

"But that's not all I want," he whispers and grabs me, pinning my arms to my sides as he plants his mouth hard on mine.

It's a nightmare as I struggle to throw him off. I can't breath. He's too big, too strong. I can't reach the pepper spray in my purse. And I know that he can do whatever he wants to me, because I won't be able to stop him.

A car door slams behind me. Footsteps hammer the pavement, and the next instant, Clancy's voice is in my ears, full of a fury I have never heard there before. He rips Gavin off of me and sinks a fist into his mouth.

"Don't you EVER lay a finger on her again!"

He's pummeling every inch of Gavin he can reach, and for a moment, I stand, stunned by the ferocity behind all his goodness. Then I realize that Gavin isn't hitting back, and I know instinctively that's a very bad sign.

"Clancy!" I throw myself at him and clamp onto his arm. Immediately, he stills, turning toward me, his breathing heavy. Gavin staggers away, clutching his nose, which is spurting blood.

"I'm calling the police," he gargles, pointing a shaking finger at Clancy as he gropes in his pocket with his other hand. "For aggravated assault."

"Do that!" Clancy snarls. "I'm sure they'll be interested to hear about the sexual harassment which precipitated the aggravated assault."

Glaring malevolently at the pair of us, Gavin taps out the number and holds the phone to his ear.

"Clancy!" My fingers are still clamped on his arm, and I shake him, terror beginning to course through me like poison. "Clancy, you can't charge him with sexual harassment."

He turns to me, cupping my face. "Chel, are you all right?" he says urgently.

I need to make him understand. I don't know how quickly the police will get here.

"Clancy, please. You can't tell them why you started beating him up. You can't charge him with anything."

"Why?" he asks, eyes trained on my face.

I never meant to tell him like this. "Gavin is the baby's father," I whisper. "He told me tonight he is going to get a paternity test and sue for custody unless I pay him off. If you try to charge him with anything tonight, he'll drag me into court tomorrow. Clancy, he just got a job at American Seafoods in HR. He'll make more than you or I ever will. A judge will be sure to grant him at least partial custody if it goes to court. I have to protect our baby." I pant, trying to swallow the sobs rising inside me. "I don't know what to do. But I need time to figure it out."

"Chel." Clancy's voice is full of an urgency I don't understand, until I hear the sound of sirens approaching. "Did you say Gavin just got a job at American Seafoods in HR?"

"Yes."

Clancy pulls me into his arms, holding me tightly. The sound of sirens is getting louder. "Take the truck and go home, Chel," he says into my hair. "There's nothing you can do tonight. They'll probably hold me for twelve to twenty-four hours before posting bail."

Through my closed eyelids, I can see flashing red and blue lights. "Do we have enough in the bank to post bail?" I whisper.

"Depends on how much they ask for." His voice holds a hint of amusement.

A voice booms across the parking lot. "Sir, I am going to ask you to raise your hands in the air and come slowly across to me."

Clancy holds me for a second longer and then slowly releases me. "Everything is going to be all right," he says, looking earnestly into my eyes as he raises his hands slowly above his head. "Do you hear me, Chel? I promise. Everything is going to be all right."

I watch him and Gavin being ushered into separate squad cars. I watch the car containing my husband turn slowly out of the parking lot and speed away on the main road. I watch raindrops begin to strike the asphalt around me in the silent parking lot.

And I don't believe him.

"Then she cried bitterly and said, 'I was terribly wrong, and am not worthy to be your wife.' But he said, 'Be comforted. The evil days are past. Now we will celebrate our wedding.'"

~Grimm

# Chapter 11
## Alone

The alarm clock in the bedroom chimes. Jerking awake on the sofa, I shove the open Bible out of my lap and race down the hallway, determined to mute the annoying sound. When silence surrounds me again, I stand in the bedroom, gazing at the neatly made bed.

After I got home last night, I sat awake on the sofa for hours alternately cudgeling my brains to think of a way out of the situation with Gavin and shooting up desperate, incoherent prayers. At 2am, still with no brain waves, I pulled Clancy's Bible toward me and began to rifle through it feverishly, hoping for some wisdom to help me. Finally, a paragraph caught my eye.

O Lord, how many are my foes! Many are rising against me; many are saying of my soul, "There is no salvation for him in God."

*That's exactly how I feel. What did this guy do?*

But you, O Lord, are a shield about me, my glory, and the lifter of my head. I cried aloud to the Lord, and he answered me from his holy hill.

*But what if God doesn't answer? What then?*

I lay down and slept; I woke again, for the Lord sustained me. I will not be afraid of many thousands of people who have set themselves against me all around.

*That's a nice sentiment.*

Arise, O Lord! Save me, O my God! For you strike all my enemies on the cheek; you break the teeth of the wicked. Salvation belongs to the Lord; your blessing be on your people!

Slumping back against the sofa, I closed my eyes. *So that's the answer? Just wait for God to somehow magically fix all your problems?*

God didn't cure Dad of cancer. What if He doesn't get Clancy safely out of jail? Or protect my baby from his psycho of a father?

But you, O Lord, are a shield about me, my glory, and the lifter of my head. I cried aloud to the Lord, and he answered me from his holy hill.

The words seemed to whisper in the air around me. *Maybe God doesn't have to answer every prayer. But He chooses to answer some.*

So, I spoke into the dark silence of the apartment. "Please, Lord. Please get Clancy out of jail. Keep him safe. God, show me what to do about Gavin. Protect my baby. Don't let Gavin get custody. Please, show me what to do, Lord. Be a shield around me. Around Clancy. Around our baby."

And now, as morning sunshine paints patterns of light and dark across the bed, I rummage in the chest of drawers for my most chic maternity clothes. I need to go and get my husband out of jail. And I think God might have answered my prayer, because I have a pretty good idea of what to do after that.

"I'm here to post bail for Clancy Jankovich," I tell the woman sitting at the front desk in the jail's lobby.

"Let me see," she responds, clicking rapidly on her computer. As I watch, fighting the urge to drum my fingers on the counter in front of me, her clicking slows, and she bites her lip, then punches something into her keyboard. "One moment, please," she says and pulls open a drawer to rifle through some files. Her face lights up as she pulls one out, then falls again as she opens it and then shoves it back among the others. "One moment," she says again, before scurrying into one of the offices behind her.

Minutes pass. Now that she's gone, I drum my fingers lightly on the countertop, rocking from toes to my heels and back again. I feel a flutter in my abdomen and smile, placing my hand over the spot.

"Don't worry, little one," I whisper. "I have a plan. Everything will be all right."

The receptionist comes scurrying back, accompanied by a tall black man whose light pink button-up bulges out slightly over the belt holding up his gray slacks.

"My name is Sergeant Trey Gillmore, ma'am," he says in a deep slow voice. "Now who is it you were looking to post bail for?"

"Clancy Jankovich," I say brightly, though I am starting to feel uneasy. "My husband."

Sergeant Gillmore sits down with a creak in the receptionist's chair and begins to click rapidly. Just as the receptionist's did, his clicking gradually slows. He pulls open the filing drawer below the desk and thumbs through the files. "And when was your husband arrested?"

"Last night."

Sergeant Gillmore squints up at me. "Ma'am, I was on duty last night, and no one of that name was brought in. Does he go by anything else?"

"Not that I know of," I say. I feel a slight kick and wonder if the baby can somehow sense my unease.

"Like I said, ma'am, no one of that name was brought in last night."

"I watched my husband get arrested last night," I say, fighting to keep my voice even. "Is there anywhere else he might have been taken?"

"Why was your husband taken into custody?"

"He was…" I search for the right words. Beating up does not sound good. "He was…having an altercation with another man."

"A physical altercation?"

"Yes," I say reluctantly.

"Was your husband injured? Could he have been taken to the hospital?"

"No, no, he wasn't injured."

"And the other man. I assume he was still alive? We're not talking about a homicide?"

"No! The other man was definitely alive. Just a little bruised."

Sergeant Gillmore thumbs through the files again. "I'm afraid no one of that name was taken in last night, ma'am."

"Could you tell me the names of the men who were brought in last night?" Maybe he gave a different name for some reason.

"I'm sorry, but that would be a violation of confidentiality."

My breathing is starting to speed up. Am I stuck in a nightmare? What the heck is going on?

"Sergeant, I need to find my husband," I say as calmly as I can. "I know he was taken into custody last night, and he should be here."

"Can you give me a physical description?"

"Medium height. Medium build. Brown eyes. Long dark-brown hair in braids. Tattoo underneath his"—I quickly hold up my hands in front of my eyes to check,—"his left eye. It's the word Redeemed. Short beard."

"Clothing he would have been wearing last night?"

I wrack my brain, trying to remember. But everything happened too fast last night for me to notice what Clancy was wearing. "I'm sorry, I'm not sure."

The sergeant snaps the notebook he has been scribbling in shut. "I will double check that no one we currently have in custody matches your description. In the meantime, I would suggest calling your husband to double check that he was not released last night or earlier this morning."

He walks away, and I reach for my phone, mentally kicking myself for not having thought of calling before.

There are no new messages. I quickly select Clancy's name in my contacts and hold the phone to my ear. One ring. Two. Three. *Please, please pick up.* Four.

His voicemail box isn't set up.

I press the red circle to hang up and stand, clenching and unclenching my hands, the nightmare-feeling intensifying. Footsteps echo on tiles, and I look up to see Sergeant Gillmore walking in from the back, shaking his head.

"We have no one in custody who matches your husband's description, ma'am. Did you try to call him?"

I nod numbly. The sergeant tilts his head sympathetically. "I would recommend reaching out to anyone who might know where he is—friends, family, work, etc.—and if he has not returned by tonight, you should come back in and file a missing person's report."

As he moves away, back into his office, I stand frozen, one hand absently caressing the curve of my stomach. Through the pounding in my brain, one thought emerges.

*We're alone, baby. We're all alone.*

# Chapter 12
## New Beginning

Hell. I'm living through hell.

After visiting the police station on Tuesday morning, I called every single person who might know where Clancy would be. I called the restaurant to see if any of the hosts or servers had seen him. I used the business card on the fridge to call the office at his church. I even riffled through the phone book and found the number for the bagel shop. Nothing.

The person I most wanted to call—Cat—I couldn't reach. By Murphy's law, this was the week she was out of the country. Her church was having a short-term mission trip to Honduras to host a VBS, and someone anonymously raised all of Cat's support so she and Serenity could go.

I thought about calling my mom and grandpa, but the tattered remains of my pride held me back. They would just say the no-good loser I married after three days has left me.

I've never met his family. His best friend, whom I've also never met, lives in Seattle. He doesn't have a gym membership. He didn't leave his wallet or any other documents at the apartment.

I called American Seafoods, and after a lot of holding, they told me no one of that name or description has ever worked for their company.

As I searched the apartment for anything that might give me a clue of where to find him, I noticed his violin case propped in a corner near the sectional. Opening it, I stared down at the dark-brown instrument, tears stinging my eyes as I remembered Clancy sitting on the couch and playing it. Suddenly my gaze caught on something propped in the corner of the case. I snatched it up. It was the sonogram I gave to Clancy after my first ultrasound. Throat constricting, I studied the little black and white image. The baby must be so much bigger now. I tried to gently prop the picture back up in the corner of the case, but it toppled forward. Only then did I notice the scribbled words on the back.

"And he will turn the hearts of fathers to their children and the hearts of children to their fathers." ~Malachi 4:6

*I will find your father, baby. I promise.*

That was a week ago. Dark fears and suspicions haunt me constantly.

I have no idea how much money there is in Clancy's bank account because he hadn't gotten around to adding me as a user yet. Luckily, he did show me the emergency cash stash behind the bottom row of books on his bookshelf. One thousand dollars. Enough to pay rent for a month and still afford some groceries.

As I am pulling off books, trying to reach the cash so I can replenish the apartment's dwindling supply of food, a small plain-covered green notebook falls to the ground. It must have been stuck between Strong's Concordance and a huge National Geographic atlas.

Wondering if it can possibly contain some clue to Clancy's whereabouts, I open it. I see a page covered in a neat, blocky print. A diary. My eyes find the date at the top of the page and my heart skips a beat. Our wedding day.

It's done. And she still has no idea who I really am. I was certain she would look down and see the signature on the marriage license, but that clearly didn't happen. And now I don't know what to do. We had a fight as soon as we got home. I knew I should tell her the truth, but I couldn't. Fighting is bad, but not speaking is worse. I just need to win her trust. Her love. Make her understand how much I care about her. This won't really hurt her. We're not sharing a bed, so if she wants to get an annulment when I tell her the truth, she'll easily be able to.

*Look down at the signature? What?*

My heart is beginning to fall into the dull, thudding beat of dread. He's clearly not who he told me he was. That's why there's no record of a Clancy Jankovich working at American Seafoods. Why I couldn't post bail for him under that name.

But if he's not Clancy Jankovich, who is he? A conman? A felon? I gnaw my lip, scanning the entry again. I draw in a sharp breath as my eyes find the last sentence.

Clearly, annulment on the grounds of not sharing a bed is off the table now.

My gut is roiling as I turn the page. The new entry is from a few days later.

She saw me without my tattoo this morning. I was sure she would figure it out. But she was just mad I hadn't told her it was fake. She said she hates it when people lie to her—that it makes her angry. I knew if I told her then, she would leave. Never speak to me again. I need more time. I'll tell her soon.

*Figure what out?* I flip the page.

She touched me tonight. I hadn't realized how badly I want her. It took everything I've got not to grab that infuriating girl and kiss her senseless. And I almost think that if I had, she might have let me. I can't tell her yet. Not when she might finally be falling for me again.

*Again?*

Next entry.

She hasn't spoken to me in four days. Should I just tell her and get it over with? How much angrier can she get? But I definitely need to tell her this in person.

*This is the most infuriatingly cryptic diary I have ever read in my life!*

What have I done? I slept with her. Oh God. She gave herself to me, not knowing who I really am. How can I tell her now? She'll hate me. She'll say I tricked her into this, and she'll be right. I'm the lowest form of trash. How could I do this to her? I love her. I'm so afraid of losing her. But lying isn't caring, like she told me.

The pages crinkle as they slip through my fingers.

I'm a coward. I keep hoping she'll put it all together. Things have been so good between us. Exactly what I hoped they would be. But I need to just tell her. Okay, Lord. By now, though, a simple confession isn't going to be enough. I need to do something amazing to make this up to her.

I rifle through the pages, but that's the last entry. The book falls closed, and I put my throbbing head in my hands. I don't understand. Clearly,

Clancy didn't tell me the truth about his identity. But it doesn't sound like he wanted to con me into anything. Except loving him. And, from his writing, which he probably thought no one would ever see, he hated lying to me. The guilt was eating him up.

But if he loved me so much, why has he vanished now? Has he left me and my baby? Or was he involved in drugs or something and is being detained somewhere against his will?

So many of his entries make it sound like I should know who he is. But I don't. I can't remember ever meeting him before that day in front of Grandpa's restaurant.

The only person he reminds me of is Bart. But I saw Bart the night I met Clancy. And he didn't have a beard. Or long hair. Or pierced ears. Or a fake tattoo, but that doesn't mean much. Clancy is amazing on the violin. Bart never played an instrument as far as I know. But the biggest thing is that Bart is getting engaged in a week. And I am as sure as I am of anything in this world that Bart would never trick me into marrying him and then go and get engaged to someone else.

I feel a twinge of excitement at the thought of the proposal. It has become the one bright spot in the dark sea in which I am swimming. Because even though it will mark the irrevocable end of anything that was ever between us, it is also the only hope I have of saving the baby whose fluttering movements I can feel just below my navel.

That was my brainwave the night Clancy was arrested. Bart works high up in HR at American Seafoods. He will be Gavin's new boss. Maybe, for the sake of an old friendship, he would be willing to use his influence with Gavin to keep him away from me and the baby. And now, I have an even bigger reason for needing to talk to him. Maybe he will have some clue as to who Clancy really is and where I can find him.

My cell phone rings, and my heart leaps, then plummets as I snatch it off the coffee table. The caller ID isn't Clancy's. It's Grandpa's.

We sit across from each other in a red leather booth in A Slice of Heaven Pizzeria—my choice of a meeting place, not Grandpa's. I watch over the top of my menu as he flips pages in his, lips puckered into a disapproving frown.

"Not finding anything, Grandpa?" I can't resist saying.

The line between his eyebrows deepens for a moment, and then he says mildly, "On the contrary, I believe I will take a Chef Salad. What about you?"

The mildness of his manner makes my conscience twinge. My life is God's now. And it isn't very Christian of me to bait him. *I'm sorry, Lord. Help me to bite my tongue. Help me to really listen to what he has to say.*

"I'm thinking the meat lover's calzone sounds good today," I respond in an equally polite tone. We close our menus and take sips of ice water in sync. Silence stretches between us. Grandpa carefully unwraps his silverware and places it neatly on the table in front of him. "Rachel," he begins, then pauses. "Your mother and I would like to help you."

"I don't need any help from you, thanks," I flash before I can stop myself.

Grandpa glances up at me, and his eyes are tired and sad. He suddenly looks very old. "I thought you might say something like that," he says heavily. "And I'm not going to pretend I don't deserve it. I've had a lot of time to think since you went away." He removes his glasses for a moment and passes a hand over his eyes. "Before you left, you accused me of only being interested in my image and my restaurant. And as I examined my life, I realized that was where I put most of my time and energy. Which made me think perhaps the reason my relationship with my granddaughter was so strained had more to do with me than with her." He sighs and then looks me in the eye. "I'm not good at apologies, Rachel. But that is why I asked if we could meet. So, I could say I am sorry. For just about everything over the last few years."

I open my mouth and then bite my tongue. Resentment swirls inside me, and I want to tell him that a few nice words over lunch one day do not make up for seven years of sarcasm and heavy-handedness and disregard. I want to say that he should have been my father when I was fatherless, but all he did was show me that I wasn't the offspring he desired.

But as I sit, struggling against the poisonous words fighting to explode from my lips, other thoughts come. Didn't I turn my back on God for seven years because He didn't live up to my expectations? And didn't He forgive everything? Didn't He accept my broken apologies when I wanted to come back?

*Lord, I don't want to forgive him. I don't want to.*

Cat's words come back to me again, the ones she murmured the night I told her about my one-night stand. "If you, O Lord, should mark iniquities, O Lord, who could stand? But with you there is forgiveness, that you may be feared."

*With You there is forgiveness.*

*With You.*

*Help me. Give me Your forgiveness.*

"I forgive you, Grandpa." The words stick in my mouth, but the second they are out, weight seems to lift off my chest. I look into his eyes and see that they are slowly filling with tears. "I forgive you," I say again and reach across the table to touch his hand. His fingers wrap around mine, and he squeezes tightly, reaching up with his other hand to dash the tears out of his eyes.

"Thank you," he says, his voice slightly muffled.

At that awkward moment, the server appears at our table with two plates and we break quickly apart, Grandpa still hurriedly wiping his eyes. We dig into our food in silence. Only when I have polished off my plate and am eyeing the breadsticks of the couple across from us with jealous interest does Grandpa speak again.

"When I said your mother and I would like to help you," he begins.

"Grandpa," I say quickly, trying desperately to keep my tone neutral, "Grandpa, I really appreciate what you're trying to do, but I don't want to be dependent on you or mom anymore."

"It isn't a question of dependence, Rachel—"

"It is to me," I say flatly.

Grandpa opens his mouth and then closes it. I watch him struggle to find words for a moment, and then he says slowly, "Rachel, please believe me when I say I am speaking out of concern for you. For you and for...your child. My great-grandchild." I open my mouth to interrupt, but he raises a hand. "Please, let me finish. I know our relationship has been rocky for years. You have been kind enough to forgive me for that, but I know that does not change seven years overnight. All I am trying to say is if you do not want assistance at this moment, that is fine but know that your mother and I are here to help you. That if ever you find yourself in a situation where you need help of any kind—be it money, time, advice, a place to stay—your mother and I want you to come to us."

A lump rises in my throat. For one awful moment, the reality that Clancy might never come back flashes across my mind. I might be raising this child alone and need any help that I can get. Then, I shove the thoughts away and meet the eyes of the man sitting across from me.

"Thank you, Grandpa," I say.

"He said to her kindly, 'Don't be afraid. I and the minstrel who has been living with you in that miserable hut are one and the same. For the love of you I disguised myself.'"

~Grimm

# Chapter 13

## Hope

The restaurant phone rings. I hesitate. I hate answering the phone at the best of times. But with my world crumbling, it's even harder to infuse peppiness into my tone.

I give myself a little shake and pick up the receiver. "The Morning Catch. Chel speaking. How may I help you?"

"Chel? Thank God."

"Clancy?" I grip the hostess stand, feeling suddenly weak at the knees. "Clancy, where have you been?"

"I'm so sorry, Chel. I tried to call you. But—" he hesitates.

"What? You lost my number?" My relief is starting to be tinged with anger.

"Yes. Seriously, Chel. I left the station so quickly that my phone got left in the impound. And I have you as a contact…I literally couldn't remember your number. I know it sounds like something out of a cheesy rom com, but it's true. I'm so sorry."

"Where are you? Why didn't you just come home? Who got you out of jail?"

There is a pause. "I got a call on the way to the police station," Clancy says. His words are measured, and I wonder if he is holding something back from me. "I got accused of stealing at American Seafoods. I—I kind of panicked. I used my phone call at the station to call Drew and asked him to come bail me out so I could go try to sort out the situation. I thought I'd be able to call you on the road to tell you it would be a bit before I could come home, but then the whole phone thing… And I've called the restaurant twice and asked them to get you a message. But that clearly didn't happen."

"You haven't said where you are."

The pause this time is even longer. "I'm in Seattle," Clancy finally says.

"You're in Seattle?" Two and a half hours away. And he couldn't have driven back to tell me he hadn't fallen off the edge of the earth?

"I don't think me saying I'm sorry again will make things any better." His words have that same measured tone, and I snap.

"What do you mean you're sorry? I've been out of my mind with worry! I thought you'd—" I can't finish the sentence. It's only the Spirit of God that keeps me from hanging up on him.

"I would never leave you." His tone is heavy. "I just—until today, I thought I was losing my job and going to jail. I haven't been thinking straight." He lets out a long breath. "I'll make it up to you, Chel. I've mostly figured things out at work. I'll need a few more days to make sure everything's squared away, but I'll be home soon."

"When can you come home?" I hate the hint of a plea in my voice.

"On Saturday night. I know you have to work, but I'll meet you at the restaurant. And I'll make everything up to you."

"You gonna take me to a food truck again?"

"I'll buy you a food truck if you want it." He pauses. "What do you want? I mean it."

"Are you George Bailey now?" I ask. "If I say the moon, are you going to rent a rocket?"

"Would it hurt you to give me a straight answer?"

"It might." My emotions are too raw, pulsing below the surface of my sarcasm. All my fear and relief and despair and joy jumbled up in a mass with my pregnancy hormones.

"Twenty questions, then."

"All right," I say as my mind whirs. *What do I want?*

"Object or experience?"

"Experience."

"Is it a concert?"

"Are you kidding me?"

"That is not an answer, sweetheart."

"Fine. Yes."

"It's a James Taylor concert, isn't it?"

"How do you know me so well?" I mean the words to be teasing, but they're not. They're raw and real, and the lump in my throat is so thick it hurts.

Clancy draws in a breath, and I tense, suddenly sure I don't want to hear what he is going to say. But then, he says, "I need go, Chel. I'll call you tomorrow, okay?"

"Okay." I don't want him to call me. I want him to walk through the door of our apartment and pull me into his arms. I want him to hold me until his nearness dispels my fears that he will one day leave me for some girl without enough baggage to fill a cargo hold.

It's like he can hear my thoughts, because he says, "You're stuck with me, kid. As long as you want me."

"That's the most sideways reference to *Casablanca* I've ever heard." I swallow. "But you couldn't do anything that would make me not want you."

"I'll remind you that you said that." His tone is light, but there's an undercurrent of seriousness, and I wonder exactly how much he is going to have to make up for on Saturday.

# Chapter 14
## The Dress

Everything is perfect. And it makes me feel sick inside.

Candles sparkle on the single round table set in the middle of the dance floor. Fairy lights glitter in scintillating ropes crossing and crisscrossing the ceiling. There is an easel set up next to the table holding a mirror with Will You Marry Me? written across it in beautiful, flowing script. There is a small stage set up to one side with instruments waiting to be played by the band Syncopation. I've loved them ever since I got into singing jazz. Apparently after he proposes, Bart wants to dance with his new fiancée. And there are white roses everywhere. He must have bought an entire florist shop.

The restaurant hasn't been open to the public at all today; instead, the staff have spent their time since noon moving all the other tables into back hallways, cleaning every stationary object, stringing lights, and arranging the decorations.

Now everyone is gone except me and my mom. Bart asked that the proposal be a beautiful, private event. He only wanted one server to wait on him and his fiancée. I have no idea why Grandpa picked me, but I didn't fight him. This might be my only chance to try to get Bart to intercede on my behalf with Gavin.

"All right, honey, I'm going to head out," Mom says, turning away from the table where she has been shifting the cutlery infinitesimal amounts, as though a perfect distance between the knife and the soup spoon are going to make all the difference while Bart Drossel is asking the most important question of his life. She looks me up and down. "Since you're the only server, I thought you could wear something a little fancier tonight." She goes to the corner where she has stashed her purse and coat and lifts up a garment bag I hadn't noticed before.

"Mom, I'm not the one getting proposed to."

She doesn't look at me, focused on fastening the buttons on her coat. "Will you just try it on? Tonight is supposed to be perfect, and, no offense, dear, but those uniforms aren't flattering on anyone."

"Okay." I put my hand on her arm. "It's all gorgeous, Mom. You did a great job."

She looks at me then, and there is something in her eyes that I don't understand. "He'll be here any minute, honey. You should go change."

I watch her push through the revolving glass doors and then take the garment bag into the ladies' room. When I unzip it, I groan. "Mom."

As usual, she's gotten too excited. This dress isn't appropriate for a server. It's deep green and floor length, with off-the-shoulder sleeves, and an empire waist that would complement my growing bump. I stare at it for a long moment, then shake my head and zip the bag back up.

It's a shame too. On a different night, I would have loved to wear a dress like that.

I hang it on the door of a stall, when an idea suddenly occurs to me. Clancy is coming to pick me up from the restaurant as soon as my shift is over. I can wear this dress for him and whatever grand gesture he's planning to make up to me the fact that he's been gone for two weeks. I had brought a different outfit, but this dress will be much better.

I leave the bathroom and head down the hall to the dining area. In the doorway, I freeze. Bart is standing there, angled away from me as he surveys the table setup. He is wearing a light-gray suit that I'm sure must have cost more than I make in an entire pay period. His dark hair is perfectly waved, and I can see the outline of his cleft chin. There is a white rose in his buttonhole, and he is holding something in his hands that I'm guessing is a ring box. My heart squeezes tight as I glance down at myself in my hostess's uniform, my belly pushing out the buttons of my turquoise shirt, feet encased in ugly, serviceable nonstick shoes. Suddenly, I wish I had worn the dress. The way I look only emphasizes the fact that we are worlds apart now, he and I. He's a king among men. And I, the girl who was once too prideful to return his calls, am a drudge, so far beneath him. I don't even know if I'll be able to get close enough to beg for his help.

I try to back away. But my stupid, nonstick shoe catches with a squeak, and Bart turns. "Chel."

"Oh, hello."

*Floor, now would be a great time to open up and swallow me.*

"Hello." He's smiling at me, his dimples carving grooves into his cheeks. The way he's looking at me is making a ball of heat expand in my chest, and I really, really need to get away from him.

"Well," I mumble, looking everywhere but into his green eyes. "I'm sure your girlfriend is about to show up so I'll just—" I gesture over my shoulder to the kitchen. "Hope it's great."

*Hope it's great? Is my brain-to-mouth connection broken?*

"Chel." He moves toward me. "I need to talk to you."

"Right now?" I glance toward the spinning glass doors.

"Yeah."

Puzzled, I join him next to the table. My eyes find the mirror, but it doesn't read Will You Marry Me? anymore. Now it reads Forgive Me?

My heartbeat is becoming painful. Pieces of the past four months start to come together in my mind, but the theory slowly coming into focus is so ludicrous that I question my own sanity for even thinking it.

"Someone messed with your sign," I say, turning to look at Bart.

But he's not standing behind me anymore.

He's on his knees.

Holding something out to me.

# Chapter 15
## The Lie

I'm dreaming. I must be. Barton Drossel, my first love, cannot be proposing to me when I'm married to someone else.

"What are you doing?" My voice sounds high in my ears. "If this is a joke, it isn't funny."

"It's not a joke."

"I'm married."

"I know."

It's only now that I see he is not holding a box or a ring. He is holding two pieces of paper.

Cautiously, I reach out and take them.

They are concert tickets. James Taylor in Portland next year.

I'm going crazy.

"What's going on?" I look around for Clancy. I don't see him, but there is music coming over the restaurant speakers now. It's Eric Clapton's "Wonderful Tonight." "Did Clancy tell you what I said? Where is he?"

"He didn't tell me, Chel. You did."

*It's not possible.*

He is still on his knees, looking up at me. Waiting for me to understand. To accept the truth. My mind adds braids and a tattoo and a beard and brown contacts, and I see Clancy staring back at me, lines of guilt etched into his face.

"No. This can't be real. You can't be…" My voice trails away.

"I'm your street musician, sweetheart."

"No." I turn away, heading for the door, but he jumps to his feet and grabs my hand.

"Not again, Chel. You can't shut me out again. We need to have this out."

I can't talk to him. The reality of the situation is crashing over me in a giant wave, and amid the devastation and anger, one thought stands out. That I'm a complete and utter fool.

His fingers tighten on my hand. "Chel, let me explain."

"You tricked me."

His shoulders tense, then slump. "Yes."

"You think some big show is going to erase the fact that you lied to me for the last four months?"

"No."

The despair in his voice makes my heart soften for an instant, before I remember the lies, the months of lies. "Why?" The single word is a barb, with sharp, curving edges.

His head whips toward me, and for the first time I see a spark of defiance. "You know why, Chel."

I glare at him. "Pretend I don't."

"You ignored me for three years! Then, we met that night, and you talked to me. You told me what was bothering you. You treated me like you used to treat me. And I saw a chance to get past your...your pigheadedness—"

"My what?" Anger explodes inside, so strongly I can barely get the words out.

"Your pigheadedness!" The words are a shout as he leans toward me, our fury seeming to collide in the air between us, sending sparks through the empty restaurant. "You love me. You've loved me since you were fifteen years old. But you just had to sabotage it because I didn't declare undying love for you the second you told me how you felt. The queen of cutting off your nose to spite your face, that's what you are!"

He's breathing heavily, clearly trying to cool off, but I don't want to calm down. "You think that justifies lying to me?" In contrast to his, my voice is quiet. Deadly and icy. "You think that tricking me into marrying you—into SLEEPING with you—was okay?"

"No." He is not shouting anymore. "No, it wasn't okay. None of it was okay."

Somehow, rather than placating me, his admission makes me angrier. "Then, *why* did you do it?"

I expect him to say he did it all out of love for me, and scathing responses are building behind my teeth, when he says quietly, "Because I have trust issues."

"What?"

The green eyes that I've missed for the past three years find mine and then slide away. "I should've believed God could bring you back to me. That He could breach the walls between us. But I didn't. So, I took matters into my own hands." A strangled sound halfway between a laugh and a groan erupts from his lips. "Clearly, that worked out great."

My anger is draining away, and I clutch at it, terrified that I am going to forgive him, that I am going to turn into the heroine of every romance novel ever, and overlook everything the hero has done, just because he says a few nice words. "How am I ever supposed to trust you again?"

He looks at me again, and this time it is I who glance away. "I don't know." The words are raw, gravelly with despair. "But how am I supposed to trust that the next time I screw up—and you know I will, Chel—you won't shut me out for years?"

The words are an arrow, an arrow that somehow finds a chink in the armor of my anger, piercing straight through and into the depths of my soul. Because he's right. While I've been busy pointing the finger at him for his sins, I've ignored my own part in this mess, the bitterness and unforgiveness that made him desperate enough to do all of this.

I remember his diary entries, his hopes that I would catch him, his guilt, his terror that admission would result in me pushing him away again.

Something brushes my pinky, and I look down to see Bart's hand. For an instant, my remaining fear and anger struggles to hold my own hand motionless. Then, my fingers twine with his, and he lets out a sigh that draws my gaze to his face.

His eyes are closed, and as I watch, twin tears slip from beneath his eyelids, tracing down his cheeks toward his cleft chin. A lump rises in my throat.

"I'm sorry," he says. "I told myself it wasn't a big deal. A harmless trick to win you back. But I broke your trust. I hurt you terribly. The person I care about more than anyone else in this world."

I want to tell him I forgive him. That I'm sorry for all the pain I caused him in three years of silence. But I can't think of words that aren't cliche or forced.

"I—I need time."

His green eyes open. They are full of despair. "I'll go then," he says quietly. He pulls his fingers out of mine and walks toward the spinning glass doors.

"Bart!" I call after him. He stops but doesn't turn around. "This isn't over," I say. "I'll call you. Soon."

I know him so well that I don't need to see his face to know he doesn't believe me.

"Take anything you want," he says. "It was all for you anyway."

Then he is gone.

# Chapter 16
## On the Docks

"So you didn't get to the ring part," are Cat's words when she opens the door and sees my face.

"What ring part?" I ask, suspicion rising inside as I follow her into her apartment.

Cat glances at me and heaves a sigh. "Bart told me the truth about three weeks ago, Chel. And he told me about his plan to have a grand apology in your grandpa's restaurant and then ask you to marry him."

"He was actually going to propose?"

Cat nods and sinks back onto her couch. "I told him that I thought you'd need some time to process. But...he's crazy about you."

I drop down next to her and lean my head back, staring at the ceiling. "He lied to me, Cat. For months."

My friend is quiet, twisting a strand of her short blonde hair. I'm sure that she is praying. After a while she says, "He was wrong to trick you, Chel. And he knows it."

"But?" I turn my head to meet her eyes.

"You froze him out for three years, Chel. The fact that he was willing to do all this—misguided as it was—for a chance to get back into your life says something."

A lump swells in my throat, and I swallow against it. "What does it say?"

Cat smiles. "That you're his ideal girl. And you always have been."

She's the only one I ever told about homecoming night. I lean my head against her shoulder. "I still don't understand how all this happened."

"You could talk to Bart," my friend says. "And also give him a years' overdue apology."

"Maybe Bart and I should write something into our vows about always listening to you."

Her fingers find mine and squeeze. "Maybe you should."

It's raining.

I look out across the Straits of Juan de Fuca toward the misty blue mountains of Canada and think of Bart and my fishing excursion to these docks years ago. Life was simpler then. But I'm daring to hope that God is going to work a happy ending out of the complicated mess Bart and I have made between us.

"Here's looking at you, kid." His voice sounds behind me.

I turn. He's wearing a tuxedo, like I asked him to when I called him yesterday and invited him to meet me on the docks.

"You stole my line," I say. I'm wearing the green dress Mom got for me that night at the restaurant. My hair hangs loose around my shoulders, but it is no longer black. Yesterday I went to the salon and had it dyed auburn again.

The corner of his mouth lifts, and one of his dimples appears. Then the smile fades, and he looks down at his feet. "I suppose you want the whole story."

"Yes," I say. "But first, I want to dance with you." I bend down and press the play button on the boombox sitting at my feet.

"As Time Goes By" fills the misty air around us. I hold out my hand to Bart. "You asked me to dance with you at homecoming," I say. "And I wouldn't dance with you. Because of my stupid pride." His expression is blank, and I'm suddenly afraid that in the two days since I last saw him, he's finally decided I'm not worth all the hassle and headache. "Will you dance with me now, Bart?"

His eyes widen behind his glasses, and he steps forward. His fingers close around mine. "Yeah," he says huskily, and relief expands in my chest. "But tell me something first." The rain is coming down harder now, ricocheting off the sodden wood of the docks. "Why didn't you speak to me for three years? Was it all because I wouldn't go with you to homecoming?"

"No," I say slowly. "I think I would have gotten over that. But then I saw you went with Sophie LaMarr, and it cemented everything I already believed. That all you wanted was a pretty face, not the baggage that would come with dating me."

"Chel, I didn't go with Sophie." Exasperation tinges his voice. "I went alone. She asked me to dance. That's when you saw us together."

"That's not all, Bart." For some reason, the words I am about to say feel heavy in my mouth, as though they don't want to be repeated. "I heard you talking to Fisher. You never once contradicted anything he said. Hot and bitchy—weren't those his words? Nobody's ideal girl."

"You really think that's what I thought of you?"

"I didn't know." My voice is small. "Not after you said you didn't want to date me."

For a long moment, he stares at me. Then he tugs on my hand, pulling me into his arms. His other hand lands on my waist, and he begins to sway. I rest my head on his shoulder and breathe in the scent of his cologne.

His lips brush my ear. "Did you ever consider that I might not have wanted to discuss my feelings for you with Fisher Davis?"

"You could have discussed them with me."

"Not then," Bart says flatly. "Chel, I remember the night my mom left my dad. I remember the words she screamed as she walked out the door. 'No woman wants to be second to a man's job, Keith. Eventually she'll find someone who will put her first.' I knew that when I started at American Seafoods, my dad would expect me to put one hundred and ten percent into my job. I would be three hours away from you. If we had started dating when you asked me, you would have been second to my job. And I was terrified that a year in you would look at me the same way my mom looked at my dad and tell me you were done."

I lift my head to meet his eyes. "Why didn't you tell me you felt this way? I would have waited for you."

A smile flashes across his face. "Really? I think you would have badgered me until I gave in and started dating you, like you and I both wanted." His voice becomes serious. "It wouldn't have been fair to you, Chel. To ask you at fifteen to promise to wait three years until you could move to Seattle so we could start dating?"

My feet slow to a stop. My hands raise to cup his neck, my thumbs tracing the line of his jaw. "I would have done it gladly," I say. "I never wanted anyone but you. Why couldn't you see that?"

His hands raise to cover mine. "Maybe for the same reason you couldn't see I was crazy about you, and that it was taking every bit of self-control I possessed to do what I thought would be best for you."

I can hear in his voice that he wants the talking part of the night to be over as badly as I do. But we have to finish this. So we can have the new beginning we both long for.

"Tell me the whole story," I say, moving to turn off the music. I sit down on the edge of the dock, dangling my feet above the water and pat the planks beside me. "The night you got arrested and disappeared. Were you really being investigated for embezzlement?"

He sits beside me, removing his rain-speckled glasses and sliding them into his pocket. "Yes. On the drive to the police station, I got a call. From the CEO of American Seafoods. He said there were discrepancies in the financial statements and that I was being suspended from my position as Chief Human Resources Officer, pending an internal investigation." He draws in a breath, and empathy courses through me. "I panicked. My whole plan had always been to win your heart as the poor street musician and then to tell you the truth and be able to offer you so much more than you had ever dreamed. There was no way I could tell you that not only had I lied to you about my identity, but I was being investigated for fraud at my job, and you might end up married to an unemployed felon. Not only did I need to deal with the situation, but I started wondering whether—in the event that I was convicted—it would be better for you and the baby to be entirely free of me. So, I crashed with Drew at his apartment while I tried to resolve the issues at work. I tried to call you to let you know not to worry, but between losing my phone and the flightiness of restaurant hosts, I wasn't able to reach you until a week later."

I grin. "I bet Camila took the messages and threw them away out of spite. She's never liked me. But you told me on the phone at the restaurant that you had mostly figured out the situation. Don't financial investigations take longer than a week?"

"Usually. In this case, the real embezzler came forward when he heard about the investigation, figuring it would be easier to get a plea bargain if he confessed than if he waited for the fraudulent charges to be traced back to him. A week after my arrest, my suspension at American Seafoods was lifted."

"Why didn't you come home after you knew you wouldn't be a felon?"

"Well, I had to deal with Gavin, to start with."

"What!" My hand goes to my stomach, and I stare at him. "How?"

"After I learned I would be keeping my job, I contacted him and informed him that we take extortion very seriously at American Seafoods and should it be discovered that any employee had attempted to blackmail someone with the threat of a custody lawsuit in order to exact money from that person, the employee in question would certainly be fired. I also informed him that there would be a court date next year where I would expect to see him sign over his parental rights as I adopted my wife's child. He seemed extremely amenable to the idea."

The fear that has been like a rock in my gut for weeks slowly dissolves, leaving a strange feeling of weightlessness. "Are you sure? He won't come back? Are you sure he cares enough about the American Seafoods job not to cause trouble before he can sign away his parental rights?"

Bart grins. "Gavin Fairchild has been applying for a job in HR at American Seafoods since he graduated high school. He's not going to throw this away after seven years."

"I guess that means he won't be filing assault charges either."

"He most certainly will not."

Relief, warm and sweet, spreads through me. The baby kicks, and I lift Bart's hand to cover the spot. "He's happy," I say.

"He?"

"It's a boy," I say. "The gender ultrasound was during the week you were missing."

"A boy." He puts his other hand on my stomach, and the baby kicks again and again, as though he's doing a victory dance inside me. Bart meets my eyes. "Our boy?"

"Our boy," I say. "You know what I think we should call him?"

His green eyes meet mine, and they hold a look that tells me he already knows what I'm going to say. "What's that, sweetheart?"

"Clancy," I say.

He laughs, deep in his throat. "I better finish this story quick. My restraint isn't going to hold out much longer."

"Start at the beginning," I say. "How did you become Clancy Jankovich in the first place?"

"It all started one day at American Seafoods," Bart says. "Drew and I were talking, and he told me he and his girlfriend had gone to see *Twelfth Night* at the local theater the night before. We got into an argument about how improbable it was for someone to be able to disguise themselves and have people who had known them before not recognize them. He thought it was impossible. I said if you had a good enough disguise and were in the right situation, it might be possible. To prove my point, the next week, I went to a hairdresser and had them put in hair extensions and apply a fake beard. I put a temporary tattoo under my left eye and clip-on diamond studs in my ears. I went to the local eyewear store and got colored contacts. I borrowed some clothes from a friend that were completely different from my usual style and showed up at Drew's office, after first looping in his secretary and asking her to make an appointment for me under a fake name. I made sure to speak in a nasal voice for the hour we talked. Then I left. The next day, I started talking to Drew and casually let fall some of the things he had said in our conversation yesterday. He was stunned when I told him I had been the 'stranger' in his office. He was impressed and said he never would have recognized me. We had a good laugh, and I put the matter out of my mind.

Then, two summers ago, my mother and I had dinner with the girl I had liked since high school. We quarreled during my senior year, and she had refused to talk to me since."

I close my eyes, feeling the pain behind the words, the scars in his soul.

"I hoped that time would have healed the wound, that she might let me apologize and tell her how I really felt about her. But she didn't look at me that whole night. I returned to my apartment in Seattle completely crushed. I remember sitting on my bed staring into the mirror on my closet door and thinking over and over, 'I wish I could be someone else. Just for one night. I wish I could be someone else.' And then the memory of the trick I had played on Drew hit me like a ton of bricks. Maybe I actually could be someone else. I got on Amazon and ordered a pack of the most expensive hair extensions I could find, seven realistic-looking fake beards, and a pack of temporary tattoos. I spent the evening developing an alter ego for myself. Clancy Jankovich—the struggling street musician."

In my mind's eye, I see Clancy, standing outside the Morning Catch with rare sunshine like a natural spotlight around him, his bow slipping back and forth across the strings of his violin, music filling the air. A hymn about a God who stays.

I force myself to speak around the lump in my throat. "Stop. Stop. How did I not know that you play the violin?"

His thumb brushes the back of my hand. "I started playing my freshman year of high school. Being a stupid, immature fourteen-year-old guy, I thought it would destroy my prestige on the football team if anybody knew I played the violin. So, I just kept it quiet. It was a hobby. I didn't compete or play in the school orchestra or anything, so it was easy to keep under my hat. I started playing more after I started my job. It just helped me to relax in the evenings. And when I got saved last year, I started playing with the church worship team."

"And you actually did become a Christian a few months before we got married?"

"Mhm." There is a brief pause before he says, "Chel, I don't think I told you a single direct lie, except that my name was Clancy Jankovich. I know that doesn't justify what I did, since I was still tricking you, but I really wanted you to figure out who I was."

My mind flies back over the past months. He's right.

"How did I not realize it was you?" I turn, looking up into his face. "It seems so obvious now. You told me your birthday was May 7th. You told me that your parents were divorced. You asked me to watch *Casablanca* with you."

"That last one should have been a dead giveaway." I purse my lips at him, and he smirks back at me, before saying more seriously, "This whole situation is a little crazy. If I had been in your shoes, I probably wouldn't have assumed my high school crush had returned in disguise and was actually my fake husband either."

When he says it like that, I feel a little less stupid.

"Tell me about the night we met," I say, leaning against his shoulder.

His arm wraps around my waist, pulling me closer. "Well, I, under the guise of Clancy Jankovich, started going out every few weekends to play on the street corners in Seattle. As time passed, I grew more and more grateful for my alter ego. I had risen in American Seafoods to become the youngest Chief Human Resources Officer in the company's history. I loved being able to leave my job completely behind and melt into obscurity as Clancy Jankovich. But something kept drawing me back to Port Angeles." His fingers squeeze my hip bone lightly. "The night after your high school graduation last year, I told my boss that I was planning to spend the summer in Port Angeles, working remotely, and I moved back."

"With your mom?"

"No, Mom spent most of last summer with friends at their beach house in Hawaii. I could have stayed at her place, but by then I was used to having my own space, so I rented a cheap apartment and started to play outside the Morning Catch every chance I got. I wanted to see you. To talk to you. I think I might have had some hairbrained scheme of posing as a friend of Bart's and trying to put in a good word for him. But I didn't manage to 'meet' you until near the end of the summer. I was still trying to figure out my game plan when I found you outside the Morning Catch that night after your grandpa's delightful dinner party."

"That's why you were upset and needed to unwind?"

His lips quirk. "I had been hoping you and I might have a chance to talk and make up. But clearly that didn't happen."

I moan and bury my head in my hands. "I'm sorry," I say through my fingers. "I was horrible that night. On purpose. I shouldn't have yelled at you. Gosh, I've been a piece of work. I don't know why you still like me. Honestly, I don't."

"Who says I like you?" he quips. "Anyway, it wasn't until we were sitting in the bagel shop, and you told me you would do anything to get away from your grandpa, that I got the idea to marry you as Clancy. I knew it was insane. And part of me knew it was wrong. But, in that moment, it felt like my only chance to get past the barrier you had put up between us for the last three years. I could marry you and make you fall in love with me again as someone else."

"But how can we really be married..." My voice trails off. "You signed your real name on the marriage certificate, didn't you? That's what the diary entry meant about thinking I'd look down and notice your signature."

"The three days between the bagel shop and our wedding gave me plenty of time to start questioning the wisdom of tricking you into marrying me. To placate my conscience, I kept telling myself you or Cat would notice my signature and call my bluff. Then you would have the option to cut me out of your life again or to choose to marry me for real."

"Why did the officiant call you Clancy if all the documents said Barton Drossel?"

Bart shifts uncomfortably. "I told him Clancy was my nickname and asked him not to call out my last name because it brought back painful memories of my father."

"And I didn't notice the signature because I was busy barfing all over the courtroom hallway." One corner of his mouth tilts in a half smile. "So, after we were married, did you keep working remotely? Or did you have to take out your hair extensions every day? Were you wearing a fake beard this whole time? Wait." I grab his forearm. "Are your ears really pierced?

In answer, he reaches up and pops the back off of one of his diamond studs, revealing a tiny hole in his ear. "The day after you agreed to marry me, I went down to Claire's and got them pierced. After that, I didn't quite have the guts to get a real tattoo." It's my turn to smile. "I've mostly been working remotely, so no, I didn't have to take out my extensions every day. And I grew out a real beard. The few times I had to travel for work, I reverted to my Bart Drossel look. So I had to use my fake beards for a bit after I came back from each trip. I thought my chin might give me away without facial hair."

A random question pops into my mind. "Do you go to church as Clancy or as Bart?"

He lets out a snort of laughter. "As Bart, of course." He sobers quickly. "And when I finally confessed to my pastor about this fake marriage, it was one of the worst conversations of my life. He told me trust is foundational to a lasting marriage. And that by lying to you, I had not only dishonored God, but that if you ever agreed to really marry me, I would have to work to regain all the trust I had destroyed." He takes a deep breath and when I look at him, I see that his eyes are closed. "And he told me something else. I shouldn't have married you as a Christian when you weren't one, Chel. Being so new to Christianity myself, I didn't know."

The despair and renewed guilt in his face wring my heart. I reach for his hand and words come, the same verse Cat spoke over me when I was wallowing in shame over my own sins. "If you, O Lord, should mark iniquities, O Lord, who could stand? But with you there is forgiveness, that you may be feared."

A small sigh escapes his lips, and he squeezes my fingers tightly. I squeeze back, awe rising inside me as I contemplate God's kindness through all of this craziness. The fact that any good came out of this situation is mind-blowing. Bart and I are train wrecks, the pair of us.

"Was it after that conversation that you decided to apologize in the restaurant?"

"I already knew I needed to tell you. But after my conversation with him, I think it really came home to me how badly I had wronged you.

That's why I planned a big fancy apology. I wanted to make it clear that I knew how big of a deal this was."

"I bet my grandpa was delighted when you confessed to him."

Bart lets out a chuckle. "On the contrary. He read me the riot act about deceiving someone you love. Your mom was nicer. I think it was easier for her to forgive me since I had made it clear that all I wanted was to love and care for her daughter for the rest of my life."

"Did Cat read you the riot act too?"

"She didn't have to." His voice is serious now. "One glance at her face told me how deeply I'd failed. I'd love to never see that look on her face again. Especially not directed toward me."

"I failed too, you know." I meet his green eyes. "I spent years clinging to bitterness toward you. I torpedoed our friendship. I hurt you. And you're not the only one who broke trust. I broke yours too. Just in a different way." I look at him, hoping for once in my life, that my heart is in my eyes. "I came to know God's forgiveness because of you. And now I need your forgiveness. I'm sorry, Bart."

"All is forgiven, sweetheart." The choked sound in his voice makes my own throat close up. "Do you forgive me?"

"Yes," I say. "'Louis, I think this is the beginning of a beautiful friendship.'"

He throws back his head and laughs. "That's what we'll build our marriage on, God's kindness and *Casablanca* quotes."

Our eyes catch, and I think I'm probably going to get butterflies every time Bart Drossel looks at me until the day I die.

"Any other questions, sweetheart?"

"Yes," I say and his face falls.

"Make it quick."

"Where's my ring?"

One hand slides away from my face to fumble in his pockets. He pulls out a small black box and opens it. Inside is a gorgeous golden band with three offset diamonds. I reach for it, but he pulls it away.

"Don't I get to propose first?"

"Do you want me to push you off this dock again?"

"There's the sweet streak I love so much," he whispers, and I feel the ring slide onto my finger as Barton Drossel kisses me beneath the lowering gray skies.

"Then the maids-in-waiting came and dressed her in the most splendid clothing, and her father and his whole court came and wished her happiness in her marriage with King Thrushbeard, and their true happiness began only now."

I wish that you and I had been there as well.

~Grimm

# Epilogue
## Clancy Drossel

**10 Years Later**

"Bethy, Lina, come on!" I stand at the bottom of the stairs in our house swinging back and forth on the round knob at the end of the banister. Mom is busy putting my baby brother Jack into his car seat, but she says without turning around, "Don't swing on that, Lance. You'll break it."

My seven-year-old sister, Beth, appears at the top of the stairs. "I'm coming, I'm coming," she sings out.

A wail sounds from upstairs. "Wait for me! Mommy, I can't find my headband!"

"Bart!" Mom calls as Jack spits up all over himself and his car seat. "Can you help her, babe?"

"Sure thing, sweetheart," my dad says, strolling out of their bedroom and down the hall toward the sound of Lina's wails. The corners of my mom's mouth twitch toward a smile as she pulls out a barf rag and starts to clean Jack up. I don't know why, but she seems to like it when my dad calls her sweetheart.

"Mom, are you going to sing tonight?"

"Not tonight, son. Tonight is for my students."

"You sound better than they do."

Mom chuckles. "Why, thank you, honey. But I've had a lot more training than most of them. I went to college for voice. Most of my students are still in high school."

Dad comes running down the stairs, roaring, with Lina slung over his shoulders, laughing hysterically. He swings her onto her feet and kisses the top of her strawberry-blonde head. He straightens and smiles at my mom, who has finished cleaning up Jack and is tickling the bottoms of his feet so that he squeals with laughter.

She looks up at him and smiles, rising and lifting Jack's car seat to the crook of her elbow. She's wearing a knee-length turquoise dress with a skirt that swishes when she moves. Her auburn hair is coiled into a soft knot at the base of her neck.

Pulling aside her unzipped trench coat, she revolves slowly on the spot. "How do I look?"

"You look wonderful tonight," my dad says, stepping forward and catching her by her slim waist as he kisses her on the lips.

"Ewwww," Beth and Lina squeal. I raise my eyebrows at them. I don't act as silly and immature as that now that I'm ten. And besides, I wouldn't admit it to anyone, but I kind of like it when Dad gets all soupy over Mom.

"Are we ready to go?" I ask in my most dignified voice.

"Lead the way, son," Dad says, gesturing to the front door. I tug it open and race down the front steps, Beth and Lina tumbling after me.

"Do we have the cake?" I shout as I clamber into my seat. That's the real reason I'm excited for tonight. Mom's recitals always have a reception afterward, and she always makes a big round carrot cake with cream cheese frosting. Mom isn't really a very good cook—Dad cooks most of the time—but she makes the best carrot cake.

"Yep, it's in the trunk," Mom says from the front seat. "Don't forget to stop by Mom's, honey. They're watching Jack Jack tonight."

"I know, I know," grumbles Dad.

"Just double checking! When he was a newborn, you forgot to stop and had to make another run across town, missing the first half of the recital which you were supposed to be filming."

As the Suburban rolls through the streets, Dad presses the power button on the CD player and violin music drifts through the car. Dad doesn't play his violin much anymore now, but he still listens to a violinist called David Oistrakh all the time.

When we pull up in front of Nana and GG's big house, I offer, "I'll carry Jack's car seat for you, Mom." I love Nana's house.

"Thanks, honey. That would be great."

"Can we come in too, Mommy?" Beth and Lina chime from the back.

"Not this time, chickadees. Lance and I are just going to run in and run out."

"Besides, I don't want to be left all alone," Dad moans from the front. The girls are giggling as I heft Jack's car seat and slam the passenger door shut. Staggering slightly, I follow Mom up the stairs and brace my arms as she rings the doorbell. Footsteps come running and Nana flings open the door.

"Hi, honey! Oh, Lance, dear, let me take that heavy car seat from you. Jackie," she coos into the car seat, "has it been so long since I've seen you, sweetie? Two whole days. Come to Nana."

She leads the way into the living room, still murmuring sweet nothings to Jack, who is crowing and pointing at everything. GG is sitting in an armchair with his reading glasses perched on his nose, a bunch of photos spread on the coffee table in front of him.

"Lance-man," he greets me. "Come on over here. I want to show you something." GG is the main reason I love coming to Nana's house. He and I talk all the time. He tells great stories about Mom when she was little, and how he fought in the Vietnam War and married my great-grandma, who my mom is named for, on a boat in the middle of the Pacific Ocean.

I run to him and lean against the edge of his chair. "What is it, GG?"

He holds up a black and white photo, so frail looking that I'm surprised it doesn't crumble to dust in his big, thick-knuckled fingers. "This is me when I was your age, Lance." I squint down at the picture and see a little boy with curly hair and a startled expression on his face. He's wearing a striped shirt and weird overalls with super skinny straps. The overalls only come to his knees, and he is wearing tall socks and clunky dark shoes.

I shake my head. "GG, you shouldn't wear tall socks with shorts. Everybody knows that."

GG throws back his head and laughs. "True, Lance-man. True. But that was the style back then. I was quite the dandy."

Mom has come over and is looking over GG's shoulder. "You were a cutie," she agrees.

"Oh, I found something for you too, Rachel." GG leans forward with a creak and a groan and begins shuffling in the photos on the table.

"Okay, Grandpa, but Lance and I do need to head out in a minute. I can't be late for my students' recital, and we need time to set up."

"Yes, yes," Grandpa waves her concerns away, still shuffling in the photos. "LeAnne, did you move… Oh, here they are. Catalina sent me a copy of the second one last week. She found it when she was spring cleaning." He hands Mom two photos. I look up and see her lips form an O as she glances between the two images.

"Can I see, Mum?"

Her voice sounds husky as she says, "Sure, honey." She hands me the pictures but continues to study them as she puts one arm around my shoulders, drawing me against her.

One of the pictures, I recognize. It's a picture from Mom and Dad's wedding. They're standing together under trees that have been strung with sparkly lights. Mom is wearing a beautiful white dress that pokes out a little over her round belly. Her auburn hair hangs in curls around her face topped with a long, gauzy veil. My dad is wearing a gray suit and smiling down at my mom. His hair doesn't have any gray streaks in it, but other than that he looks exactly the same as he does now.

I've actually been to the vineyard where Mom and Dad got married. If the girl I marry wants our wedding to be there too, I wouldn't mind. The trees and grapevines make me think of an Elven forest. Mom once said something about Dad wanting to get married at GG's restaurant, but I think he's happy now that they went to the vineyard instead. He told me once that God must have approved their wedding since the weather felt like June even though it was the middle of November.

In the second picture, Mom is sitting on a park bench next to a guy I don't recognize. It must have been windy when the picture was taken because Mom's black hair and her pinkish shirt are all ruffled out in the picture. The guy beside her has hair in lots of long dark braids. Diamond studs glint in his ears, and his smile makes the tattoo under his eye crinkle up into a black line. His dimples make his smile look like Dad's.

I think I hear GG mutter something like, "Both big days," to Mom, but I don't know what he's talking about.

"Who's this?" I ask her, pointing at the guy in the park picture.

"His name was Clancy, honey. He's who you were named after."

"Clancy Gerald Drossel," GG booms proudly. My middle name is after him.

"Does Dad know this guy?" I ask suspiciously.

Mom's lips twitch. "He does. They were very close."

"You're not telling me something, Mom. I don't understand what's special about these two pictures."

Mom smiles down at me. Her eyes hold a wry expression. "Someday I'll tell you the story, honey. And you'll get to see that God was extremely kind to your parents, who made a lot of mistakes." She puts her arm around me and gives me a squeeze. "The fact that it's a story with a happy ending is crazy. Almost like a fairy tale."

# Acknowledgements

This book is actually the second manuscript I ever wrote. And four years ago, after many rejections, I decided to shelve it for a while because I was unsure if I would ever find a publisher who would want it. But I never stopped loving Chel and Bart and praying that I would someday be able to share their story with the world.

And God answered my prayers. Amanda Wright—the incredible acquisitions editor at Firebrand—read *Nobody's Ideal* and offered it a publishing home. So the first thank you goes to her, for taking in this query-tossed book and giving it a place on Quill & Flame's shelves.

To my husband, Kyle—my first and forever love—no matter what life has thrown our way, you have never stopped fighting for me and for us. It is the greatest privilege in my life to get to be "your ideal girl."

Mom, your support through this crazy writing journey has meant everything. Thank you for all the babysitting, the marketing talks, and the encouragement.

To Helena, Bec, Mattie, and Andrea, thank you for being my first readers. The fact that you made it through the messiest version of this book means a lot.

AJ, thank you for making a home for gritty, life-giving stories. I can't wait to continue to watch what God does through you and Quill and Flame.

To Micah, Caleb, Jules, and baby #4, I can't believe I get the joy and honor of being your mom. Love you forever and always, dear ones.

To the incredible authors who took the time to read and endorse this book, I am more grateful than I can say for your support.

My editors, Jennifer Frankovic and Lori Ann Nelson—you honed this story and made it better. I am so grateful for your help and perspective.

And to my Father God, thank you for always running down the road to meet me when I come home. Your forgiveness and grace to this wrestler are extravagant. All glory to You, Lord.

# Bibliography

Aliki. *A Weed Is a Flower*. Simon & Schuster Books for Young Readers, 1988.

Capra, Frank. It's a Wonderful Life. RKO, 1946.

Clapton, Eric. *Wonderful Tonight*. 25 Nov. 1977, .

Crossway, and Crossway Bibles. *ESV Study Bible*. Crossway Books, 2014.

Curtiz, Michael. Casablanca. Warner Bros., 1942.

Dylan, Bob. *Mr. Tambourine Man*. 22 Mar. 1965, .

Miller, George. The Man from Snowy River. 20th Century Fox, 1982.

Rowling, J. K. *Harry Potter and the Chamber of Secrets*. Arthur a Levine, 1999.

Sullivan, Daniel G., and Fredric Lebow. *While You Were Sleeping*. Directed by Jon Turteltaub, N/A, 1995, N/A.

Taylor, James. *Fire and Rain*. 1 Feb. 1970, .

Wyler, William. How to Steal a Million. 20th Century Fox, 1966.

Zemeckis, Robert, and Bob Gale. *Back to the Future*. Directed by Robert Zemeckis, N/A, 1985, N/A.

IF YOU LIKED *NOBODY'S IDEAL*

CONSIDER CHECKING OUT MORE QUILL & FLAME PUBLISHING HOUSE TITLES

HEAT WITHOUT THE SCORCH

WWW.QUILLANDFLAME.COM

www.ingramcontent.com/pod-product-compliance
Lightning Source LLC
LaVergne TN
LVHW012015060526
838201LV00061B/4323